HaiLOS

BY DAVID PEROZO

Copyright © 2024 by David Perozo

All rights reserved.

No portion of this book may be reproduced in any form without written permission from the publisher or author, except as permitted by U.S. copyright law. For permission requests, contact david@hailosthebook.com.

This novel is entirely a work of fiction. The names, characters and incidents portrayed in it are the work of the author's imagination. Any resemblance to actual persons, living or dead, events or localities is entirely coincidental.

Book Cover by Lucia Canale.

"The Changing Light" by Lawrence Ferlinghetti, from HOW TO PAINT SUNLIGHT, copyright ©2001 by Lawrence Ferlinghetti. Reprinted by permission of New Directions Publishing Corp.

Contents

Part 1

1. The Grey Man — 2
2. The Machine — 7
3. Corroboration — 17
4. The Changing Light — 29
5. The Lonely Man — 39
6. The Pitch — 49
7. Small Coffees — 60

Part 2

8. Mick — 70
9. Windows — 84
10. Steam Train — 96
11. Vision — 110
12. The Light Brigade — 121
13. Continuing Education — 136
14. In the Morning Light — 143

Part 3

15. Sid — 152

16. DSL	164
17. Artificial	178
18. Lisp	188
19. The Rainforest	199
20. On the Inevitability of Fate and the Plight of Good Intentions	214
21. Penumbra	226
Epilogue	238

<PART 1>

⟨ 1 ⟩

The Grey Man

I still remember where I was the first time I saw it. It was past dark and starting to get crowded. I was at McNally's, which is where I usually was if I went out anywhere. I had started feeling a buzz and knew I should be heading home soon before the college kids and twenty-somethings looking for love and a good time showed up.

I used to think going out was fun. It was a nice enough crowd there, normally. There's a sense of community when you live in a place like Oakland, and people there just wanted to have a good time. But the last few years, I found the whole scene annoying and wanted to avoid the hassle, even if it meant leaving earlier than usual. Pretty soon, earlier than usual became the new usual.

He was an older guy and he didn't look well. He was wrapped in a wool overcoat even though fall was months away. Or fall here, anyway, it doesn't start to get cold in the Bay Area until November. But there he was in charcoal grey with an untied black scarf draped over his slumped shoulders.

His face was...well, it was grey, or greyish and stubbly, even though he seemed like the kind of guy who shaved every day. He had straight, greying black hair, and although I guessed he was 60 years old, he had plenty of it left. He looked like the kind of man who had face-to-face conversations and told things to you straight, someone who carried a briefcase and might offer a word of advice. He was neither short nor tall, neither heavy nor thin, in all respects but the one, unremarkable.

He was just sitting at the other end of the bar, looking straight ahead. He was drinking something brown, which added to the air of solemnity. He was alone, staring at his drink or the bar, or, in all likelihood, he was seeing something no one else could see because it wasn't in the room. He was bathed in light, or so it appeared to me, backlit by a lamp hanging from a cord over the table behind him. That's what made it difficult to see at first. Plus, I didn't want to stare at him. Not that he was looking at me or up at all for that matter, it's just that I feel self-conscious staring at someone. What if somebody said something, or what if Tiny noticed?

Tiny was the bartender, and of course he was about six foot four, bald as a bowling ball and ripped. The nickname was so ironic that it was unironic, which was the way the guys at McNally's always tried to play it. They were so counterculture that they were mainstream, but they didn't even notice. The whole San Francisco Bay Area is like that now and nobody realizes it. Some people do, I guess. Whatever.

I thought maybe it was the booze, but I counted the drinks. Four. Not that many, but not exactly judicial sobriety, either, I understood that. Everyone has a magic number and four was a pretty good one for me. I liked to keep it around there. On occasion – tough day, perhaps – it could end up being one or two more, or, if the college kids showed up early, perhaps one or two less.

I tried to make a rule for myself – no more drinking at home. That had the effect of forcing me to spend more time around other people, which, in theory, I knew was a good thing. I know the great Walt Whitman wrote, "Have patience and indulgence toward the people," but did he mean these people? (I sometimes wonder whether he might rewrite the preface to his great poetic masterpiece were he alive today.) As it happens, though, my "rule" also acted as a curb on my alcohol intake due to my general dislike of crowds. I could have solitude or alcohol, but not both. It was sometimes frustrating, but intellectually, I believed it was necessary.

The next thing I considered was that something was wrong with my eyes. I looked away. I looked back (a few seconds later). I rubbed them. I dabbed them. I tried to distract myself and forget about it. I saw it again, I rubbed my eyes again, etc.

After thirty or forty minutes, I fumbled for my glasses, which I always carry with me but never wear. I put them on and all that did was make the image more crisp and undeniable. I guess I must have almost given the whole thing away because –

"What's wrong?" Tiny asked, walking over, wiping a glass.

"Nothing."

"Why'd you put on your specs? Leaving early?"

"No. No, I just...thought that woman was someone I saw last week," I said, nodding towards a slender blonde woman on the other side of the Grey Man.

"First timer," he answered. "Tinder date for Mr. Handsome looks like," he added.

I looked at the guy next to the blonde. Too old to be one of the college kids, too young to be a regular. Probably lived in one of the million-dollar shacks in the neighborhood. I say shacks because that's what they are, hundred-year-old Craftsman 2 and 3-bedroom houses that for the life of me I can't tell how they're worth so much.

I moved into the neighborhood when rent was cheap and the restaurants were fantastic, crowded, noisy, small places with excellent food. Now, the restaurants almost all are parodies of themselves, all aesthetics and no character, like giant iPhone restaurants serving more of what people wish they were than actual food.

I took off the glasses. "Oh, I guess not."

Tiny moved away. I think his real name was Mike or Mikey and I made a mental note to remember and to start calling him that instead of Tiny, and then I realized that was dumb and I would just call him what I'd always called him, except that was dumb, too. I got mad at myself for being so drunk that I was tying myself in knots and starting to see things.

I caught Tiny's attention and asked for some water and chugged it down. Tiny refilled it and looked in my face. That's the last thing I wanted because you don't have to be a genius to know how observant he is and I hate it when people ask me too many questions. I have very particular opinions about asking questions. I am a lawyer, after all. So I just sipped the new glass of water and set it aside.

"Thanks," I said.

"Don't mention it," he replied and I guess it would be redundant if I told you that he said it ironically.

It occurred to me to ask Tiny if he saw what I saw, but I didn't want to get cut off and possibly never be allowed into McNally's again. It was the only bar in the neighborhood that had a whiff of authenticity left to it and if I had to go sit at B45 or Le Plume, I would rather just say to hell with all my rules and drink myself silly out of a paper bag on my front stoop like the old timers that used to live in the neighborhood.

So I did the only remaining thing that there was left to do. I got up to walk past the Grey Man and go to the bathroom.

This was a bit of a high-risk maneuver, but I didn't see any way around it. I thought of just finishing my drink and leaving, which is probably what I should have done, but I was too invested at that point. I mind my own business anymore as much as anyone, but even I couldn't handle walking away from this. The light, the overcoat, the thousand-yard stare. The guy hadn't looked up in forty-five minutes and I needed to know, I had to know, what I was really seeing. How could I be seeing it? How could I *not* be seeing it?

So, up I stood. I made an effort to steady myself, and then walked around the bar and toward the bathroom in the back, attempting to be as casual as possible. I passed Jim, the finance guy who works at Google and comes in to watch the Warriors (only the Warriors weren't playing). I passed two older neighborhood guys that I see now and then. I passed the first of the college kids, with their beautiful skin, full heads of hair and not-a-care-in-the-world smiles. I passed the blonde and Mr. Handsome and a couple of empty barstools. And then I got to him. The Grey Man.

I was looking down at the ground, trying hard to be discreet. I was pretending like I wasn't paying attention to anyone so nobody would pay attention to me. But I knew that when the moment came, there would be no getting around it. When I got there, when I got to him, I would have to look up and would have to do so deliberately. So, that's what I did.

And when I did, I saw it. I saw it up close and without any doubt, sure as I was standing there. All of my concerns about being unassuming went out the window. In that moment, I didn't care if everyone in the entire place saw me staring as I walked past him, my mouth open. Because right there above his head, unmistakable fact, bright, gleaming circle. The Grey Man had a halo.

< 2 >

The Machine

I didn't know at the time, but I know now that the halos always looked pretty much the same. They hovered about six to eight inches above their subject's head and appeared as a circle of radiant white light, with what you might call a golden or a golden bronze tint to them. There was little to no discernible variation in color between them; the only way they differed from one another was in intensity. I would later realize that the Grey Man's halo had been considerably brighter than average when I saw it, which was probably why I could recognize it for what it was.

That night, after I walked past the Grey Man and saw his halo up close and in detail, there wasn't much left to do. I came out of the bathroom a minute later, nearly killed myself falling over a bar stool while doing a double and triple take, then stumbled back to my spot at the bar.

"You ok?" Tiny asked when I sat down. I could only muster a grunt in response. This is the benefit of this type of relationship, of course. A grunt is a perfectly acceptable answer. I didn't have to worry about hurting his feelings and he didn't worry about hurting mine. Tiny wasn't going to go home after work and wonder why I was "emotionally unavailable." He poured them. I drank them.

I held up a finger and he brought me another drink without making eye contact. I gulped it down quickly because I was having a hard time not staring at the halo. I was in sort of a confusion-induced panic and I had no idea what to do, which was unusual and stressful in and of itself. I had exhausted all the potential solutions and ideas I could come up with to confront the circumstances and was still perplexed. So I did the only thing I could think of: I closed out my tab and went home.

When I got home, I showered and tried to go to sleep, but I couldn't. The image of the halo may as well have been burned into my retinas. I saw it with my eyes open and with my eyes closed. I saw the Grey Man's face sitting there, impossibly illuminated. I attempted to replicate the halo vision in my apartment. I turned on different lights in different sequences and different combinations, opening and closing my eyes. I stared out the window to see if there were halos above the people walking by, all to no effect.

Eventually, I gave up. I thought of going back to McNally's but that seemed ridiculous. What was that going to accomplish? Instead, I went to bed and laid there, seeing the same things and going through all of the same thoughts as I had for the previous hours. Eventually, I told myself that I couldn't have really seen what I had absolutely seen. I knew I was lying to myself, or at least I was *pretty sure* I was, but that was enough to fall asleep.

I woke up the next day and did what I do every morning, I pissed in a cup and passed it through a filter. I know that sounds strange, but it's a filter I invented, or, I should say, I was *inventing*.

Once the urine had completely filtered through the cup, I removed a strip of the filter and put it into an analytics machine, which I called Nina. I built Nina from scratch. She ran a program that I also developed. If everything went according to plan, Nina and the program would all be integrated with the toilet, because pissing in a cup is gross, but I hadn't gotten that far yet. That sort of integrated development required expertise that I didn't have and I hadn't found anyone yet who was willing to help me with it. The most important part anyway was to get the prototype right. After that, everything would fall into place.

After a few seconds, the program sent out an analysis directly to an app I had installed on my phone. I received an alert, opened the app, and read the analysis. I'd had too many drinks last night and I was dehydrated (duh). I had low levels of a few essential minerals, probably because of what I'd eaten the day before, but other than that, everything was normal. Nina recommended I take a supplement, eat something rich in iron and minerals during the day and take a magnesium pill before I went to bed in the evening. Basic.

Ever since I'd gotten the program up and running, I had been in steadily improving health. I couldn't remember the last time I had gotten sick, and for the past few weeks, I felt much better than usual all the time. It was hard to pinpoint exactly when things began improving after I started using Nina and how much marginally better each iteration had been than the previous version. It hardly mattered, though. Everything was moving in the right direction.

When I started all of this almost a year ago, it was based on an intuitive feeling that had been gnawing at me for years: We should be able to know, at all times, through a simple procedure, what is happening inside our bodies. We inhabit our bodies and yet what is happening inside of us can be as mysterious as what is happening in a galaxy millions of light years away. It seems preposterous. We're right here. How can we not know what is going on inside of us?

From this initial impetus, I started doing some research and focused on urine as a simple method of analysis. Urine is abundantly available, can be collected in a non-invasive manner, and is already part of our daily routine, with or without science. Collection would be seamlessly integrated with our lives. I believed that was a key element. Additional research confirmed urine as a promising path for analysis. There are hundreds of organic compounds that can be detected in urine and research is uncovering more all the time.

Originally, with Nina 1.0, you might call it, my preliminary attempt at simply detecting what was happening inside of our bodies was inadequate from a commercial standpoint. I was told (by venture capitalists, mostly) that the product was just another part of the "Quantifiable Self" movement (know your heartbeat, know how many steps you take, know how you slept last night), which was going out of fashion or being controlled by a few dominant players. What was needed was "actionable" (I fucking hate that word) data that people could do something with.

I thought that was bullshit. You can take a three thousand dollar blood test that will tell you if you have a DNA marker for cancer, but we all know by now that doesn't mean anything. Fine, it means something, but we have no idea how many people have that marker for cancer. Maybe it means something. Maybe it doesn't mean anything. What means something is when that marker activates and cancer cells start replicating in your body. That's what my machine would tell you, ideally, once it was built out. Admittedly, I wasn't there yet, but that's what I felt Nina had the potential to do.

With that feedback, though, I'll begrudgingly admit that I made several changes that helped improve Nina significantly. I added a recommendation engine, which took the biometric information and turned it into suggestions for how to improve your health. It seems obvious now, but that was definitely new ground. I was careful to access multiple medical databases, both typical western medicine and more holistic resources. I felt further progress could be made there, but I'm not a doctor and so my work was based on material I had previously worked on, research I had done and assets I had been able to license (cheaply) in the market.

Another breakthrough occurred when I added DNA reading capabilities into the prototype and related databases into the program. This would enable the product to be tailored to each individual, as opposed to just providing blanket, one-size-fits-all medical information. And finally, I would say the latest milestone was incorporating a piece of AI software into the program. The artificial intelligence piece would allow the product to learn from past experience and improve its recommendations and advice over time based on its assessment of previous advice, user behavior and the latest measurements. It was fantastic.

Every morning you could wake up, take care of your business, and get a sort of status update about yourself. "Good morning, Mr. Percy. I see you had a good nights' sleep last night (melatonin). Your diet seems to be going extremely well (proteins). Take a multivitamin and we'll see you tomorrow." The machine would be able to provide better and more constant care than your own doctor. It would have complete, seamless, up-to-date information and you would have total transparency into everything happening inside of you and what you could do about it. Admittedly, it had become a bit of an obsession.

Nina had now developed to a point where I was ready to try again to raise venture capital so I could start limited production and take it to market. I hate talking like that because I live in a city full of VC and tech douchebags. It's no secret why the Bay Area is so popular and attracts all these people. The weather is amazing, the access to nature is incredible, and many of the people are entertaining, but I can't deny that it has gotten annoying. Having been born in San Francisco, I can remember when it wasn't like this, but the tech industry has turned Oakland, San Francisco and the Peninsula into an annoying hub of douchebaggery. And here I was, doing exactly the same thing.

What's more, I was a beneficiary of the very industry I complained about. I had gotten a job in the legal department of a biotech company by accident. That company turned out to be a cancer analytics firm – scan your blood for signs of cancer so you don't have to get a finger or a tube up your ass – we were acquired, I got a hefty paycheck and a pink slip and now I'm talking like them. But I thought the problem that I was working on was…well, it was different, so I was exempt, in a way. At least that's how I felt at the time.

I spent the morning working on my investor presentation in the small desk area I had set up in the living room of my one bedroom apartment. I was still stuck in this fourplex I rented, two units on the bottom, two units (including mine) on top. I told myself it was too overpriced to buy anything then. I had waited too long. Maybe after I had some investors lined up and my product started selling a little bit. It was hard to say. It was hard to see that far into the future.

As morning turned into noon, with several hours of work under my belt, I went to Black Tavern for lunch. It's walking distance from my apartment and they have the best burger in the East Bay. Nina had identified the lack of minerals, so I thought getting some red meat would be good for me (yes, I know eating beef is bad for the environment and the animals are slaughtered inhumanely, but I can only tackle one problem at a time).

Lunch at the Black Tavern has been a complete nightmare since about two months after it opened because of the chef (previously opened several successful restaurants) and the great reviews it received. I had been going there since Day 1, though, and I know the bartender from when he worked at Swordfish, another local joint, so he usually finds me a spot at the bar. He saw me walk in, made some space for me in the corner, and put in my order before I even sat down.

After lunch, I went back home and worked all afternoon on the several aspects of the Nina program. I rarely go to McNally's two nights in a row. If I really need a drink, I'll sometimes go to the Golden Bear, this place under the stairs on College Avenue. It's bright and wide open, and it's hard to find a quiet corner there to have a drink by yourself. But it has a big bar and a dartboard and it'll do in a pinch. There's also Swordfish, which I frequented back in my college days at Cal. It's dark, crowded and falling apart, hence its popularity.

But that night I went back to McNally's for obvious reasons. Tiny was surprised to see me, but didn't ask any questions. I sat down in my usual spot, with my back to the front door, and ordered a drink. I was getting nervous inside like a little kid and I chided myself for being so immature. Seeing everything in the same spot as last night, as every night, and everything looking so normal, emboldened the small part of me that had been so ready to believe that I'd made the whole thing up and it was now perhaps 5% of my brain, instead of the previous night's 1%.

Tiny handed me my drink.

"Hey, you remember the older guy in the grey overcoat sitting over there last night?" I asked, pointing to the opposite corner from where I was sitting.

I recognized a knowing look flash in his eyes – so that was your problem. "Yeah, why?" he responded.

"Have you ever seen him before?"

Tiny shook his head. "Why do you ask?"

"Did he seem…unusual to you?" I asked him.

"Unusual. Unusual…" He let the word marinate in the air in a way that let me know exactly what he was thinking. What the fuck does "unusual" mean? Especially in this town. Multiple piercings and tattoos on your face and neck? Not unusual. Gaping holes in your ears from where your ear spacers used to be? Not unusual. Pink or blue or green hair, black patent leather lace up knee high boots and a tight black mini skirt with black makeup and eye liner so thick it looks like it was drawn on with crayon? Not unusual. People of every race, shape, size, gender (or lack thereof), sexual orientation (or lack thereof) and inclination? Not unusual. Nothing, in this place, is unusual. So he had every right to ask me what the fuck I had meant by "unusual."

But he felt sorry for me, I guess, and he was his normal, generous self. It's why everybody likes him and why he does so well as a bartender. It's not easy to draw the line between being a people person and being a fake, between being attentive and giving people their space – which is essential in a bar—and between being smart and being a smart ass.

"No," he responded, wiping down the bar in front of me. "Nothing unusual."

"Thanks," I said. And I meant it.

Laughter rang out from a small table in front of the bar where two women were engaged in lively conversation. A blonde was listening attentively to the details of the story her friend, a brunette, was telling, and she looked around, embarrassed at how loudly she had just laughed. They were both nice looking with the standard demeanor of attractive, professional women. They were clearly successful people of some sort or other. The blonde was dressed somewhat more casually, perhaps. Her friend, the brunette, looked like she had come straight from the office. She had short, straight, dark hair and was wearing mismatched earrings, with one much longer than the other, a feather or a golden net of some kind. It was hard to see. Normally, I wouldn't go for that sort of faux fashion, but it looked nice on her and gave her an interesting aspect. Neither of them had on much in the way of makeup, but that's the common standard in the Bay Area. I like it, to be honest.

Tiny noticed me looking. "Send her a drink?" he asked.

"Which one?"

"Which one do you like?"

I took a sip of mine. As a man, you have to get used to not being manly enough for your fellow man. You have to get used to disappointing people by not being willing to aspire to the cinematic standard of manhood. "No thanks," I answered. "I can't get into anything right now. I'm pretty busy with work."

It was such an absurd comment that even Tiny couldn't help himself. "Dude, I said a drink, not a ring."

"Yeah. Yeah. I know what you mean." The women looked over. They knew we were talking about them and, as the brunette smiled at me, I felt a warmness rush into my head and I looked quickly back at Tiny. I was aware I was being ridiculous.

In the old days, this was part of the attraction of a place like this. I would come here, meet people, go on dates or meet for coffee, sometimes something would come of it, more often than not nothing, but I was involved, I was a participating member of the human race. Unfortunately, though (or fortunately, depending on how you look at it), I just didn't have it in me anymore. I was tired. I was tired of the same old routine of meeting people, and I was tired of having to think about it. It was all the same, anyway. People, relationships, evenings, all fell into the same categories after a while. This woman reminds me of that one. This conversation is going like the one three years ago. This is what I should say now.

Pretty soon, it's like playing some video game you're tired of. It just gets boring. I could try this thing or that thing, but it all leads to the same place. And after a while, the monotony becomes too much to take and it's not just plain monotony but monotony laced with rejection and disappointment. I couldn't bring myself to do it. It felt like lifting a thousand pounds.

"I appreciate it, but I can't."

"Hey, man. It doesn't bother me," he said, walking away.

I paid the bill and left after that. It was pretty early, before even the first college kids showed up. The brunette didn't look at me anymore and it was clear that ship had sailed. It was just as well. And the Grey Man? I never saw him again. Of course.

< 3 >

Corroboration

The second time I saw a halo was a week later on Market Street at 9:30 in the morning. I was coming out of the Montgomery Street BART station with the throng of people rushing out into the heart of downtown San Francisco. I was remembering when that used to be me and the thousands of times I had been in a hurry to join a call or make a meeting. Why was I always so worried about being late?

On the long escalator ride, I started to go around the person in front of me and inadvertently stepped into a river of people speed-walking past us up the same escalator. The guy I accidentally cut off nearly ran me over from behind, knocking the phone out of my hands.

"Sorry about that," I said, picking up my phone. But he didn't hear me, he was listening to something other than actual life on his earbuds and looking past me with an impatient stare. Over his shoulder, I saw several other commuters casting condescending glances in my general direction. People in this city are so judgmental. It's one thing to appreciate about New York, actually. A New Yorker would tell me to go to hell on the spot and straight to my face, and then never give it another thought. On the West Coast, we express displeasure politely with "steely" glances and a look that menacingly says: I'm definitely going to tell someone about this later when you're not around. They say the differences in cultures are disappearing. I can promise you they're not.

As I looked into the long line of passive aggressive faces, I caught a glimpse of it – a halo – running past me, up the stairs next to the escalator. My head whipped around. Deep down, I knew I hadn't invented the Grey Man out of whole cloth, but the confusion of that night and the days since had caused doubt to settle in. But here, passing me on the stairs, was corroborative proof.

A suit from behind Earbuds Guy finally mustered the courage to say something. "Come on! Move!" he shouted. I snapped back to reality and darted up the escalator steps, two at a time, straining to see what I could through the crowd. The woman (it was a woman this time) with the halo was making good time up the stairs – she was in excellent shape – and I was straining to keep up.

In fact, I was unable to keep up. The halo, and the woman beneath it, disappeared at the top of the stairs out into the bright fogshine of the morning. I bounded off of the escalator moments later, making a concerted effort not to bump into anyone, and ran onto Market Street, with its red bricks and electrified overhead transit lines. I passed a guy carrying his bicycle down into the station, passed a homeless man with a few bills in a paper coffee cup and passed a throng of people walking while staring hungrily at their phones.

She was gone, though. I looked left, right, up, down, but the haloed woman was nowhere in sight. What had she been wearing? A suit, a navy suit. She was in her fifties, probably, thin, elegant. Short, streaked blonde hair. Had she slipped down the alley? I hustled over. Nothing there. Had she gone down New Montgomery? I ran to the corner. Didn't see her. Walked to Third Street? Not up that way, either. I checked into a couple of coffee shops, but I had lost track of her. I stood there on Market

Street, surrounded by people rushing past me, out of ideas, and caught my breath. I was at once disappointed and relieved. I had lost the halo, but found the evidence I needed to confirm my gnawing suspicions. All the doubt in my mind vanished in an instant.

After a few minutes, and with a couple of backward glances hoping to catch sight of the halo, I reluctantly turned and walked up Montgomery Street (so as not to be late to my meeting). I was meeting with a patent attorney to make sure we finally had enough information to file a provisional patent for Nina, a step I'd been working on for months.

A provisional patent is like a placeholder for an actual patent. It preserves your patent filing date (for one year), which could be important, and it doesn't need to be as detailed or thorough as a complete utility patent application. For this reason, it is also significantly cheaper. I wanted to show investors that I was making progress with my product, that I was moving forward with my business, but I needed to preserve my own money in the process. A provisional patent would, in theory, make Nina a more attractive investment, which would then make a utility patent easier to obtain (financially).

The law office was what you would expect from a small, boutique patent law firm in the City. It was modest but nice, with tasteful decorations carefully updated, nothing extravagant, yet still elegant. My patent lawyer, Ken, is a likable guy in his late 40s, on the short side, beard, smart man. He looked old for his age, though, with the telltale sign of dark circles under his eyes. Sometimes, I wanted to ask him why the hell he kept doing what he was doing, coming into the office every day, chasing work, chasing clients. The hours are impossibly long, the pressure and the stress incredibly real. He seemed like a decent guy and I wanted a better life for him.

It's the main reason that, after five years, I left the law firm where I first started practicing law. I looked around at all the partners and realized I didn't want their houses in Pacific Heights or vacations at the Royal Hawaiian in Waikiki. Their lives were consumed by billable hours and partner-associate leverage, chasing deals and clients, on and on for all of eternity. I saw their faces, the miserable stress wrinkling their skin, their heavy scowls during the long elevator rides, and couldn't figure out for the life of me who would sign up for a lifetime of that.

Ken's associate, Julie, didn't fall into that category. At least not yet. She was still relatively fresh-faced and bright-eyed. She was very pretty in a restrained way. Straight dirty blonde hair pulled back in a single ponytail, no makeup. Early 30s. East coast law school (I didn't ask her, I looked it up because professionally it's important), specialized in patents, which seemed like a strange choice for her. I asked her once why she didn't work in a more general intellectual property related practice. She said that patents are what interested her, but I couldn't tell if she meant it or it's just what she had told herself once she found herself working there.

"This is quite a product you have here," Ken said after we sat down in a small conference room. The views of the City weren't quite like you would get at a bigger firm with big budgets for first-class office space. There was just a slim shot up Sutter Street out of the window – no Telegraph Hill or downtown skyline. There was no burst of blue or grey from the bay.

"Thanks. I appreciate that. I've been working on it long enough."

"Impressive that a lawyer could come up with this," quipped Julie. "It gives me hope!" We chuckled. She reminded me of someone I'd met in the dorms at Cal. Everything about her beamed positivity and hopefulness except the calm expression she always wore on her face. It was something about her eyes, I guess? They seemed to turn down at the edges, so they counterbalanced and neutralized her smile. I wondered what she did for fun, what she did on the weekends (or the weekends she wasn't working, I should say).

"I think we have what we need with what you sent over last week," Ken said. "Julie is working out the details, but we should be all set."

"That's great," I said.

"You're hoping to try and raise money again once we get this filed?" asked Ken.

"That's right. Most VCs told me to check back in with them if I achieved any milestones. I've also compiled a list of other firms that are active in this space, either from checking on their website or through their recent investments."

Ken nodded. He had something to say and was trying to figure out a nice way to say it. I wish I could have told him that he could say anything to me, that I genuinely liked him, but it probably wouldn't have mattered. He was too busy trying to say something without offending me. "You mentioned that some of the feedback last time was regarding, uh, your background? Or a cofounder? Something along those lines?"

"Nobody believes a lawyer could invent something meaningful in the biotech space. I get it. The truth is that there is a lot more we can do once I find someone with the right technical background. But unfortunately, I haven't made a lot of progress there. I'm hoping that if I'm able to raise money, that will help."

"I'm surprised you can't lean on your network from BlueLabs," he said, referring to the cancer analytics company I used to work for.

This was a fair point. I knew dozens if not hundreds of people in the biotech field, doctors, engineers, the gamut. I had called some of them, of course, but nobody was willing to jump into an unpaid side project with a lawyer. Only Sid, an old friend of mine from Cal and a BlueLabs engineer, had entertained it. But, when I asked him directly, he balked at the idea of joining me and pursuing an actual startup ourselves. I pressed him on the topic, but was never able to convince him. To make up for it (I think), he had recently pointed me in the direction of some of the most useful databases and libraries that I had ever added to Nina.

There were other people who could have helped me, but the truth is that I was avoiding seriously pursuing it. I don't know if it was that I didn't want someone to criticize my work or if I didn't want to get distracted or veered off course with somebody else's stupid ideas. I wholeheartedly believed that I had the ability to get where I needed to go and I wanted to prove I could get there. I wanted to show that my idea had merit, that you could quantify your biological metrics using ordinary activity and that you could improve your health and your life on that basis.

"It's a valid concern. I guess I've been mostly focused on the technology. I'll get to the team next."

"I don't want to rain on your parade," he added, "And I'm sure you know this given your experience in the field, but you don't usually get unlimited bites at the apple. How many times have you gone out and pitched this concept, this product?"

"This will be my third time."

"Right. Eventually, those doors will close for good."

"You mean they're not serious when they tell me to keep in touch?" I asked. Everyone laughed.

Ken was one hundred percent right. VCs will tell you how much they love you and how interested they are, but the truth is that they're only really interested if they know everyone else is interested. Why is that, you might ask? Because they're dumb. Money is dumb.

There is even a saying in finance about this, which is to refer to certain investors as "dumb money." When people in tech and finance refer to dumb money, they are referring to non-professional investors or investors who aren't specialists in the field and, therefore, can be fooled easily because they don't know the right questions to ask. But the dirty little secret I've discovered is this: All money is dumb money.

Money eats well and sleeps at nice hotels. Money gets into the premiere and money gets front row seats. Money drives a Range Rover or (God forbid) a G-Wagon. It's exclusive, it skips the line and it avoids the crowds. Money likes nice sheets and a comfortable bed. Money likes those things so much, has grown so accustomed to the luxury it can acquire, that money does everything possible to keep itself away from the problems caused by its own scarcity. Because what money fears most, what keeps money up at night, is disappearing. And fear is a very powerful motivator.

Hungry, on the other hand, isn't afraid, because hungry is already fucking hungry, isn't it? What are you going to be afraid of losing when you don't have anything to lose? Money is afraid of hungry. Extremely afraid of it. So much so that money does everything possible to keep hungry at bay, to keep hungry down. The best way to do that, of course, is what money spends most of its time doing: Making more money.

It's precisely this fear of its own scarcity that leads to an incredible lack of originality. What would be the easiest way to make money? Copy it. Money copies money because if it tried something new, well, it might not work. Things that have worked before have a greater chance of working again, money tells itself. So money copies. Relentlessly, endlessly, tediously, monotonously copies.

There are two, maybe three, good ideas in Silicon Valley *all year*. That's it. Out of everyone. Out of the billions of dollars and millions of people in this place, in this giant enormous place, two, maybe three. Everything else is copied. Copy this. Copy that. Copy the user interface, copy the product flow. Copy the investment thesis. Create this derivative of this, make this similar to that. Copy the product, copy the market trends. Copy everyfuckingthing. It's all they do, all day, in their extravagantly elegant and beautiful offices. Copy, paste. Copy, paste. Copy. Fucking. Paste.

"I know," I told Ken eventually, "And that's a great point. I have a pitch set up in a few days, so maybe that will tell me a little bit. Either way, I really appreciate your feedback. I knew I came to the right guy."

I said goodbye to Ken and Julie and made my way back into the downtown air. It was late morning, almost noon, the clouds were thinning and the sun was threatening to make an early appearance into the San Francisco day. It's a beautiful city, but it is a gorgeous city when the sun is out and you don't have to be Emily Dickinson to appreciate dramatic beauty, even when constrained by industry, society and circumstance. So, I stopped in a coffee shop and ordered a Gibraltar. I stood to the side and watched the barista prepare my drink on a La Marzocco machine. He had a striking armband tattoo on his upper right arm and a handsomely shaped head with cropped, dark hair. He had probably spent ten thousand dollars to have someone draw on his body, and, in that moment, it made perfect sense to me. He called my name and I thanked him, grabbed my drink and walked back into the cool air, looking for a bench or somewhere to sit and enjoy the coffee and the coming sun.

San Francisco is not a big place, but it's still a city, with a sizeable downtown and hundreds of thousands of people who come in and out on a daily basis. But it's as quiet as any city you'll ever visit. Outside, during the middle of the workday, it felt like Christmas break on a college campus. A handful of people moved about noiselessly. A few cars moved quietly down the street. A couple of techies walked past me with their lattes, talking about product churn rates and "growth." (Normally, hearing the unabashed vernacular of tech on the San Francisco streets would have sent me into a mental tailspin, but I was feeling hopeful, if not good.)

That's when I saw the third halo get onto an escalator going back down into the BART station.

This time, I didn't hesitate. I tossed my drink into the nearest garbage can (no food or drinks allowed on BART) and ran to the escalator as fast as I could while fumbling in my bag for my BART card. I sprinted down the escalator stairs and came out onto the main ticketing level. I pressed my card against the gate's card entry reader, opening the gates. Once inside, I looked around feverishly and saw the haloed man, older, perhaps early 60s, heading down the internal escalator onto the train platforms.

As I ran for the escalator, I heard a train approaching from the north side. I had to hurry. I ran down the stairs, two and three at a time, past a few people (who were politely and neatly standing on the side of the escalator) and onto the platform as the train pulled up. It was a San Francisco Airport train, headed toward the south city and Daly City, the opposite direction from my apartment, but I saw the haloed man board, so I jumped on as well, two cars down from him.

The doors closed behind me and suddenly inside it was quiet again. The train pulled away from the station and I steadied myself and walked in the direction of the halo, holding out my arms to keep my balance. I used the internal doors to move down to the next car, less crowded than the first, and walked through it. I paused for a moment before going through the next set of internal doors. I was full of adrenaline and expectations, hoping to see the haloed man.

I was not disappointed. There he was, sitting in the yellow seats reserved for handicapped and elderly people. He didn't look up as I walked in, he didn't move at all, actually. He was staring into his lap, catching his breath.

The train was almost empty, perhaps seven or eight other passengers in our car. I sat two rows behind him. Nobody else in the car seemed to notice the halo or the man, and he didn't seem to notice me, so this time I studied him without remorse or hesitation. His halo was similar to the Grey Man's, but quite a bit brighter than the Navy Suit Woman, and he didn't look well at all. He was sweating and dabbing at his forehead with a handkerchief, into which he would also occasionally cough.

I took a long, close look at the halo. It shimmered and shined. It seemed futuristic or supernatural, with a radiance independent from its brightness. It was a white so pure it looked gold and there it was, hanging in the air, a few inches above his head, shimmering like a thin, circular lightsaber. I thought I could just walk over and touch it, but of course I didn't dare.

In my mind, he was a salesman, this man. He had on wool trousers, even though it was going to be a warm day by our standards, an ill-fitting long-sleeved shirt, and a jacket that was too big for the time of year. He had a likable face that had momentarily dropped its pretense. He looked tired, he looked like he did not feel well, and most of all he looked sad. He didn't pull out his phone, he didn't read anything, he just sat there as if any movement would cause him great discomfort. He moved only as the train moved and swayed when the train swayed.

After 15 minutes, the train emerged from its underground route through San Francisco and up into the fog south of the city. The Salesman got up as the train approached the Colma station and he walked towards the door. He held onto a handrail as the train lurched to a complete stop and the doors opened. He walked out, and when he did, I stood up and followed him, getting out just as the doors closed behind me.

I had been so distracted I hadn't even made sure I left with all of my belongings, and for a moment I panicked, thinking I had left something on the train. I took a quick inventory of everything. Bag – check, wallet – check, phone – got it. I breathed a sigh of relief and followed the Salesman down the escalator.

He was looking down at his phone and shuffling his way slowly out of the station and toward the street. I followed, but when the Uber pulled up in front of him, I realized my plans were foiled. All of the possibilities quickly rushed through my mind. The taxis that would have been waiting around the station five years ago were no longer there. An Uber would take several minutes to get to me, at best, and Uber doesn't have a "Follow that car" feature, as far as I remembered.

I briefly considered hopping on an electric scooter and just the thought made me chuckle. First of all, I (thankfully) don't have any of those apps installed on my phone and even then, those things must max out at 10 or 15 miles per hour. I pictured myself crouched down for aerodynamics on a brightly colored scooter, zipping down the street at 12 mph, losing sight of the Toyota Prius as it wound its way through the pulsing streets of sleepy grey suburbia. A modern day Charlie Chaplin. There were no other options.

I stood helplessly on the sidewalk as I watched the haloed salesman step into his ride, close the door, buckle up, and drive (noiselessly) away. The car drifted down the street, past the shops and sidewalk cafes, over the sloping hill of the avenue and down into the day.

Where was he going? Why was he coughing and sad and cold? And, most importantly, why did he and the Navy Suit Woman and the Grey

Man all have halos? Where were they coming from? Could anybody else see them?

I was about to find out.

< 4 >

The Changing Light

The next morning, I decided my best chance of seeing more halos was going back to the City. Around my Oakland neighborhood, I probably saw no more than 10 or 20 of the same people every day. I might see a handful of different individuals at lunch or dinner, but in a lot of cases, these were the same people over and over, as well. Same thing at McNally's. Seeing the halos in San Francisco made me realize that I needed to maximize the number of people I saw to get to the bottom of this mystery. I planned on venturing back into the City after lunch for an afternoon of walking around.

While brushing my teeth that morning, I stared closely above my head in the mirror. There was nothing there (except the reflection of the wall behind me). I looked for any evidence of a halo, but there was none. No light or luminescence, no golden white brightness, nothing. I moved my hand slowly back and forth over the space where a halo might be and studied my hands during the process. They were completely unchanged.

I spat out the toothpaste and drank cool water from the faucet. I cupped my hands under the water and splashed it on my face and ran my hands through my hair. I turned off the faucet and lifted my head, looking at myself in the mirror. The water glistened on my skin. I looked good, I thought, for myself anyway, and I took pride in my appearance and in taking care of myself. I examined my face and looked closely at my skin, my eyes, my hairline. It all looked...good, pretty good. I was just past 40, but I thought maybe I looked younger than that and this recommitted me to my project and to self-improvement through quantification and analytics.

I got dressed and prepared a supplement mix recommended by Nina, I had the feeling that she was getting to know me. She wasn't recommending food I didn't like (pork, squash) and wasn't telling me to do things I found annoying (pilates, which is like yoga for yuppies). I had made sure to tap Nina into a wide variety of methods and strategies for self-improvement. There were dietary recommendations, behavioral and exercise recommendations, and lifestyle recommendations, in addition to vitamins, minerals, supplements and even medication.

I wasn't sure whether to attribute Nina's recent advances to the newly incorporated AI or the novel databases and libraries that Sid had obtained for me. It would have taken me decades to amass the kind of information that was already neatly assembled in these massive files, carefully documented by scientists somewhere. Some of the information was open source, meaning that it could be freely used by anybody, and some of it was proprietary, but in those cases, Sid had helped me obtain a test license for very little money. Finally, there was a category of more exploratory (beta) information that he tapped into, where I was an early adopter. Either way, I recently noticed a marked change in the suggestions made by the Nina engine, particularly with certain products that I needed to research and order online, obscure supplements that I had never heard of, and the like.

I was hoping Sid's involvement would be enough to pique his interest in joining me on the Nina project full-time. He was the kind of guy potential investors love to see, Cal undergrad, a Masters from Johns Hopkins. I needed someone like that on my team, as Ken had hinted, but Sid had said that, at this stage in his career, it wasn't the right move for him. He wanted to focus on his earning potential, and given the kinds of salaries plus equity that biotech firms were throwing at people like him, I couldn't blame him. He ended up at BioTechM, one of these ridiculously well-funded biotech companies focused on medical devices.

Sometimes you will hear executives or older "wise" men (and it's always the men) say things like, "Smart people want to work on exciting projects. They don't care about the money." Those people are fucking liars. Everybody in this business cares about the money. Maybe it's not the only thing they care about or even what they care about the most (even though it usually is), but who doesn't want to be the next Steve Jobs, someone admired as much for his innovation and talent as for his wealth? Stories of the friend of a friend, one of the first dozen employees at some hot startup, who made millions and retired in their thirties, are ubiquitous around here, and people are chasing that dream.

There was still a ton of work to do on Nina, obviously. In general, all of the finer points were shit. The user interface was non-existent and all user-facing components needed to be far more robust. I needed to make the recommendations easier to comprehend and contextualize, so a user would get feedback that explained everything in a way that made sense. But the engine was there. The product was working. And I was collecting data and fine-tuning the algorithm. I felt good.

When my eyes glossed over from the code, I worked on my investor presentation. My first pitch meeting was in two days and although I was optimistic, I wanted all of my materials to be flawless. I had seen, worked on and watched hundreds of these investor presentations in a support role and now it was my turn to drive. I hired a designer to create a minimalist background design for the pitch deck and picked a font that was serious but not boring. I selected the most compelling information to present, careful not to jam too many words or numbers onto any one page. I felt like I was ready.

Even as I focused on Nina that morning, my thoughts never wavered far from the halos. I was excited when it came time to head out and optimistic about what I might discover that afternoon. I knew immediately I had picked a good day to venture into the City. The cloud layer was burning off and it was getting warm. The sun will come out in Oakland hours before it does in San Francisco, so it was a harbinger of the good weather to come across the bay. Seventies and sunshine. There's nothing like it. Days like this are a reminder of why so many people want to live here. You can write all the articles you want about the "next" tech hub, but none of those places have our weather.

I saw Juan Pablo, my across-the-hall neighbor, leave at the same time as I did. He waved to me and smiled and I lifted my hand in response. Although we had lived in the same small building for almost two years, I had only spoken to him a handful of times, and briefly at that. He was an Argentine guy, worked in tech after getting an MBA at Stanford. He had a senior position in the finance group of some software company, having previously worked at one of the big investment banks, as I recalled.

I ducked down the street as he got into his car and pulled away. I thought of driving, myself, but I owned one of those new electric cars and while I enjoyed driving it, I wasn't yet totally familiar with everything it could do. At times, I felt like I was driving a computer more than a vehicle and it made me nervous to leave it parked in San Francisco all day. Plus, I needed to be on foot, so, I took BART into the City again and got off at the first stop, Embarcadero, and as I always do if given the chance, I headed for the water.

The changing light of San Francisco
is none of your East Coast light

That was Lawrence Ferlinghetti, of course, not a native San Franciscan, but we've gone ahead and given him the honorary degree. He was right about the light and I have a theory that it starts with the water. Depending on the time of year and what the sky looks like, the bay can give you brilliant blues, greens or steel grey. The water itself varies. It can be choppy, still, murky, muddy, dirty or clean and clear. Sailboats are out almost any time of year. Ferries go back and forth to Oakland, Alameda, Vallejo, Marin. Cargo ships are piloted under the Bay Bridge. I could watch it for hours. And I have.

Once in San Francisco, I walked to the Ferry Building. This was in the years before the pandemic, so there were still a good number of people loitering and literally lying around and the health and hygiene was, shall we say, lacking. Inside, I walked amidst the locals and tourists, through the coffee shops and the bread stores. No sign of a halo, but I didn't mind. I was having a good time perusing the shops and people watching, something I rarely (never) did.

I grabbed something to eat and walked back outside. The last of the fluffy grey and white clouds were thinning out, dissolving with the sunlight, and whisping away with the wind. The sun would be out any minute. I took off my sweatshirt and looked at the water. I turned north up towards the piers and then I cut back inland to visit Lawrence's neighborhood, walking up the Greenwich Steps toward North Beach and heading to Coit Tower.

San Francisco transplants have a habit of bragging about never going to the landmarks of the City, places like Coit Tower and the Palace of Fine Arts. I have it in for those people. Imagine someone in New York saying, "Oh no, I *never* go see shows on Broadway," like it's some kind of badge of honor. Or a Chicagoan bragging about how they never go to the lake. It would never happen. San Francisco attracts its own special kind of asshole.

You think the Beat poets avoided spending time in Coit Tower, with its Depression-era WPA murals depicting the labor movement and life in the cities? Give me a break. I imagine those colorful cats sneaking in a bottle of something, spending an hour or so discovering some new, hidden part of the murals, and then going home or to some park and pouring their soul onto a blank piece of paper. Most people hate poetry because they say it's dense, obtuse, indecipherable or boring. But what could be more dramatic than expressing yourself publicly as clearly and concisely as possible? I stood there, at the base of the tower on top of the hill, with its incredible views of the Bay and Alcatraz, and thought of what Lawrence had to say about it.

The light of San Francisco
          is a sea light
                    an island light

Yes. After a momentary reminiscence, I left Coit Tower, walking into North Beach, and stood in line for a coffee next to City Lights. I chatted with the person behind me (something I never do) about the flower arrangements across the street in front of a little shop. I got my coffee, raised my cup to Lawrence's memory, and walked back outside. I meandered through the neighborhoods, turning randomly up and down different streets until all of the two and three-story apartment buildings felt like home again. I walked for another hour or so through the neighborhoods, without any luck on the halos front, and then decided I needed a change of pace, so I headed down Leavenworth toward Market Street.

Leavenworth Street runs all the way from the Marina to Market and cuts through about five neighborhoods on the way, but the name has only ever meant one thing to me: the Tenderloin District. The Tenderloin has a higher sketch factor than any other neighborhood in the City, and one of the highest in the Bay Area. Anything goes here, all day and every day, and this is where I finally arrived. There were people hustling around, opening stores, catching busses. There was the usual collection of homeless and drug addicts and people who didn't fit neatly into the Venn Diagram of those two populations.

I turned a corner and finally saw what I came to see: another halo. This time, it hung over the head of a fairly overweight man in his fifties, big and tall, wearing a red jacket and jet-black shoes. He had a big bald head with a small crop of nearly completely grey hair around the sides. I was neither surprised nor caught off guard by the halo this time and I immediately got on his tail and followed him into a corner market to get a better look. I stayed a comfortable distance behind him as he fumbled through the medicine aisle, flipping past pain relievers, and grabbed a bottle of something I couldn't quite make out. His halo was the brightest I'd ever seen. It was so bright I wondered if it would somehow turn into flame and burn this rickety store to the ground. The Red Jacket Man walked to the cashier, breathing heavily, paid and left, hastily shoving his wallet and change into his front pocket on his way out the door.

I followed him down Ellis Street, where he walked into a five-story brick apartment building on the corner. He was struggling a little bit as he fumbled with his keys and stood for a long moment at the door. I watched from across the street and glanced around to see that nobody else seemed to notice this man, which is not saying much for this part of town. Eventually, the Red Jacket Man disappeared inside the building.

I thought of walking over and seeing if I could get in, but I wasn't sure what that would get me. "Excuse me sir, may I observe you?" So, I decided to stay put. I wasn't going to let this opportunity pass me by. There was a little joint across the street from his building that served food, so I grabbed an aluminum chair on the sidewalk and began my vigil. I pulled out my phone, put some headphones on and fiddled online while keeping an eye on the front door of the apartment building.

About an hour passed and I was starting to get hungry. I was weighing the pros and cons of ordering a sandwich from the place when the sound of a siren in the distance caught my attention. This isn't New York. You don't hear sirens on an hourly basis and this particular siren was getting extremely loud. So loud. So much for the silent city I thought and covered my ears as a fire truck drove past me.

Only it didn't drive past me. A small, red medic unit fire truck stopped right in front of me. When its siren turned off, I heard a second siren approaching. The paramedics got calmly out of the truck while a young woman emerged from the Red Jacket man's apartment building and anxiously held the door open. The firemen walked in, calmly, confidently, yet seriously, the way only a fireman can do. A few minutes later, an ambulance arrived and they, too, went inside.

Then, silence again. I was alone and noticed I was on my feet now, though I didn't remember standing up. I started pacing the sidewalk. I thought of buying a bag of potato chips, but I wasn't hungry anymore. I stared at the firetruck, the ambulance, the buildings, the walls, the trees. It seemed like hours went by. I looked for different exits through where they might have gone. Had I missed them? I checked my phone and local apps related to emergencies to see if I could determine what was happening inside.

When they finally emerged from the building, I couldn't believe what I was seeing. The entire group was somber. The paramedics were pulling a body on a gurney. A white sheet covered it from head to toe. An older woman, not the young woman who had held the door open earlier, was walking behind the gurney in tears, sobbing, crying out vocally and screaming in a way you would only hear in a neighborhood like this. Behind her, the firemen came out and walked slowly back to their truck.

A small crowd had begun to gather on the street and I felt myself crossing over and pushing past them. In a daze, I walked past everyone and right up to the gurney, surprised by how easy it was. It was so easy. Next thing I knew, I was standing next to the lump of a cadaver. I wasn't thinking logically or consciously, I was just acting on instinct. Could it really be what I thought it was? Did I know all along what it would be?

"What are you doing?" I heard a voice say. I had my hand on the gurney at that point and felt the soft texture of the sheet and the hard rubberized cover of the cushion underneath it. Other voices rang out, but I ignored them. With the flick of my arm, I cast aside any doubt and uncovered the impossible answer to everything right there before me.

"What the fuck are you *doing*?!" It was a voice loud enough to ring through to my senses.

"You animal!" screamed the crying woman.

"Who the fuck are you, man?!" came another voice. And then others yelling various recriminations at me.

It didn't matter. I barely heard them anymore, anyway, the buzzing in my ears had become so loud. I was jostled as I backed away. The paramedic covered the body back up. A fireman as big as the building itself, and with gear that weighed as much as I did, stepped in front of me, saying something that was threatening or lecturing or both, but I didn't hear. I didn't care. I saw what I had needed to see. I saw it for only a moment, but it was enough. It was indisputable.

Beneath the sheet, on the cot, I had seen it. I looked down at him and there he was. Motionless, sunken, transformed in a way, but the evidence was indisputable. I saw the red jacket. I saw the jet-black shoes. It was him, laying there on the stretcher, still and lifeless. His halo, gone. The Red Jacket man, dead.

The enormous fireman yelled something more at me and pushed me back, hard. I reeled backward, off the curb and onto the street, backpedaling, stunned and adrift

anchorless upon the ocean

< 5 >

The Lonely Man

I have only one rule for bars in San Francisco: They must be on a hill. It doesn't have to be a steep hill or a long hill, and it doesn't matter what side you're on — going up or going down. A simple incline will do the trick. I'm not saying there's not a single good bar on flat ground in the City, it's just my rule and it's always served me well. There's something about walking onto a flat floor from a tilted street that will settle the mind.

That's exactly what I needed at that moment – something to slow me down – and I knew immediately I had picked a good spot. There are bars for drinking early and bars for drinking late. There are bars for drinking alone and for drinking with big groups of people. There are bars for starting the day, bars for lunchtime and bars for finishing the day. This particular bar was a bar for drinking a lot and that's exactly what I did.

The bartender was perfect. He was in his 30s, black t-shirt, short dark hair and skinny arms. He wasn't short and he wasn't tall and he wasn't at all surprised when I finished my first drink before he had time to put the bottle away. He hit me again and watched me closer this time to see if he needed to keep the bottle out, but the first drink calmed my nerves enough for me to slow down. He relaxed a bit and put up the bottle and got back to restocking.

I can't really express how dumbfounded I was to see that first dead body, even though I'd had a sinking suspicion in the back of my mind that this is where it would lead me all along. It seems extremely obvious in retrospect, of course. They were halos after all. But there is a difference between suspecting and knowing, and the truth, the terrible truth, had revealed itself. I needed to come to terms with it. I knew that immediately. I don't remember walking or stumbling from the corner to the bar, but it didn't matter. There wasn't far to go.

So, death. Death. That is where the halos had led me. But why and for what purpose? I quickly waved that thought away. There is no purpose. Funny how we always default to fate and that kind of weak-minded thinking. There was no point in it, in any of it. But there could still be meaning and the meaning is what I needed to focus on.

I went over what I knew about halos in my head. They had been around since the Greeks and were present in other cultures before being adopted in full force by the early Christians. I was used to seeing them in pre-renaissance religious paintings, not around real people, though. My art history knowledge was not spectacular and I sat with my phone for a bit and did some cursory research.

I asked skinny arms for another drink and he obliged. "You play guitar?" I asked stupidly. He nodded. "You?"

"Not a chance," I answered, and he laughed.

Four halos, three of whom looked particularly unwell, and the subject of one of them was now confirmed dead. I could easily imagine two of the others, at least, would have already or would soon meet the same fate. The Grey Man and the Salesman both looked to be in pretty bad shape.

Struggling. The halos, then, could be some sort of harbinger of death? That seemed to be the likeliest explanation, as impossible as it sounded.

The woman in the navy suit looked fit and healthy, though, double timing it up the steps as she bypassed all of us tools on the escalator. She was probably hiking around Fort Funston by now. It was possible that the Red Jacket Man's demise was some kind of coincidence. What if there was another explanation? And why was I the only person who appeared to see them?

I looked around the bar. There were two tech bros at a table in the corner who were consoling themselves about why their careers were in the shitter. They seemed to be coming up with every answer but the one they were pouring down their throats. Asshole bosses, incompetent colleagues, unsympathetic wives, you name it. Pour me another drink, though, while the sun's still out, there's time to get back to the office later.

San Francisco used to have a real personality that had nothing to do with technology. It was based, I don't know, on the gold rush, of course, and the 1906 earthquake and the Navy and the war. That was the foundation, but it was also the 49ers (football team), the hippies and the free movement, flowers in your hair, Tony Bennet's heart and it was the Castro. It was foggy mornings and cold summers. It was the Presidio, Ocean Beach and Alcatraz, tourists wearing sweatshirts in July and locals wearing anything (or nothing, perhaps). It was Haight Ashbury, Golden Gate Park and North Beach. It was the Embarcadero Freeway, which everybody hated, and which the '89 quake finally took care of, and it was Market Street and the Mission. It was all of those things.

I remember the first time I heard a conversation on the street that I was used to hearing at the office. I was with my cousin having coffee near the Panhandle and two people at a table next to us were talking about stock options in their new startup. It was shocking. I was very used to hearing the words but I was not used to them being said outside, blocks from where the Dead and Grace Slick used to spend time expanding their consciousness. It felt sacrilegious.

Now, it's uncommon not to see people like that everywhere, in the markets and in the bars, on BART and Muni. Everywhere. Like zombies from the apocalypse, infecting every bit of the City until they overwhelmed the living soul of everything. It became an entire "dot com" city overnight, it seems like, and the very people complaining about it the loudest (like me) were a significant part of the problem.

But these two guys who had moved into my city without knowing any of this were not going to help me solve my problem. I had to get back out to where there were people, where there was life and death. There was no chance I would find the navy suited woman, I guessed, but I needed to confirm my hypothesis. Ok, it wasn't a hypothesis yet, it was a supposition. I didn't want to create a hypothesis as chilling as that one if there could be a different explanation.

I paid skinny arms and stumbled out into the bright day like a kid walking out of a mid-summer matinee. My head was positively humming with chatter and sunlight and vodka as the bricks passed quickly under my feet. I gained steam as I walked down the hill toward crowded Market Street and past the homeless people begging for money, sleeping off a bad trip or trying to keep what was left of their lives together. I passed the tourists piling into the shopping malls, past the bakeries and the mediocre restaurants that wouldn't last 5 years, past the glitzy tech shops that didn't pretend to be established, all beneath the offices and bank buildings of the old world.

I was all the way down Market Street before I knew it, without passing a single halo, and found myself in the ferry building again. I caught the ferry to Oakland for a nice change of pace. The bay was invigorating, as it always is, with the late afternoon sun bouncing off the waves. It cleared my head and gave me energy. I love passing underneath the shadow of the Bay Bridge on a sunny day as the seagulls swoop and glide lazily around. People stood on the deck of the ferry taking pictures, taking in the sunlight. I made a note to myself to take the ferry more often even though I knew I wouldn't do it.

Back on the Oakland side, I walked past the new, vibrant waterfront restaurants in Jack London Square, past the original cabin of Jack himself, built in the 1900s, and then stepped into Heinold's First and Last Chance Saloon for a pick-me-up. There aren't a lot of bars over 100 years old on the west coast and they should be visited often. Christina, my ex-girlfriend, had turned me onto this joint and I found it funny to be passing it now. Ernesto Sabato said there are no coincidences, only destiny, so I walked in, sat down in the dark and surprisingly crowded interior, and ordered a drink.

I had come in a lot during those 2 years and 8 months of my life but now it was just a pit stop. Marx said that religion is the opiate of the masses, but he would've said the same thing about love if he hadn't been so fucking unattractive. Who was going to get with that guy and his crazy ass beard? Sure, he was probably married, but did they love each other? Did she enjoy picking food out of that mass of facial hair? Anyway, love, religion, whatever. It's what some people need to believe in to justify other unhappy things in their lives.

I paid my bill and walked outside, surprised to see it was almost dinner time. I walked uptown, turned on Telegraph and started walking the fifty something blocks to my apartment. Christina, the Red Jacket man and halos were all playing in a loop inside my mind as uptown Oakland gave way to Pill Hill and I approached Temescal. That's what was so compelling about Nina, about quantifying the status of your body and health. Science is just that, it's science. Two plus two is always going to equal four. You're not going to wake up one day in a bad mood and discover that two plus two equals three and a half that day. It is what it is and it will always be that. It's math. It is objective. These are facts. They are knowable.

Not like this mystery before me, I thought. But as I passed near the MacArthur Bart station, I saw another halo which snapped me out of my mental machinations. A brightly lit one that hovered over an old, quiet man. It surprised me the least of all of the halos I had seen. Perhaps I was getting used to them.

The subject of this halo was walking past a homeless encampment under the freeway and even though I was in no condition to undertake any scientific observations, I immediately followed him. He was an African American man, could have been anywhere from 60 to 80, I couldn't tell, and he was hunched over at the shoulders and shuffled his feet so that he was barely picking them up at all. He seemed to move without making a sound. He was entirely distant, his eyes were elsewhere, his expression was somewhere else and so were his thoughts. What this man radiated more than anything was solitude. He was completely alone amidst the people and the traffic and the busses and the trains, moving as though in his own bubble of thought.

From the sidewalk, he turned in at a very old and rather undesirable looking motel on MacArthur, just a block from the BART station. The reddish building had a sign in front that said "Rooms Available" and "Internet" the way old motels would advertise cable tv or air conditioning. The small, 2-story, U-shaped building had maybe 12 rooms and surrounded a parking lot with just three cars in it. It was a throwback to another time in Oakland and I was sure it had been there before both BART and the freeway.

But it was a dump now. The Lonely Man walked up to one of the rooms, all of which faced the street. He stood at the door a while, opened it, walked in and closed the door behind him. I walked over slowly, looking around the area to see who might be watching. Nobody. The brown door to his room looked like I could have knocked it over by blowing on it, but it did prevent me from seeing inside. The curtains were obviously closed.

Other than the bus stop across the street, there was no place to sit and watch the door. There is a lot of traffic at the Macarthur BART bus stop and I didn't want to be distracted or miss anything, so I went inside the office and got a room on the ground floor for forty-five dollars.

The inside of the dark room was not so disgusting as it was just old. It smelled like grandparents and the fabric on everything was worn to the point of thinning completely through. I didn't care, though, because I wasn't planning on living there. I opened the drapes, turned a stuffed, re-upholstered and lumpy chair towards the window and watched.

Hours passed without a word or a sighting of the Lonely Man. I had a pizza delivered and after the delivery driver handed me the box, he stood looking at me, then looked around the motel, then looked back at me.

"There were no rooms at the Claremont," I said and he didn't get the joke. But he did get the hint and left quickly.

When the sun set, the Lonely Man's door opened and he shuffled slowly outside. He was holding a folded, nylon patio chair, the kind with fabric that made criss cross shapes. This one was white and blue and the nylon material was badly fraying. He, opened it up, set it down outside his door and sat down.

He could've seen me if he had looked across the parking lot, but he wasn't looking. He sat down and his face and his eyes pointed toward the street, but he wasn't looking there either. I had never seen anyone so completely lost in their thoughts. That's not true, he wasn't lost in his thoughts, he was found in them, he was there on purpose. He knew exactly where in his thoughts he was and he visited there frequently, he lived there and not in this old motel on Macarthur.

He sat motionless for hours as the sun went down and evening came over Oakland, hands clasped in front of his face, then hands on his lap, one hand on his chin. Back and forth, slowly, with his thoughts. I finished my pizza and watched him. It felt like I was watching a long, compelling piece of performance art. I imagined the Lonely Man as a father, a husband, I thought of different things he might have done for a living. I imagined him having successes and failures, maybe starting his own company, a car wash, for example. And I imagined people leaving him one by one until finally he ended up here, on a loud corner of a dodgy street in The Town across The Bay. After it had been dark for a while, he pulled up his chair and slowly walked inside, closing the door behind him.

That was the last time I saw him. The next morning, the Lonely Man was dead. I woke up before 5 a.m. to the flickering lights of an ambulance in the parking lot in the twilight. They were loading his body onto the truck when I walked outside. The door to his room was open and I peered in. He must have been living there for quite a while because the room was full of stuff, clothes, boxes, suitcases and things spread out all over the floor and the counters.

"What happened?" I asked the paramedic.

He looked at me a bit surprised to see me there. "Passed away," he said, very matter-of-factly.

"From what?"

"Natural causes," he shrugged.

"Vernon was 86 years old." I turned around and an old, overweight woman was standing on the balcony in a robe, the door to her room open behind her.

"Eighty-six?" I said aloud.

"Eight-six. And now at last he can go be with all his people. He talked about them all the time. His wife. His children. All gone. Everybody gone. Now he can go be with them."

"Amen," came a man's voice from inside her room. "And with the Lord."

"Amen," the woman replied. "He with the Lord now." The woman turned around and walked back toward her room, nodding her head slowly and saying something to the man inside.

I had a sort of clarity, a terrible clarity in that moment of finding what I had been looking for and what I was terrified of finding all along. I went home without even going back into my room. Once there, I collapsed in my bed and fell instantly asleep.

Somewhere in that morning, I dreamt I was visiting one of those nursing facilities or retirement homes. I walked in but there was nobody in the lobby. The reception desk was empty and there was nobody behind the counter. To my right, I saw the backs of several people walking shakily down a dimly lit hallway. An attendant or a nurse of some kind was pushing an old woman in a wheelchair along worn-out carpet. An even older man walked slowly behind them. I followed them down the hall as they walked through a set of interior double doors and into a dining room.

It was breakfast time. The dining room was full of people, sitting at tables with red trays, juices and coffee, some were lucid and others not.

Some were hunched over, barely moving. I looked around in amazement and awe. I stopped counting. I couldn't count them all, it would have been impossible. There, in the dining hall, floating in the air at every table, there were dozens and dozens of halos.

< 6 >

The Pitch

The next day, I had my first investor meeting for the new Nina. This was my first pitch with a functioning prototype. I was caught between excitement for my project and visions of halos and the people I had seen. I was enthusiastic about my hard work and good prospects, but haunted by the Lonely Man's eyes, walking down the street, sitting on his motel porch.

I wrestled with these thoughts but eventually came back to the fundamental point–I couldn't let it interfere with my life, my work. Not now. I had finally gotten Nina to the point where I could legitimately raise money and ramp up the project and the company the way I had always hoped, the way I had laid out. It felt like I had real momentum. Everything else was just a distraction and I needed to focus.

How could I explore the halos further, even if I wanted to? What would the next step even be? I had to live my life. I had priorities. What I needed was progress on my ultimate mission–to quantify what is happening inside of our bodies and guide myself, guide everyone to a more healthy and potentially happy life. The halos would have to wait. Or maybe they would go away. Or maybe the answers would present themselves. In any event, it was clear, I had to move forward as planned with Nina and figure out the halos if and when I could.

That morning, I showered and shaved, though I'm not sure why because nobody cares about facial hair anymore, and put on a collared shirt, though I'm not sure why because entrepreneurs aren't supposed to get dressed up anymore, either. Old habits die hard, though, and it was hard for me to give up the "business" in business casual. I still remember when my dad would wear suits to work every day. I remember sitting with him as a boy as he shined his shoes once a month. I would watch him carefully, trying to learn and memorize a craft it turns out I would never use. I had imagined a future where I was an engineer, like him, and I wore suits and tie clips and polished my shoes in the morning before heading in to the office. I would never have believed in a future where engineers wore shorts to work and tennis shoes that didn't need to be shined. I probably also would never have believed a future where my dad would leave me to be raised by my grandparents, but that one happened, too.

I made the one hour (non-rush hour) drive across the bay on the San Mateo Bridge and the sudden change in architecture and surroundings helped me focus on my upcoming meeting. Maybe it was just the energy of the place, driving by the offices of stalwart tech companies and shiny new office buildings. Silicon Valley, or the Peninsula, as we call it, is home to the highest concentration of venture capital wealth in the entire world. Also, it's home to the highest concentration of douchebags in the solar system. The richest few people in this area have as much money as half of the entire population on the other end of the spectrum. And they didn't inherit any of it, as they like to tell you (wink, wink). They made it. Quickly.

The dirty secret is that very few of these people would have made any of their money without at least some financial help from a friend or relative, but let's not be impolite here. It's true that this lightning fast accumulation of staggering wealth is the staple currency of the entire Bay Area economy. It's what makes it tick. No, it's what makes it hum. And the pride of this New Money isn't difficult to suss out. People are very proud of what *they* accomplished, of what *they* did, how much money *they* raised.

At the offices of PA Bio Ventures, I was greeted politely and led to a sleek, modern conference room in the middle of the ground floor. Not many tall office buildings in this part of the Bay Area. Eschewing the ostentatious style of Old Money, Silicon Valley money is displayed in an entirely different style than in New York. You won't see the massive marble entry ways or the ornate, dark wood and dark leather conference rooms. Here, you've got minimalistic design, lots of light, and clean lines. Simple, New Money says, snubbing its nose at Old Money. It doesn't take generations and the exploitation of millions to accumulate wealth, New Money says, snapping its fingers.

Marc with a "c" was a perfectly nice and respectable human being, even for a venture capitalist. He walked in with a big smile. "It's nice to see you again, Drew," he said as I stood up. He shook my hand with a firm grip, looking directly, but non-threateningly, into my eyes.

"Thanks for making time to see me," I replied.

He looked impeccable. He wasn't classically handsome, but he was nice to look at. Every possible physical feature that could be improved upon had received very specific attention. His teeth were right out of a Colgate commercial, as white as a snowfall in Lake Tahoe, where he probably owned a second home. He had a perfect, hundred dollar haircut, a smooth face from regular facials, and manicured and buffed fingernails. He had probably been an athlete of some kind, playing baseball or lacrosse at his Ivy League college.

He was dressed, without any irony, in khakis, a long sleeve collared shirt and a sweater vest, the official, unofficial uniform of venture capitalists. All of his clothes looked tailored to fit him exactly, without being too tight or fitted. His shoes were less than a month old and completely uncreased. He radiated success and confidence, like he could reach into his pocket and pull out a wad of hundred dollar bills, and then reach back into the same pocket and come out with another identical wad as they regenerated in his pocket in perpetuity.

We chatted as we got comfortable sitting around the table and I set up the presentation, some people we knew in common, a partner at my former law firm that had done work for PA Bio Ventures and the like. We talked about some former colleagues at BlueLabs, where PA Bio had been an early investor and he asked me about things in Oakland, an exotic location when you're on this side of the Bay. It seemed strange, the two of us sitting alone in this immense conference room, but Marc was extremely comfortable and this relaxed me. I projected my presentation onto the big screen and he leaned back in his chair as if settling in to read a book or solve a puzzle and his eyes peered at the screen curiously, but with a healthy dose of standard VC skepticism.

I went through the usual initial slides about the problem I was intending to solve, the addressable market for my product, competition and other standard boilerplate VCs want to see. Marc listened politely. After a few minutes, I arrived at the part of the presentation that focused on Nina. The moment had finally arrived. I was in the exact situation I had been waiting for, anticipating, for months. Rehearsal time was over. This was the big show.

"Last time we met you said you wanted to see me build a prototype," I began.

"And?"

"I'm happy to report that I have a fully functioning prototype. And the first user: Me."

I clicked over to a slide showing some of the initial sample test results Nina produced, along with the associated product recommendations I had received, focused on diet, supplements and exercise.

"Interesting," Marc said, leaning forward.

The next set of slides focused on the backend engine that had produced the product readouts and the database where a user's information was stored, including the recommendations that had been provided over time. I clicked through the deck slowly, giving him a chance to see the evolution of information in a way that made sense, and at a pace that would give him plenty of time to read. I was confident, but nervously and anxiously awaiting his feedback.

"You built this yourself?" he asked.

"Yes, I did. I think I told you last time about my background in programming?"

"I remember vaguely."

"It might not be typical, but it's been enough to get me here. Of course, I'm just building the product layer. The recommendations come through a sophisticated combination of medical databases, libraries and other resources."

"So, this is a medical device."

"Not exactly..."

"Well, it's going to need FDA approval," he interrupted. "That could take years."

"It's possible we'll need FDA approval. I'd say that remains to be seen. I would argue that the key product feature here is the software program. It's the combination of biological information from the user with the available medical information and a layer of artificial intelligence that learns to fine tune the recommendations over time."

He looked at me and then back at the presentation. "How can you be sure that urine is the right substance to analyze? Won't a blood test tell you so much more?"

"Who wants to get a blood test?" I answered, using a line I had thought of and rehearsed a hundred times. "Nobody likes it. On the other hand, we urinate all the time, every day. In addition, urine is the byproduct of the greatest filter ever invented, the kidneys. They filter toxins and other biological substances which makes urine ideal to analyze and assess subtle changes in your body functions. I can show you medical research that proves that many disease markers appear in urine *before* they appear in blood and frequently before symptoms occur. Plus, it's seamless, it's part of us and who we are already. Urine analysis is completely non-invasive, and once Nina is integrated with the toilet, people won't even know they're using it."

Marc nodded, and then continued after a moment. "Tell me about the AI," he said, the way some interviewers might ask you to tell them a little about yourself.

"Well, I'm just one person. I'm not a data engineer and even if I were, I couldn't build it in the amount of time I've had." I said and paused. "I licensed an AI engine and built my application on top of it."

"Licensed from whom?" Marc asked. "Microsoft? One of the open source companies?"

"No. I looked at those, but I ended up going with a startup product. It was easier to work with and had a lot of the interfaces I was looking for."

"Why would you do that? Why would you put yourself in the hands of a startup?! What if they go out of business? What if they pull the license?"

The urgent tone of his voice made me panic somewhat, I'll admit. My pulse quickened notably, but I tried to remain calm knowing that he was making an error in judgment that he would surely soon identify. "Pull the license? Why would they…Look, the AI is just a layer, it's not the entire product."

"But it's a layer in the product you're trying to get me to invest in right now. How do you know the output wouldn't be different if you used a different AI? It could affect everything."

"I…I… Look, AI or machine learning isn't the secret sauce here. It's not a secret how to tell machines to extrapolate and learn."

"Still," he said. "That's risky."

"Risky," I repeated. "Risky." My anxiety was making me go a bit off script and veer into some emotions bordering on anger. I was thinking about that word and what it meant. What is risky? What did Marc know, sitting at this conference table that probably cost half a million dollars, about risk?

"This is the opposite of risk," I heard myself say with more disbelief in my voice than I intended. "Risk is not knowing about yourself. Risk is not knowing what you're doing, what you're eating or drinking, and how it is affecting you, your sleep, your activities, your brain, your life. Nina will change all of that, all of it, in a completely seamless way that's integrated with your life and normal activities.

"You can't control your feelings," I added without thinking. "You can't control your mind. But you can control your body. It's physical. It's real. Palpable. There's a science to it. It's like math. Right now, we could, in theory, know everything that's going on physically inside of you, your proteins, your amino acids, how that affects your heart rate, the level of blood in your oxygen. And…and, this is no small thing, what you can do about it. Today. Right now. What you can do to fix it. To make it better. Improve.

"Maybe you can't control different things going on in your life. Maybe what's left of your family sucks. Maybe your best friend from college doesn't talk to you anymore. Maybe your girlfriend cheated on you after three years or you think you see weird shit everywhere you go. But this. This. This you can control. Your body. Your physical being. And we can optimize it, optimize your health, so you can be the best version of yourself you possibly can be."

Marc was looking at me intently, he was looking into me, past my eyes, with his hands clasped together in front of his face. He sat for several seconds like that as my words hung in the air. At least I knew better than to keep talking.

"Well, that's very compelling," he said finally. "I like the way you think. We invest in founders, you know, not just companies or products, but in people. We invest in people we believe in."

"Good," I said. "I'm happy to hear that."

He sat for a moment, quietly thinking, contemplating some unknown (to me) thoughts, conflicts, ideas, opinions. And when he started speaking again, I waited to hear more along those lines, more of the catch phrases of interest that are bandied about in these parts like spare change. But there wasn't more. Not for me, not that day. Instead, he started talking about PA Bio Ventures and their investment philosophy and how they add so much value to their portfolio companies. After a moment it was all just background noise as I let the facts settle in. He sat there, calmly, his mouth was moving, but I wasn't sure exactly what he was saying.

Marc with a "c" was blowing me off. I had been to enough meetings to know this. He liked me or he liked something, at least, had heard something, perhaps, but there was none of the typical follow-up actions, bringing in additional members of the team, setting meetings, discussion of a term sheet, plans for the future. After a few minutes, he stood up and thanked me for coming. He shook my hand and showed me more of that perfectly symmetrical smile. He walked me to the door and said goodbye.

I drove home in silence, replaying the meeting in my mind and how he had reacted to various things. Where had I gone wrong? What could it have been? Was it the medical device issue? The FDA? This is something Sid had mentioned as well, but if Nina was delivering, wouldn't it be worth it? Was it the AI license? That seemed like a silly thing to focus on. Maybe Marc understood less about software than I thought.

After a while, I started mentally going over the list of other investors I put together and reprioritizing them in my mind based on my meeting with PA Bio. It couldn't just be a standard MedTech fund, maybe I needed more of a tech fund that had some crossover into bio sciences? Names slid up and down in rankings in my mind as the miles ticked by.

When I got home, I needed a drink, but I didn't feel like seeing anyone I knew. I went to the Golden Bear on College Avenue so I could at least watch people playing darts. It would be a distraction, even if it was a little too bright in there and the food was nothing to write home about.

Four drinks later, with my mind endlessly replaying the presentation and Marc's comments, the college crowd had completely taken over the

Golden Bear. With them came the miscellaneous collection of happy people looking for a good time. Normally, I would have left by then, but that night, I felt even more invisible than usual amidst this collection of happiness and hormones. I needed to be alone in the company of people and the collective sound of all of that conversation. The loud drone of the voices had a soothing effect on me (along with the alcohol).

Marc with a "c" was just one investor, I told myself. There were others. I hadn't really anticipated rejection, as silly as that sounds, because of how much I believed in the project, but I had sent out other emails, made some connections and thought I could set up some other meetings in relatively short order. I could do that while staying in the top tier of VC firms, and if that didn't work, I would continue on to the second-tier firms and so on. What did I care how I raised money? People talk about having the "right" investors, but I can produce a list just as long of successful companies that didn't have them. In fact, perhaps a longer list. The "right" investors only mattered if you were a shit company. Great companies can succeed with an investor that produces dollar bills, which is to say any investor.

Amidst this sea of thinking, as if in the background, I could hear the soft sound of women's voices and female laughter. I was looking up to order another drink as the bartender set down a bowl of house popcorn on the bar next to me. I reached for it instinctively and my hand hit the bowl at the exact same time as the soft hand of the woman sitting next to me.

My eyes went from the popcorn to her light purple painted fingernails, up to the slender wrist with a small tattoo of a rose on the underside, then up the rolled-up sleeves of a loose-fitting white blouse, up to the shoulders, the long, straight chestnut-colored hair, and finally to the smiling face and bright brown eyes of the woman sitting next to me.

"I'll arm wrestle you for it," she said.

I laughed.

"Oh look, Kelly, a smile." She turned to her friend. "I think that's the first one in 45 minutes." Kelly laughed.

"Yeah, I'm not exactly known for that," I replied, straightening my posture and trying instinctively to pay attention to reality after hours of being lost in my head.

"What are you known for?"

I laughed again. "I'm not sure yet."

She smiled a big smile and said, "I'm Susan," and held out her hand.

"Drew," I said, and shook it.

She was all smiles and positivity. I felt suddenly perkier just from her attention. As she shook my hand, smiling, her eyes went over me from top to bottom, quickly, unobtrusively, but without question, lingering on my face, my eyes.

She was light as a feather, it seemed. Her mannerisms, her expressions, her clothes, her friend, the drink in front of her, everything looked like a good time. She caught me completely off guard and drew me in by some indescribable aspect of a magnetic personality. There was no question that Susan made friends everywhere she went and left a good time in her wake.

She opened her mouth to say something to me and I could feel myself getting ready to laugh. I let go of her hand somewhat reluctantly, but observing appropriate etiquette, and my focus shifted from her face to her whole aspect, wide angle if you will. And as her voice rang out with a clever quip, that's when I noticed it. Clean and bright, clear and unmistakable, there was a bright, beaming halo glowing steadily above her head.

< 7 >

Small Coffees

I'm not super proud of what happened next, but it's not like I would change anything, either.

The halo threw me off at first. "What do you keep looking at?" Susan asked me, looking over her head and behind her.

But the intensity of the distraction didn't last very long. "Sorry. I keep glancing at the dart game over there."

"You play?"

"A little. I used to."

"We'll be back," Susan said to Kelly, standing up, and she walked over toward the dart boards with a bounce of her hair but without looking back. For her part, Kelly simply laughed and shook her head. I couldn't help but smile, too, as I got up to follow Susan. She was funny, confident. I hurried to catch her and then walked slowly behind her as we weaved through the crowd of people. As I did, I got a good, long look at the halo over her head, just to make sure it was really there. There was no denying it.

She grabbed a short piece of chalk and scratched our names for next game on the small chalkboard in the corner and we chatted while we waited. She was in marketing, worked in tech, lived in the City and was out visiting her friend, Kelly, who lived in my neighborhood. She had been there before, but not too many times. She liked Oakland. Did I? What did I like about it? What did I do? What kind of product was I working on? That's so interesting.

The whole time we chatted, I had a river of thoughts flowing through my head. Of course that happens all the time, but this time the river was louder and more evocative than usual. She didn't seem to be sick. She was more like the Navy Suit woman than the Lonely Man or the Grey Man. She wasn't a smoker, she didn't seem to have any bad habits. I wasn't going to ask her if she'd been to the doctor lately or anything, but it didn't really make sense. Then again, none of it made sense. Could Susan really be about to die?

I had two competing, although not necessarily conflicting, feelings fighting for position in my brain as we waited for our first game. The first was an intense morbid curiosity. Here she was, a person with a halo. I had spent the better part of the last few days looking for people like her. Here was my opportunity to learn something about a subject I was keenly interested in. That feeling came with some moral or ethical baggage, however. I liked Susan far more than most people I tended to meet at the time, and I was uneasy treating her as some sort of experiment.

The second feeling I had was that I liked her. Plain and simple. The more we talked, the more free and easy I felt around her. I found that I wasn't second guessing anything I said to her. I wasn't concerned about the ramifications of our conversation or of taking a position on something that I might later change my mind about. I wasn't thinking about being intellectually inconsistent. I wasn't comparing every little thing about her to Christina (something I did for years after that breakup). All of the usual things that had been keeping me from having easy interactions with women were gone. It was just her and I and the conversation we were having right then, at that moment. It was liberating and those feelings combined with her face and her voice and her personality were literally exhilarating. I felt almost like I was walking on air.

After a while, I forgot about the halo entirely. She made me laugh and she made the people around us laugh. When it came our turn to play (Cricket), the first dart she threw was a triple 20. The small crowd around us erupted in cheers. She was a ringer, and even though I played darts regularly in college, she carried us to victory in the first game and there's no telling how many more after that, laughing and having a blast the whole time. We never lost.

We closed the bar down and stumbled back to my place, laughing more. The alcohol had done away with my earlier moral conflicts and besides, I didn't even ask her to come home with me, it's just what we did. It was natural. It's what was going to happen. I had lost track of Kelly and wasn't sure at all what had become of her, but it didn't matter and Susan never seemed interested in finding her.

"I love the Craftsman architecture," she marveled, as we passed a little white house with a quaint garden on the walk home. "It's so different from the Victorians in the City."

"They're very solid," I added in agreement. "This style is super trendy now," I said, pointing out a freshly sanded brown shingle, two-story house. She nodded approvingly but then made fun of the fact that it shared a driveway with the house next door. "At least they have parking," I said and she laughed.

A few minutes later, we were standing at the front door of my apartment as I fumbled with the keys. I opened the door and motioned for her to go in first. "Oh, I love your apartment," she said, stepping in. She dropped her bag on a table and just as I closed the door she turned around and kissed me.

The kiss was everything I would have hoped for if I had hoped for that kind of thing back then. We kissed for several minutes right there at the door. Hard, deep kisses, the kind that I hadn't experienced in years, and I felt a rush of things in me that I had long before forgotten.

Was it wrong? I've asked myself that a lot since then. At the time, when the thought did creep into my head, I didn't have an answer. There didn't seem to be a way to broach the topic logically. "No. Look, stop. You're about to die," seemed like an awkward conversation starter. And everything I thought of saying ended with her walking abruptly out of my apartment.

Instead, we stumbled back into my room, shedding keys, phones, layers of clothing. She was laughing. I was laughing. We were having a great time and I was enjoying it tremendously with only perhaps a small, but gnawing sense of guilt, inside me. I was starving for human touch and intimacy and the caveat that it was somehow based on false pretenses felt like a technicality. I wasn't doing anything wrong. There was no non-crazy way to address the situation. I was no good at enduring human relationships and a kind of loophole had presented itself to me and I intended to explore it.

We fell back onto my bed with more laughter and more kissing. Of all the things going through my mind, I hadn't given a single thought to my messy apartment, how I barely ever made my bed anymore, the fact that I hadn't cleaned my bathroom in months, Nina equipment being everywhere, the mess at my work station, the living room, what was the last channel I'd had on my TV, the blinds – were they opened or closed? None of the usual things I would obsess about constantly were concerning me. It was just a sort of light exhilaration. I allowed myself to get lost in the moment with her and eventually my only thoughts were of her face, her neck, her skin.

It felt fantastic to touch someone and be touched by them. I'm not going to pretend I'm some sort of amazing lover or anything, but it felt natural. It felt like what people did and I could understand why. And when it was over, the softness of her body next to mine felt incredible with the distant sound of traffic on Telegraph Avenue, and darkness. We fell asleep like that.

In the morning, I woke up with the twinge of a feeling that I had gotten away with something. There was a note on the pillow next to me. It said, "Went in search of big pastries, small coffees. Back soon." A heart, and her name, Susan. The heart was loopy and full, with the two lines at the bottom overlapping a bit. Her name, so alive there, on the paper, stood out to me so clearly.

The sun was coming in through the windows and I laid there for a moment thinking about the night before, processing everything. I was smiling, happier than I remembered being in years, but I began to worry a bit again about the implications of everything. I wondered if the halo would still be there when she got back and I tried to imagine ways in which I could bring it up that wouldn't make me sound like a complete lunatic. Some time passed and I got up. I went to the bathroom, used Nina, and stood there eating an apple while I reviewed the results.

I decided I would tell Susan about Nina when she got back, to see what she would think about it and maybe ask her some questions. Maybe she could use it? No, that would throw everything off. Nina wasn't set up to be used by anyone else. I would have to establish an entirely new user profile and while that seems trivial, I didn't even have Nina set up to understand different users and segregate information like that.

But I could create it.

I pulled out a piece of paper and sketched the architecture of what a user-based system would look like within the program. It wasn't complicated, but I still needed to map it out so I could understand the implications, where things fit, how they would interact and so on.

When that was done, I sat down and immediately set to work on coding the user system. This would be tremendous. It would give me a head start on something I needed to do anyway, and I would be able to conduct my first experiments on a second user. Dozens of ideas flowed so quickly through my head, I had to start jotting some of them down on a side pad of paper. I casually wished I could replicate myself ten times so I could make progress on all of the different work streams as quickly and efficiently as possible. Maybe that was another product idea.

Susan seemed genuinely interested in what I was doing. Maybe she would have some interesting ideas for Nina given her experience in marketing. Marc with a "c" was going to really regret blowing me off, I was sure of it. And, most importantly, perhaps we could figure out what was causing Susan's halo and maybe she could get to the doctor and do something about it? Certainly there was something that could be done about it. I couldn't type fast enough. The programming was coming out of me faster than a sentence in English normally would.

As I worked, I started to feel the gentle pangs of hunger coming on, at first as though only in the background, as though I was just hearing about it second hand. When that feeling got stronger, I wondered what kind of coffee Susan would get. Would she walk to Philz for some pour-over coffee or Cole Coffee for some dark espresso? Maybe she was more mainstream and would go to Peet's. They were all on the same block on College Avenue. She'd be able to choose whatever she wanted. But given the "small coffee" clue, I guessed she would go with Cole. It would be the most original choice to go with in the neighborhood.

I was coding faster than I had since I first started working on the program. Occasionally, I would laugh to myself thinking about how

Susan would react to Nina, in general, and to different usage aspects. She was sure to come up with something funny. It had been a fun night. Something about her made her easy to be around and so she was pleasant to be around. It wasn't complicated or high maintenance. There was no second guessing of anything. Everything just flowed.

I was starting to feel hungry in earnest, and I needed coffee. I wasn't sure how long the line must have been at Cole, but it seemed like Susan was taking a long time. I looked up from my work and realized that somehow it was 10:30 a.m. Susan had been gone for almost two hours. I stopped coding and stood up at my desk.

I looked in the dining room and her purse was gone, as was her sweater from the night before. This was natural, though, because she would need her purse to buy coffee and it was always chilly in the morning in the Bay Area as anyone who lives in San Francisco would know. Or had she had second thoughts and just left? That seemed unlike her. But I didn't even know her so what the hell did I know?

I looked around and couldn't find anything else belonging to her, but I was convinced she wouldn't just leave and not say goodbye. Finally, I threw on some jeans and a sweatshirt and walked out without even brushing my teeth. My mind was still focused on the user profile program and different work streams were flying through my mind when I opened the front door.

The cold morning air went right through me. I stepped off the porch and sensed immediately that something was wrong. Everything seemed different. There was no flow to the street. There was no movement on the block. And the moment I turned to walk east, I knew why.

About a block and a half up, there were cars stopped on the street, hazard lights on, and a group of people congregating on the corner. I started quickly up towards College Avenue, walking faster and faster until, finally, I broke into a kind of jog. I got to the corner and saw three police cars and an ambulance parked in the middle of the street, blocking access. The police had blocked off the street with yellow tape. Dozens of people stood by, watching.

"What happened?" I asked the first person I reached.

"I don't know. I can't tell if that woman was hit by that car or what."

"I don't think she was hit. I think she fell," came another voice. But others thought she may have been hit before she fell.

There was a general sense of confusion and so I went to get answers for myself. I walked past one group of bystanders after another, onto the street, past an officer taking measurements and over to where paramedics were loading a gurney onto their ambulance.

There's a sound that coin-operated machines make when the internal mechanism releases the inserted coin, just before the machine performs whatever function it was designed to perform and the coin drops into the collection basket. That's the sound my mind was making when I saw Kelly across the street. She was in a sweatshirt and sweats, standing next to a man I didn't recognize, crying and talking into her phone, her eyes red and swollen. She probably wouldn't have recognized me even if she saw me, but she didn't see me.

A police officer was on the street taking measurements and writing things down in a small notepad. Below him, on the street, a small bag of pastries lay in a circle of white chalk. Likewise, two cups of Cole coffee, now empty, on the pavement. A Honda Civic was stopped in the middle of the street, the driver of which appeared to be talking to the police.

The body on the gurney was covered from top to bottom with a white sheet. Only an arm hung down from the covered body. At the end of the arm, just under the slender wrist was Susan's small rose tattoo.

The first thing that occurred to me was that I had meant to ask her what the tattoo represented or what it meant, but I never got the chance. And now I never would.

＜PART 2＞

< 8 >

Mick

I slinked away from the scene without talking to anybody. You could blame me for that, I suppose. It crossed my mind for a brief moment to approach Kelly and talk to her, but what would I have said? And who was the guy she was with? I didn't see how I had any information relevant to any kind of investigation and my involvement, or the mere sight of me, might have only served to hurt people Susan cared about. There was no turning back the events that occurred on the street that morning. I was only entangled through some metaphysical or cosmic anomaly of some sort.

I walked the short distance back home in somewhat of a state of shock about what had transpired and the way it all unfolded. I can't say I was completely surprised, of course. The moment I saw the halo, it seemed like a *fait accompli*. There had been some element of uncertainty, maybe, but it felt more like watching a movie where someone had already spoiled the ending. Only in this movie, I got to sleep with one of the characters, I guess. It's an imperfect analogy, but my point is that I didn't understand my role in all of this and I felt kind of like an innocent bystander, or a bystander in any event, not a protagonist. I'm not trying to rationalize my behavior. I'm only trying to explain my actions.

I got back to my apartment and looked around. It was so empty. It felt more empty than it had ever been, even the day I moved in. What was worse, or better (I couldn't decide): There was no evidence Susan had ever been there. Had she ever been there? I looked around.

I instinctively ran my hand along the dining room table and fumbled among the things on it searching for something of hers. There was nothing. I went into the living room looking for her sweater, for discarded clothes on the floor, but there was nothing. So much had happened – in many ways I felt like a different person – but where was the proof? I went back into my room and the rumpled sheets on my bed and the scent of her perfume on my pillow were all I needed to confirm what I knew to be true.

I laid there for a moment enveloped in her sad perfume. All those questions I might normally have had – when should I call her, when is appropriate to text, etc. – were mute now. There would be no second date (was there a first one?), there would be no letting someone down or being let down by them. It was just kind of over in a clean break that didn't hurt anyone's feelings. Clean breaks were never my specialty, but there I was. It was a clean break in a way. We'd had a relationship, and now it was over. It was tragic, of course, but it wasn't unexpected. And it happened.

I sat up in bed. I still hadn't eaten, though I couldn't say I was still hungry. It felt like there was something I should be doing, but there was nothing to do. What I sensed in myself was an urge to be with other people, which was an unusual feeling for me in those days. So, I got up and changed my clothes methodically, half expecting to hear a knock on my door that never came. I brushed my teeth and washed my face, still waiting, but for nothing, and finally finished getting ready to see about possibly getting some food, even if it was just a bite.

I opened my front door, which led to a small interior hallway in the fourplex, and then to some stairs down to the exterior door. My upstairs neighbor, Juan Pablo, had his front door open and so I reflexively looked into his apartment. He was sitting down on a chair in his living room, facing in an awkward direction toward the wall. This caught my eye and I paused there for a second in the hall and before I realized what I was doing and could walk away, he looked up.

"Hey. There he is!" Juan Pablo looked at me from his chair with a big grin.

"Hey, Juan Pablo. How are you?"

"Good. Good. But the question is, how are *you*?"

I hesitated for a moment, unsure what he was talking about. Well, actually, I kind of had an idea of what he was talking about, but I wasn't sure how he could be talking about it and I was hoping that's not what he was actually talking about.

"It got pretty loud over there last night, if you know what I mean," he said at last.

I must have blushed or had some other expression that gave me away.

"Alright! I knew it! You are the man!" he said, standing up. He walked over and stuck out his hand to shake mine.

"Okay..." I answered, still pretending I didn't know what he was referring to but doing a bad job of it. When I shook his hand, he grabbed my hand, held it up, and high fived me. It was extremely uncomfortable, but somehow I seemed to be trapped in an unexpected conversation with my next door neighbor.

"Don't play dumb with me, Drew. We live right next to each other. I hear everything."

"It's not a matter of playing dumb," I began.

"There is nothing to be ashamed of," he added. "It's natural. It is all natural. I am honestly very relieved. I was beginning to worry about you."

"Why would anybody worry about me?"

"Dude! You are never with anyone. You live by yourself. And I don't just mean that you have your own apartment. I mean you live your entire life by yourself."

I was completely taken aback. I opened my mouth to say something, but no words came out. Before I could think of anything to say, he spoke again.

"Where is she?" he asked.

I hesitated. Susan. "She had to leave."

"Okay, well I'm very happy for you."

I looked nervously around his apartment hoping at least to change the subject. It was then that I noticed he was holding a small, wooden mousetrap, the kind you can buy by the dozen at the hardware store, and at the foot of the chair in which he had been sitting was an open jar of peanut butter. In the corner of the apartment, staring intently into the closet, by his chair, was the orange cat that lived next door, Wanda.

"What are you doing?" I asked.

"Ah, fuck. Wanda brought a mouse in here," he said, walking back to his chair. "She dropped it right here to show me, but it was still alive and it ran in my closet. So now," he said, sitting down and returning his focus to the mousetrap, "I'm trying to get rid of the mouse." He tried unsuccessfully to set the trap and it slammed shut, just missing his fingers.

"*Hijo de puta*," he said. He struggled several more times to set it, but each time the trap slammed shut with a loud snap. Snap. Snap!

"Don't do that," I said finally.

"What?"

"You keep making the trap go off."

"I'm trying to set it."

"You're going to scare the mouse."

"Scare the mouse?" he asked.

"Yeah, it keeps hearing the snapping, it's not going to go for the peanut butter."

"You're crazy. It's a mouse, dude."

"So what?"

"So, it doesn't know what the snapping is, obviously," he answered. "It just smells the peanut butter and when it's quiet and dark it will go get it."

The mouse trap snapped shut another time and I felt like I might snap myself if it happened again. I don't know why it was bothering me so much. It's not like Juan Pablo is a bad or noisy neighbor, in fact, he was an exemplary one. "Not if the peanut butter keeps snapping at it," I answered.

He just waved me off and tried again to set the trap. "I'm not a mouse expert, personally, but I don't see another solution."

The mouse trap snapped shut again. I couldn't help myself and walked into his apartment. "Look, if you were really hungry and you saw a McDonald's, but then you saw a huge explosion in the building, would you go eat there?"

"I wouldn't eat at McDonald's. We hate McDonalds in Argentina."

"Shut up, I've been to Argentina. There are McDonald's everywhere. People flock to McDonald's like it's the sacred wall."

"And like with the sacred wall, they're mostly tourists."

"That's ridiculous. I've eaten there. It was full of Argentines."

"Well, maybe. But it's not cool to eat McDonald's in Argentina."

"It's not cool to eat McDonald's here either," I said. "Unless you're like 7 years old."

"Yeah, dude, but it's an American company."

"Well, so what, so is Disney, but that doesn't mean that that's Mickey fucking Mouse in your closet."

He just shrugged at me and went back to looking at the trap, turning it over in his hands and studying its mechanism. He was a handsome guy. The way the light was coming in through the window highlighted his dark brown hair, light white skin and blue eyes. He had a beard that looked at once scruffy and thin, like a young man might have the very first time he grew his facial hair out. I crossed paths with him several times a week, every week, but this seemed like the first time I had ever looked at him closely and it was without question the longest conversation I had ever had with him.

He suddenly stopped fidgeting with the trap and sat still. Then he looked at it closely, set it down, and then looked over at me. "I didn't know that, by the way," he said. "How come you never told me before?"

I shrugged.

"What were you doing in Argentina?"

I sighed. I looked back at my front door, still open, and thought of closing it to keep Mickey out. I looked back at Juan Pablo but didn't even know where to begin. I hadn't talked about it in years. "My dad lived there. He moved there with his girlfriend when I was in high school."

"Holy shit. You were living with your mom, then?"

"My mom died when I was three. I was living with my grandparents."

He paused for a long time. "Fuck dude. I'm really sorry. Is that why you never talk to me?"

"Don't take it personally. I never talk to anyone."

He nodded and seemed to understand, which struck me as incredibly compassionate at the time. But I was at a loss as to what to say next and, in fact, for the first time, neither of us were sure about what to do. We both looked at Wanda, who was staring intently into the closet. There were no other sounds coming from behind the half-open closet door.

"Do you think it's dead?" I asked.

"Wanda doesn't think it's dead."

"I think she's upset that it got away," I said.

"She's a cat, dude."

"Cats can't be upset?"

Juan Pablo looked up at me. "It's just that animals don't feel emotions the way people do. She's not upset because she made a mistake. She just wants the mouse."

"You're probably right," I answered. I looked around his apartment. It all suddenly looked so interesting, so connected to another life. He had a few pictures on his mantle, different faces, little decorations. I at once wanted to leave, but didn't want the conversation to be over. I wanted to be with people right now, but not necessarily him, or maybe him and I didn't know and I wasn't sure how to go about it exactly.

"Can I show you something?" I asked him suddenly.

"Of course, anything."

"Here. Come to my apartment."

"I don't know if I should take my eyes off the mouse."

"You don't have to watch the mouse. You can just look at Wanda. That mouse can't take half a step without Wanda knowing about it."

"But it's not your closet, dude. I don't want Mickey living in my house."

"It's just going to take a minute."

"Okay, but only because it's you, Drew, and you have never invited me inside of your tiny apartment before, even though I live like 2 meters from you, and I take this as a very significant step in our personal relationship."

He was a funny guy. That made me laugh and he patted me on the back as we walked across the hallway. "See, that wasn't so hard," he said.

We walked into my apartment and, at his request, I showed him briefly around, even though we have the exact same fucking apartment. After remarking about this obvious fact, that our apartments were mirror reflections of each other, and after commenting on the set up in my kitchen and everything from my espresso maker to my cups to the tea kettle on the stove, he followed me to the bathroom.

"This is Nina," I said, showing him the product.

"You mean *niña*?" he asked.

"No. It's like that, but it's 'Nina,' without the *ñ* thing."

"Oh, okay. Nina."

"Right." I explained the project to him and he seemed genuinely interested and asked questions in a way that boosted my confidence. It felt good to talk about Nina to another person who wasn't a lawyer or a venture capitalist and I realized that this was probably almost the same conversation I was going to have with Susan, but here he was, Juan Pablo, my neighbor for the last couple years with whom I seldom spoke.

"That's so cool, Drew. Really cool. And at least now I know what you're doing in here all the time. You're on the toilet!"

I laughed. "You're pretty funny," I said stupidly.

He smiled. "Thank you for showing me, really. That's very interesting." He started to head back to his own apartment.

"Look," I blurted out, in a way that was totally uncharacteristic of me. "I started creating a second user account earlier. When I'm finished with it, I...I would really like it if you could use it. And help me out."

"Is this important to you?" he asked.

"It's my life."

He paused for a moment but then continued walking back into his own apartment. "I hope that toilet thing is not your life, dude. That is a terrible symbol."

I walked after him, surprised by his frankness. "What do you mean? Don't you think it would be useful to know everything in your body right now. You can get a machine that will tell you everything that's going on with you and what you need."

"It's my own body. I know what I need."

"No, nobody does. That's the point. This machine can tell you if you're sick or if you're getting sick or if you've slipped off your diet or if you're doing great. You can know so much more about yourself."

"I don't need more information about myself. I am already me!" he said, with his hands out and a huge smile, as if saying hello to the world.

"You don't think you need to go to the doctor?"

"The doctor, yes, but not the toilet. Ok, well, yes, I go to the toilet, but I don't want it to give me a goddamn consultation. I just want it to do its job."

"I think you're missing the point."

"No, I think *you* are missing the point," he added. "I knew you were...what would you call it? Eccentric. But I had no idea."

I followed him into his apartment and we both noticed immediately that Wanda was gone. He looked at me and I at him and then we both heard a quiet sound in the closet as if something was moving slowly, items rustling as they were being pushed gently out of the way. Then another sound, another step, and another. Then there was the very brief sound of a scuffle, some soft and muffled swatting and a faint squeak.

We both watched as Wanda walked out of the closet, tail high in the air, meowing, with a grey lump in her mouth. She stopped in the middle of the living room, meowing loudly, and once again set the lump in the middle of the floor. This time, it didn't move.

"Oh no!" Juan Pablo said. "What is she doing?" He was looking around, unsure what to do.

I wasn't ecstatic about the sight of the mouse, either, but at least it wasn't my apartment. I walked backwards without taking my eye off the thing, closed my front door, and then walked back into Juan Pablo's place. "I think cats do this sometimes. Play with their prey, you know."

"But not in my apartment!"

Wanda was staring at the mouse with a detached bemusement. She lifted her paw and swatted it again. The mouse moved its head back slightly, but it had nowhere to go.

"It's still alive," Juan Pablo said. "It's breathing."

Wanda stared at it, then nudged it until it moved ever so slightly, then she swatted it again with a thump. The mouse cowered underneath her.

"Go get me something," I finally said, walking into his living room. "A bag. Something!"

He ran into his kitchen and came back with a sack and a paper towel.

"Give them to me," I said. I put the paper towel over my hand, opened the sack and walked slowly over to Wanda, who meowed again as I approached.

The mouse was indeed alive, but it looked very weak, and very much as though it had accepted its fate. Moving quickly, I bent over and used the paper towel to gently scoop the small, grey mouse into the sack, then

I quickly folded the top of the paper sack over to prevent Mickey from escaping.

"Got you," I said.

Juan Pablo gave a huge sigh of relief and walked over and gave me my second high five of the day. We walked outside into our common backyard with Wanda on our heels. He asked me what I was going to do with the mouse. "I don't know. I'm making this up as I go along," I said.

When we got outside, Wanda jumped to the top of the side fence between our yard and hers, gave a look back, and then disappeared over the fence.

"Thanks a lot, Wanda. Come back any time," Juan Pablo said sarcastically. "That fucking cat comes over every day. This is the first time she brings me a present."

"She never comes to my apartment," I said.

We looked around the backyard and Juan Pablo led the way to our back fence, which abutted a small, grassy field. "Here," he called to me. "This is a good place."

I walked to the back fence and looked over. There was nothing in the field except tall grass – one of the few undeveloped lots left in Oakland, it seemed. I looked up to check, and there were no birds in the sky, either. This was going to be as good of a place as any.

Bag in hand, I reached over the fence, turned the bag over and gently unfolded it. I shook it slightly and Mickey dropped without a sound into the tall grass. It sat there for a moment without moving.

"*Andate boludo*," Juan Pablo said. Mickey sat in the grass, cowering, as if expecting more thundering cat fire paws. When none came, it moved, at first a little, and then in earnest and it burrowed between the blades of tall grass and then was gone.

"I forget what that word means," I said to him. "*Boludo*."

"It means a lot of things."

"Really?"

"Yes."

We turned back to our yard and stood there in the sunlight and looked around. Our landlord always did a great job of taking care of the garden and there were a few rose bushes and other late season flowers in bloom, contrasted against the deep green of the ivy on the fence and the green of several other potted plants. We walked into the middle of the yard. Everything looked fantastic and it was warm with only a few puffs of white clouds in the sky.

"Let's make an *asado*, dude," he said to me, suddenly, as if he had just had the best idea of his life.

"Really?" I answered.

"Yes, it will be amazing. It will be just like home. We will go and get meats and red wine and bread and it will be fantastic. You will see. I am an excellent chef."

Perhaps I was hungry, after all, and I had wanted company. Normally, I would have avoided one-on-one situations like this at all cost, but that day, it didn't seem like a bad idea. It had the added bonus that I would be near my apartment and if things got awkward or for whatever reason, I didn't feel like staying, I could just go into my place and close the door.

I agreed to the *asado*, which is kind of an Argentine way of saying a barbeque, and we went to a Uruguayan butcher shop in Berkeley that Juan Pablo said had the best meat in the East Bay. He had a long, animated conversation in Spanish with the butcher that I only partly understood. We left with what seemed like half a cow and some other animals. We bought wine at Vino, this perfectly acceptable wine shop on College Avenue and a baguette at La Farine, and came back to the apartment where he set up a grill with wood charcoal and cooked more meat than two people could eat in a week.

We talked about the places I had been to in Buenos Aires, how my dad had told me that moving to Argentina with his girlfriend was his one true shot at happiness and how I would love living with my grandparents. Juan Pablo was furious in a way that surprised me, but which I found oddly comforting. He told me about his family back home, their apartment in the Palermo district and their house in the country. And he told me about his frustrations with living in the Bay Area as both an expatriate and a Latino.

After we finished the bottle of wine, I went in and got another from my apartment and we did our best at putting a dent in the grilled meat he had amazingly prepared, different cuts of beef and sausage. Delicious, every bite. After we had eaten, my phone buzzed. I looked at it and saw it was a text from Marc with a "c."

"Hey Drew. We just got out of a meeting to prepare for Monday's partner meeting and I have some bad news. I love your idea and your progress, but I don't think I can get the partners on board. We're going to pass on Nina for now. Best of luck."

"Fuck that guy," Juan Pablo said. "Who sends a message like that by text?"

Exactly, I thought.

"Look, if it's important to you, I will do the pee thing. I will use your machine. And you will find another investor. You'll see. That machine is going to be fucking amazing, dude. I totally believe it. And fuck that guy."

I thanked him and after we cleaned up, I excused myself and went back inside my apartment, surprised that it was past 7pm. It felt like a lifetime had passed since I was sitting in there 36 hours prior, getting ready for my meeting with PacBio. So much had happened. It was exhausting to think about.

I sat down at my computer and opened it up to continue working on the second user profile program, because that's all I did in those days was think of Nina. But my heart wasn't in it. I was full and a little bit dizzy and very tired and oddly happy. But mostly, I was exhausted. I closed the lid of my laptop and sat down on my couch, staring at the wall. Familiar words came to mind.

> *I know that I shall meet my fate*
> *Somewhere among the clouds above;*
> *Those that I fight I do not hate,*
> *Those that I guard I do not love;*

That was Yeats and his lyrical and melancholy expression of a perhaps depressed Irish airman who foresaw his own death in World War I. Maybe it was like that with Susan. Maybe what happened didn't matter for its own sake. Maybe it was just part of something bigger, some element in the universe of which we were all apart. Some sort of destiny. It was hard to make sense of it all.

I fell asleep on the couch and woke up around 2am when a car passed in front of my apartment blaring music at levels that are clinically unhealthy for human ears. I got up sleepily and walked into my bedroom. I didn't bother changing clothes. I laid down on top of the sheets and was back asleep, as they say, before my head hit the pillow.

‹ 9 ›

Windows

I woke up the next morning determined to get back to work. I was feeling reinvigorated, like I had been given a new opportunity to refocus on the task at hand, and hungry. After my usual Nina analysis, and with the blessing of her results, I had a small piece of sausage Juan Pablo had wrapped for me from the night before and an egg white omelet. I ate in the kitchen, looking out of the small window over the kitchen sink, and drank a cup of hot black coffee. When I was done eating, I poured myself another cup and took it to my work station.

I sat down at my desk and resumed coding the multiple user system. At first, I struggled to focus and push the events from the previous morning out of my mind, but it got easier after a while. I worked for several hours without taking my eyes off the screen or my hands from the keyboard. There was so much to do it felt like I could work for a week straight without stopping, and this kept me focused and productive.

I made myself a sandwich for lunch and then spent a few hours working on the business side of the project. I pulled up my spreadsheet of potential investors and reorganized them according to my train of thought from the drive home from PacBio. I researched a few of the firms, focusing on particular partners I had identified, and added other firms to the list. I sent emails to the next five investors on my priority ranking and then worked on the presentation, highlighting some recent progress. In addition, I added a few slides to preemptively address some of the issues Marc had raised. Finally, I made relevant notations in my workstreams checklist, updating the document to keep it current.

After that, I dove into the libraries and database issue and was surprised by what I found. In addition to the usual and recognizable medical sources there was a significant amount of information from and references to institutions and entities I had never heard of. These sources all appeared to have been part of the most recent data dump from Sid. This, in and of itself, was not necessarily alarming, but when I tried locating more information online, I couldn't find what I would consider to be appropriate disclosures and information. Several of the sources were from, or referred to one lab in particular, an establishment called DSL Labs.

The information on DSL that I was able to locate seemed slightly unusual and unlike your standard medical or biotech reference. The company appeared to be focused on marketing and selling a supplement derived from a plant called *Dulcinea Galdamesiana*. This plant grew in abundance in only one location, the Panamanian rainforest. But I was unable to find absolutely any information about the plant, or its biology, online. I checked my collection of pills and supplements and, sure enough, it was an ingredient in one of the products I had purchased based on a recommendation from Nina.

I called Sid but his phone went through to voice mail, as usual lately. I sent him a text message: "Hey man. A couple of questions on the materials you provided. Call me, please." And then I sent him a longer email:

"Hey Sid. Thanks again for helping out with the Project Nina. Everything is working great and I feel like I'm close to making a breakthrough. The lab work aspect is functioning perfectly. Product analysis is creative and differentiating. But I'd like to look into some of the sources you provided. I've had to special order some obscure supplements and, in some instances, I can't quite figure out how the sources are coming up with this indication. I don't have any reason to suspect that its inapplicable or erroneous, I would just like to look into it further so I can give more complete information to potential investors and because I'm pretty curious about some of the science. Can you give me a call?"

I stared at the body of the email for a while, and then added:

"I'm sorry if I haven't been myself lately or if I did or said something wrong. But I really need a hand with this. I'm sorry to bother you, I know you must be super busy. I promise not to bug you anymore about helping out. I just really need this info.

Best,

Drew"

I could give an entire lecture about the evolution of "Best" as a way to sign off on emails. I still remember the first time I saw it: "Best." Best what? Best regards of course, but this is an email and the 21st century so we don't have enough time to write it all out. But it's genius in a way because it is such a non-threatening closing that it's difficult to take issue with it. I'm wishing you the best. I'm sending you my best. It's the best. You're the best. What are you going to do? It's better than "Sincerely" which is anything but sincere and "Yours Truly" always felt like closing Civil War era correspondence. If you say "Cheers" and you're not from England, Australia or South Africa, I have some words for you. So...now, it's best. And everybody around here uses it.

I worked all night on Nina, feverishly at times, and made good progress. The next day I worked equally as hard and accomplished just as much, if not more. In addition, I received replies from two potential investors and I was giddy about it. "Sounds promising. Would love to learn more." Also, "This is right in our wheelhouse. Would love to meet you." I was able to schedule meetings with BT Ventures and Pacific NeoBiolabs, and was still waiting to hear back from some of the other funds, who were familiar names in the industry.

After two days working at a feverish pace, though, I needed a break. I headed to McNally's, but a little later than usual, purposefully timing it so that I'd catch some of the college crowd and see what everyone was up to. Ever since the evening with Susan, and perhaps somewhat prior to that, I couldn't shake a certain curiosity of being around people. It suddenly seemed interesting, instead of annoying, not knowing what might happen or what some other person might say. It occurred to me that maybe something funny would happen if I were out with people.

I felt a pang of something, though (regret?), thinking of the Golden Bear and the evening with Susan. Had I moved on too quickly from the events of that night? That seemed preposterous, I barely knew her. Still, she was a human being and now she was gone. Every person's death was worth acknowledging, Hemmingway had taught us that. Then I remembered he was quoting John Donne and it was Donne who had said, "No man is an island, Entire of itself." That's a tremendously impactful idea, but I was distracting myself again. Sometimes, it's hard to get your brain focused on the right things. It's like moving a boulder.

I managed to force those thoughts from my mind and settle into a spot at the bar in McNally's. What I would describe as the usual crowd was there and Tiny saw me and asked with a nod what I wanted to drink. "Gin," I said and he started to turn around. "And...tonic," I added.

He froze and turned partially back towards me, a puzzled look flashing ever so briefly behind his eyes with the order of such a garden variety drink. But after a slight hesitation, he turned right around and poured my g&t and slid it over to me as if nothing had ever happened because he's Tiny, or Mike or whoever he is, and he's great at his job.

"Thanks," I said. I felt like telling him, "Hey, look at me! I'm different now. I've had these experiences I want to tell you about," but I'm not ridiculous and I'm not going to be one of those sad stools who pours their heart out to a bartender every stinking night. Forget about that. So I sat there and swallowed my emotions like a big boy.

From my college days, I remembered guys who chewed tobacco would occasionally swallow their bitter, thick tobacco spit when they had to, instead of spitting it into a cup. Maybe they lost their spitting cup or were in a place where you weren't supposed to be chewing. Whatever it was, they swallowed their spit if they had to, bitter as it might be. It went with the territory. Whenever I had to swallow a particularly painful thought or emotion, I just thought of those guys. It felt like doing the same thing. I reflexively took a sip of my gin and tonic. It was refreshing and sweet, just like I remembered, and it got the taste of the non-existent tobacco spit out of my mouth.

I looked around McNally's and consciously checked for halos. There were none. I looked down at the spot where they Grey Man had been. A couple of tech bro looking dudes were sitting in his spot drinking beer – IPAs, no doubt. And the memory of that first halo made me wish I had ordered something stronger.

Jim from Google was there, Warriors hat on. You can tell a lot about a guy by which sport he favors, actually. You have your baseball guys. They can talk your ear off about various subjects, are generally very observant and if you mention anything related to a statistic to them, forget it. There goes your whole night. You have your basketball guys, like Jim. They tend to be more into pop culture, the goings on about town, if you will, movies and concerts. They're a pretty good time (as long as they're not watching basketball).

Football guys, on the other hand, they will run you over. It's always 3rd and 10 to a football guy and God help you if you're in their way. These guys know how to eat, though, I'll hand it to them there. If you're going out to dinner, you could do worse than having a football guy organizing things (and they love to be in charge of those things). Hockey, don't get me started. I'm a west coast guy, so I don't really know much about hockey and the hockey guys always seem like they're from a different planet. Soccer? Those guys are just trying to be different. Just kidding, but they usually are a little different and it's hard to put them into a box. (Are they international soccer guys? World cup soccer guys? Etc.).

"Hey, Jim, who they playing tonight?" I asked him before I realized that I was even talking.

Jim looked at me, then looked around and behind him to make sure I wasn't talking to someone else. "Hey, man. What's going on?" he answered, "I didn't even know you followed the Warriors."

I shrugged.

"How do you know they're even playing?" he asked, ribbing me.

I smiled and pointed to the place on my head where a hat would be if I had been wearing one. "The hat," I said. "You only wear the hat when they play."

He looked totally discombobulated, like I had just told him the name of his first high school girlfriend and the names of the websites he visits when his wife's not around. "Wow. Ok...Um, the Clippers. They're playing the Clippers," he said, and took a long drink from the beer in his pint glass. It looked like a dark ale. Jim was too smart to modify his tastes with the changing trends.

"Should be a good game, then. Season is getting underway, right?"

"Uh...yeah. Yeah, and we get...you know, our whole team back tonight. Healthy."

"Totally," I said.

Now when I say Jim was a basketball guy, I mean it in the best way. He could sort talent like a pro scout and had original opinions on everything from the development of the 3-point shot to free throws and zone defenses. He could see a back pick coming a mile away and would react to what was happening in the game before it actually happened. And not in a braggy or show off kind of way, but in a legitimate, he-just-cared-about-the-game-more-than-you-did sort of way.

He played pick-up basketball on Tuesdays down at the Presbyterian Church on College Avenue but had blown out his achilles two years ago and had to give it up. He was from Indianapolis or somewhere in Indiana, but had moved here for school and loved the Warriors, because who didn't love the Warriors back then. They owned the Town and the face of the team was somebody that nobody could say a bad word about anyway.

I had gathered all this without ever really having much in the way of a conversation with Jim. Sure, we talked now and then, especially in the old days, but never about any of that. It was just information I knew from being at that particular bar repeatedly, overhearing conversations, observing things (Jim on crutches for two months) and in general not being a complete dumbass.

I picked up my gin and tonic and carried it over and sat next to Jim, which didn't surprise him at that point as much as it did Tiny. It was kind of funny, out of the corner of my eye, seeing Tiny do like a double take in slow motion as I walked over and sat on the stool next to Jim and in front of the television.

"Fill me in," I said to Jim. He proceeded to tell me everything. How the season was shaping up, who was doing what, where it fit in the arc of that player's particular career and how that bode for the playoffs for the team and maybe a championship. He talked about the coach and the assistant coaches and their responsibilities and why that was important. He talked about the Clippers and how they were a pain in the ass, but they were going to be terrible until at least the trade deadline and what was the General Manager thinking in the offseason, it was obvious what they needed but that's why the Clippers are always going to be the Clippers. It was great. It was better than any goddamned analysis on the entire planet this side of Bill Simmons. And it was free. This information is free out there, I thought. You can just get it by talking. Incredible.

I ordered another g&t when the game started and I was sipping on that and following along until about halfway through the second quarter when a group of three women walked in. They were very nice looking, especially one who was a little taller than the others, and they took the last free table in the bar area. Jim didn't notice, of course, because he was watching out for the next back pick, but I noticed and missed a key point in the game apparently because Jim shouted, "NO!!! Ah, damn. Did you see that?"

"Can you fucking believe it?" I said. I figured that was a pretty good response to just about anything.

But I wasn't following the game anymore because at that particular moment I was thinking about the tall woman in the corner and what I might say to her. I wasn't afraid of rejection, exactly. Anybody who is anybody will tell you that rejection and failure are a part of life and I had learned to deal with it, both professionally and personally. You never know what's going to happen. If some woman doesn't want to talk to you, it sometimes has nothing to do with you. (Sometimes it does, of course, but who knows and it doesn't really help to focus on that part of it.) You have to have the courage to confront life and not think about the consequences. I told myself this over and over and over.

Halftime came and Jim patted me on the back and went to use the restroom.

"Another drink, boss?" Tiny asked.

"No," I said. "I'm going to wait a bit."

He nodded politely and walked away.

I thought of different things I might say or circumstances that might lead to a conversation with the tall woman. Maybe I would run into her near the restroom. Maybe something else would come up. But after thinking about it for a while, a sort of laziness fell over me and I didn't want to think about it anymore. It all suddenly seemed less interesting or perhaps less *compelling*. It wasn't the tall woman, it was the situation maybe. It didn't seem as easy and natural as it had been the other night with Susan. Or maybe I just wasn't ready. That's a stupid way to think. Had I just gone through a divorce? Of course not. Either way, I decided to abandon the idea.

"Tiny! Sure," I said and he turned around. "Hit me. Only this time, maker's rocks," I said.

That's more like it, he thought, or at least I'm 99.9% sure he thought, and then just smiled and turned around to pour me a drink. Dangerous to mix booze, but what did I care? I hadn't had a hangover in months, it seemed like, and I was starting to feel indestructible in that regard.

Jim came back and so did the Warriors, pulling away late in the 4th quarter, as they always did back then. I bought Jim a beer, even though he didn't need me to, because he works at Google. "Cheaper than a subscription to the Chronicle," I told him, and he laughed.

I left after the game and decided to take a long walk home since it was a perfect late summer night. (Technically, it was early fall, but we don't even do seasons the normal way here in the Bay.) Sometimes, I feel like the cold and the fog are only here to make us appreciate the sun and the warmth. That's how it could feel on a night like this. It felt like Los Angeles weather without the traffic or the smog or the fake ass bullshit. Just the weather, just for tonight, and leave the rest. I walked down College Avenue in the opposite direction of my apartment, just smiling and looking around. I walked past the new, fancy pizza and pasta place with the big windows and the white tablecloths. Something caught my attention and I looked inside more closely and saw the unmistakable, yet relatively faint sight of a golden white halo.

It was an older woman, but not too old, maybe 64 or something like that. She had short grey and white hair, cropped at the sides, and was sitting with five other women at a round table in the middle of the restaurant. There was a big bottle of white wine in a silver bucket in the middle of the table, and, by the looks of it, at least three or four others in the tank. They were all talking, in very animated fashion, and laughing and looking at one another, except the grey haired woman. She was smiling, sure, but she was talking a little less frequently, laughing a little more quietly and observing slightly more closely than the others. She looked content, I would say. She was contented.

She was somebody's mom, no doubt. Somebody's mom who lived to be past the age of 27. She got to raise her kid or kids, probably still talked to them out there somewhere. I'm working at an investment bank, mom, I just got a job at a new firm. I've been promoted to Head Copywriter mom, everything is going great. She sent her kids care packages when they lived in the dorms that made the other students jealous, no doubt. She wrote meaningful messages inside of birthday cards and everyone recognized her neat handwriting. Maybe was still even married to the dad. No, she wore the short hair like a kind of independence. She was divorced from the old bastard, but they still had a cordial relationship. She disliked him, but was tolerant of him in front of others, never saying a bad word about him to her kids.

I don't know how long I was staring at her, at them, but it must have been quite a long time because the maître d' eventually came outside and confronted me.

"Excuse me! What are you doing? Can I help you with something?"

I snapped back to reality and looked at him.

"I'm not doing anything," I responded.

"Your hand is on the window and you're staring at my customers."

I looked at the maître d' and then refocused on the table of women. Their expressions had all changed and they had scowls on their faces and were looking at me, pointing, saying things to each other that I couldn't hear.

I jumped back from the window instinctively, shaking my head. "No. No. I...uh...Sorry. I'll leave," I said, stumbling backwards on the sidewalk. "I didn't mean to stand there and stare. I wasn't doing anything wrong. I'm sorry."

Inside, the grey haired woman wasn't looking at me in the same way as the others. She was looking through the window and directly into my eyes, plaintively. The halo, glowing, encircled her head. I could not peel myself away from her gaze as I tried to regain my balance, reaching out behind me feeling for a parked car or something to fall back on. After a moment, an eternity, she looked away. I stood there catching my breath.

"I thought you said you were leaving?"

"I am. I am. I don't want any trouble."

⟨ 10 ⟩

Steam Train

That next week, I went to two investor presentations, but neither led to anything. The first VC never responded to me after the meeting (during which he was looking at his phone half the time). The second just kept asking for more information for weeks after we met. Please send me your presentation deck. Can you please send me financial projections? Send me your product roadmap, etc.

I know what investors are doing when they do that. They're gathering data, but not necessarily the stuff you're sending them. They're measuring you up, trying to see how you'll respond to the different requests and delays and life. It's all a stupid game. I feel like two reasonable people should be able to just sit in a room, be honest and direct, and hash things out. That's never how it goes, though. You have to do the *kabuki*, as Governor Schwarzenegger used to say. It was a waste of time is what it was because at the end of the day, he told me thanks but no thanks. At least he had the courtesy to do it by email.

I was feeling more zen about the fundraising process, though. I felt like I was showing good traction with investors, in general, and although perhaps my expectations were coming back down to Earth, I was still optimistic. I had four more meetings set up over the next ten days and

I was getting responses to my emails. Some of that may have been due to the fact that I was really leveraging my relationships. I was calling in every favor I was ever owed and many that I wasn't and never would be. I needed to pull out all the stops. If I was ever going to make it happen, this was the time. It was the moment I had been working toward for years.

Sid never got back to me and it was starting to get annoying. My options to further explore some of those product and database issues without him involved getting on an airplane and visiting some of these entities, foundations and non-profits myself. It would involve a couple of days in Seattle, perhaps, some time in Austin and a trip to Northern Virginia. Even if I could get in front of some of these people, I wasn't sure I would know what to ask them. I really needed someone with medical expertise to help me figure out what I was looking for. I much preferred he just return my calls.

That weekend Juan Pablo suggested we hit up the Sutter Hotel, this slick joint in the City that was somewhere between a bar and a club. I hadn't been there in 10 years but decided to go because of the fond memories I had of the place. When we were getting ready to leave, he told me the news that our landlord was thinking of selling our fourplex.

"I was out back reading on one of those chairs on the patio," Juan Pablo said. "Mike was back there doing the gardening, you know. And he casually mentions to me that he and his sister would probably sell the building in the next year."

We agreed that it was a tremendously cavalier way to broach a very sensitive subject to a tenant. "Did he give you any context?" I asked.

"No. None. He is so weird, that guy. It was like he was talking to someone who didn't live there or something. He seemed surprised that I reacted the way that I did."

"How did you react?"

"I don't remember exactly, but I stood up and started asking him tons of questions. I was like wait, wait, wait and saying things like that, you know?"

"What did he say?"

"He was saying like the market *this* and when we bought the place *that* and blah blah blah."

"I can't believe it."

"It reminds me of a story my friend's dad used to tell. He was a prison guard in Argentina. There is a golfer golfing with another guy and he is about to tee off on the first hole, when all of a sudden, the other guy comes up behind him and kicks him in the balls. Prafff! The golfer crumples down and is laying there in total agony and everything and then the kicker says, 'I use two of those during each round of golf. And I won't tell you when I'm going to use the other one.' So for the rest of the match, the golfer hits terrible all of his tee shots, because he is always waiting for the PRAFF in his balls."

"Sounds like a story you would hear in prison."

"No, but it's true. Come on! We have to live now like this..." his hands were going crazy with gestures that I vaguely remembered seeing before, but no longer understood. "Is he going to sell the place or not? We can't have any peace, because any minute now..."

"Praff," I said, imitating Juan Pablo, who didn't even notice.

"Exactly."

He had a point. Not that I was expecting to live there for another ten years, but what did I know? Time seemed to be slipping through my fingertips. And now, that time, or at least my time at that apartment, had an expiration date.

We drove into the city across the Bay Bridge in my computer of an electric car. Juan Pablo was figuring things out that I had not yet had time to learn about the car and he was impressed with several of its modern features.

"I can't believe you would buy a car without knowing how it works," he said.

"Tell me everything about how your phone works," I responded.

"That's different," he answered.

"No," I said. "It's the same thing."

"I don't drive my phone at 70 miles per hour across the bridge."

I just laughed and we looked out the window as the light was changing over the bay. The water was absolutely shimmering in the twilight. Alcatraz was still visible, engulfed in shadows, and the twinkling lights of restaurants and houses was visible across the bay in quaint and picturesque Sausalito as the sun set beyond the Golden Gate.

"My father used to tell me that happiness was over there," I said, pointing to the sunset.

"On the Golden Gate?"

"No, further on. You know, in the sunset."

He shook his head.

"In the U.S., it's a cliché. All of the classic movies end with the protagonist heading off into the sunset. That's how you knew it was a happy ending."

"That's very sad," he said.

"No, I liked it."

"The story is nice," he said. "I meant the part about your dad."

"Yeah, I guess so."

It was quiet for a moment, so he started messing with the car's voice interface and soon the car was speaking to us as a man, instead of a woman, in a way that made us laugh. He said he didn't like this voice, though, so he changed it so that the car was speaking to us with, first, an Australian accent and then a British accent.

"Fuck that, it might tell me to drive on the wrong side of the road," I said.

We laughed some more. He kept switching languages. The car was speaking to us in French, which we both agreed sounded sophisticated, like perhaps the car wasn't going to tell us everything it knew, and then German, which I'll admit was a little intimidating ("What if it starts criticizing the way I drive?"). Neither of us could make heads or tails of some of the languages, though. He switched the language to Spanish and listened for a while, paying close attention to what the vehicle said.

"I wonder how it's localized," he said. "What country they use for the base language."

"You mean translation?" I asked.

"No, translation is just the beginning. Translation just puts the words in general Spanish. But there are different words for each country."

"Why wouldn't the same word be the same in every country?"

"Let me ask you a question," he began. "Would you go to an office supply store and ask for rubbers?"

"Not unless I was totally desperate."

"Exactly. But in England, the office supplies are full of rubbers because that is the common word they use for 'eraser.' You only have three or four different main English-speaking countries. Imagine Spanish. We have over 20."

"Fair point."

"For example, the Spanish verb most countries use for to 'take' in my country means to fuck. So, depending on where you are, to 'take' a taxi could have very different meanings!"

"I'll never take a taxi again without considering the potentially grave consequences."

I couldn't believe it had taken me a year to get to know Juan Pablo. He was funny. He was interesting. He seemed genuinely kind. What more can you ask from a person? I remembered when he moved in, the first day I saw him, he introduced himself and had this look on his face like he wanted to have a conversation. But I just said hello and put my head down and walked past him. After that I might run into him at the mailbox or going up the steps and he was always very pleasant. He never gave up on me, I thought, but I found it a strange thing to think about a person you had just met.

The Sutter Hotel was built in the refurbished lobby of an old hotel. It had a long, modern bar, ceilings that must have been 25 feet high and plenty of places to sit and talk in red velvet armchairs and overstuffed sofas. There was an exceptionally large separate room for dancing or milling about, depending on the hour. It had other interesting features, like enormously long, full-body portraits of random people dressed in steam punk fashion with eyes and faces that magically followed you around the room. Given the hip space and its popularity, it was always able to attract high quality DJs and so the music (some version of EDM on most nights) was almost always top notch.

We ordered drinks and spent some time walking around the club. It felt a lot like the kinds of nights I used to have and I was enjoying this unusual feeling of liking being around people. There were still plenty of idiots there that deserved criticism, mind you, but I just didn't feel like I needed to be the one criticizing them. I was happy listening to the music and being out. It felt in a way like I was taking a type of trip down memory lane.

We had been there for a couple of hours and it had definitely gotten crowded. Juan Pablo ran into some people he knew, some expats and some software people. It looked like a curious group. He excused himself and left to go talk to someone or do something, I couldn't really tell because it was loud and I wasn't too concerned about it. I walked back towards the front door to where most of the cool air was and came face to face with an unannounced, surprise guest. But it wasn't a visiting DJ.

It was a young woman in her 30s, on the thin side with pale skin and brown freckles and short brown hair cut in a sort of bob. Her features were very fine. I would say that she had a fragile quality to her and I thought that she was almost classically pretty. She sat by herself on a lounge near the door with her legs crossed next to a pile of purses and sweaters and a jacket or two. She was holding a phone in front of her, but not looking at it, in a pose that made her look tired. Above her head, faint though it was at first, was the distinctive glow of a halo.

My pulse spiked immediately and I felt a rush of adrenaline and other emotions. Everything in front of me went sort of out of focus and then quickly back into focus. My breathing quickened. I felt instantly sorry for her, yes. It was terrible that someone so young could be in the situation she was in, whatever it was. The halo was obviously not a sign of good news. But I also found in a way that you might call perverse (but it wasn't, and still isn't, to me) that the halo made her interesting to me. It added something to her persona, which was already very appealing. She had a vulnerability to her that was almost magnetic to me.

Like Susan, she had nothing observably wrong with her. She didn't look as robust or full of life as Susan had, but what was someone so young and pretty doing with a potential expiration date so proximate? Unlike when I met Susan, though, I had my full wits about me and I wanted to be able to use my judgment and a clear mind. Here was another chance to understand what was happening to me or around me.

I wished I could just walk up and talk to her, but that almost never works. Why was everything always so difficult and complicated? I tried to collect my thoughts, but found myself in a metacognitive process about the entire situation and me and everything and that led to feelings of panic at the realization that I might be blowing my only opportunity to ever speak to her. I needed to seriously calm down. I couldn't remember the last time I so desperately wanted to talk to someone I hadn't even met.

I took a few deep breaths to steady myself. Ok, this wasn't that important, I thought. It really doesn't matter in the long run. This is just a situation I was in and the only way past it was through, as they say. I told myself the butterflies in my stomach were just a physical process that had nothing to do with reality. I had faced my nervousness before, many times before, in many different circumstances. Why would this be any different? I could do it. This was no problem.

By the looks of her, I needed to be very careful in my approach. I thought back to when I was single – well, I was still single, but now I was single like a noun as opposed to before when I was single more like a verb – and I remembered thinking of just jumping into a swimming pool. You just hold your breath and jump. So, I closed my eyes for a moment, pursed my lips together, and approached the chair next to her as casually as I could.

"Mind if I sit here?" I asked her.

"No, that's fine."

"Thanks." I sat down and she began looking at her phone out of nervousness.

Well, I was there. I was next to her. Step 1! Now I needed to figure out what to do next. I looked around at the people still pouring in and those milling around. I made an effort to sort of examine what I was feeling so that I might say something that sounded authentic. "My friend took off and it makes me feel better to at least be sitting near someone," I finally said, staring straight ahead.

She gave a sort of smile that made me relax a bit. "I know what you mean."

A smile! A beautiful smile, it was a simple acknowledgment, a shared moment together. And perhaps, some small encouragement to continue the conversation? "What's your name?" I asked.

"I'm Laura."

"Hi, Laura. I'm Drew," I said, leaning towards her a tiny bit so she could hear me. "I came out here with this crazy guy. He's my neighbor. But he's more of a party animal than I am. He likes to go out all the time, I think."

She moved modestly, almost imperceptibly closer to the edge of her seat. "I know what you mean. My girlfriends go out all the time," she said loudly, talking over the music. And smiled again, much to my satisfaction.

I smiled back at her. A wave of calmness rushed over me, taking the edge off of my anxiety. It could be seen as abnormal, or deviant, I'll admit. Being attracted to a woman with a halo is not going to give me the reputation of being a gentleman. Yet, it was undeniable – that is what was happening – and I was cognizant of it at the time. I don't know what to call it. It was exciting?

There was no saying anything about it, of course, and I had to resist the urge to do so. This is what I'll say in my defense. Even if I had said something, even if I had grabbed her hands, looked her straight in the eyes and said, "Laura, I have something to tell you, and it's going to sound weird, but you have to listen to me," she would've hit the exit faster than an investment banker in a bear market. This is San Francisco, after all. There are crazy people everywhere. While it was plausible that I was now one of said crazy people, I needed to above all keep my emotions under control and see where this was going. At some point, if possible, maybe I could use my knowledge to assist or advise her. But for now, it felt fantastic just being in her presence and having the opportunity to talk to someone new. I needed to keep cool.

We spoke for almost half an hour. I asked her where she was from, always a safe question around here, and she told me about a small town in rural Nebraska. I had always wondered what it would be like to be from a small town. She told me in some detail. What had attracted her to San Francisco, I asked. She had just always been drawn to coming here. She came here without a plan or a job, she just got off the plane and started looking.

What was it like to be from here? I couldn't really say because I'm not from anywhere else (she laughed). I told her about growing up in the City, I told her about the night after Mayor Moscone and Harvey Milk were shot and why I would always have a soft spot for Dianne Feinstein. I told her what I remembered about watching the AIDS epidemic develop firsthand, how I remembered when they closed the bath houses and how I hadn't really understood what that meant. She asked me about Oakland and confessed she hadn't explored very much of the Bay Area outside of the City, but she said it in a way that was more apologetic than condescending and so I found that totally acceptable.

She looked at me the way you might look at a memory, if it were unfolding before you. She smiled at me pleasantly and I found her eager to talk and ask me questions and answer mine. But eventually, as was bound to happen, her friends showed up. Laura stood up abruptly and nervously got ready to leave.

"I'm sorry to see you go. I had a nice time," I said.

"Me, too. I really appreciated having someone to talk to. It was…it was very nice."

"Would you mind if I asked for your number? I'd like to take you to coffee or something."

She said she'd enjoy that and so I took out my phone and typed her number into my contacts. Ten minutes after she left, I sent her a quick message. "Hi, this is Drew. I mean it, I'm going to call you tomorrow. There are some great places for you to check out if you're willing to leave the cold and foggy confines of the City."

She waited a few minutes to reply with one letter: "K." And then a moment later a winky face emoji.

About that time, Juan Pablo came around the corner with one of his friends. "What have you been up to?" he asked.

"I met the nicest woman," I said. "Very cute."

"Really?" he asked. "Where is she?"

"She had to go."

"Okay," he said.

"What?" I asked him. He had a strange look on his face that appeared to be somewhere between curiosity and concern. "Why are you looking at me like that?"

"Nothing," he replied. "I just never get the chance to meet your girlfriends."

I shrugged.

Three days later, I took Laura to Cro Café in the Temescal Alley in Oakland, the best coffee in the East Bay before it closed down during the Pandemic. From there, we went around the corner for a creme-filled donut at Donut Dolly and walked the Peralta Creek in and out of the neighborhoods.

She came from a cattle ranching family, she said, but never felt at home with either the cattle or the family. She was "different than they are," she said without elaborating and I didn't press her. We talked about how tech was something like the opposite of being a farmer. Whereas one deals with the physical world, the natural elements, the other deals with the digital world of purely manmade elements. Whereas one is grounded in the very real limitations of man and nature, yields, weather patterns, etc., the other is limitless in grasp and scope, multiplied by infinity in every way possible.

On a whim, I drove her up into the Oakland and Berkeley Hills and we rode the miniature steam trains through the redwoods with nothing but new parents and toddlers around us. The steam trains have been there for as long as I can remember, miniature versions of the real thing, with coal powered engines and a steam whistle that lets out puffs of steam that can be heard around the park as you ride around in open aired cars on a miniature track past the occasional miniature town. The only thing not miniature are the redwoods, tall and majestic beauties, drinking in the fog and looming large overhead. We sat in the front by the engine. She loved it.

We drove down Grizzly Peak and stopped at a turnout with majestic views overlooking the bay, Oakland and San Francisco, and watched as the fog began its evening procession under the Golden Gate, over Alcatraz, along the Marina and into the East and South Bay. I'm not sure what had come over me, not since my ex-girlfriend would I ever have done anything so romantic. But it was beautiful and enjoyable and we talked for over an hour while the sun set into the Pacific beyond the hills and threw red and orange streaked clouds across the San Francisco sky.

We kissed in the front seat of my car like a couple of adolescents. She kissed me in a way that made me want to look after her and care for her needs and desires. I wanted to get her things that she liked and bring her small flower arrangements to make her smile. I wanted to know her favorite color and buy her things that reminded her of me or of pleasant memories. I wanted to rub my fingers over her hand and arm and gently trace lines across her neck and shoulders.

After we kissed for a few minutes, she pulled away from me and apologized. She told me that she actually really liked me but that she hadn't been feeling well. I looked into her eyes, but couldn't tell if she knew what I knew. What I could see in the deep part of her eyes was bravery. Whether it was from what lay ahead of her or behind her, I never knew.

I suppose I still feel guilty that I never told her. At several points that afternoon, I did consider different scenarios, ways that I could tell her, but I never found the right one. And honestly, I was so smitten with her, that for most of the time, I forgot about the halo entirely.

I offered to drive her home, but she insisted I drop her off at BART. It would be a two to three-hour round trip for me with traffic and she wouldn't hear of it. I obviously should have done it anyway, but I didn't realize it was the last time I would ever see her and I didn't want to seem overly paternalistic.

We exchanged texts over the next couple of days, but after a while, she stopped responding to my messages. I tried calling her, but it went through to voice mail. I texted her periodically for several weeks after that and eventually got a call from Riley, one of her friends who had been with her that night at the Sutter Hotel.

Laura was in the ICU with a rare form of cancer. It had metastasized and the doctors had only given her days to live. She had been living with severe pain in recent months, but refused to talk about it or go to the doctor until she collapsed at home. It had been almost two years since a bad break up of an 8-year relationship had caused Laura to slip into a deep depression, from which she never fully recovered. Riley apologized for the awkward situation and then thanked me and told me that Laura really liked me. I was the first guy since her break up that she had cared about. Laura had told her of the drive we took through the Berkeley Hills and watching the sun set behind the Golden Gate Bridge and Riley thanked me for being kind to her.

I asked if I could do anything, but there was nothing to be done. I asked if I could see her, but she said it was family only. I thanked her and told her I appreciated the phone call.

Three days later I received a text from Riley that Laura had passed away quietly in her sleep. I was lying in bed when I got the text and I stayed there for a long time after that. I just set the phone back down and stared at the ceiling. My life seemed to be spinning out of control when, in all actuality, nothing had really changed. I was still there, in my apartment, and still alone. I had my project and my things and that was all.

I thought for a long time about riding on the Steam Train next to Laura that sunny afternoon, the tracks winding through the forest of majestic redwoods. I remembered specifically a bright patch of blue sky at the end of a dark tunnel and the sound of children laughing under the trees. We seemed to be flying through the air together, all of us, through a slow, warm breeze, as the steam from the train's whistle misted droplets of water onto our hair and faces.

⟨ 11 ⟩

Vision

If I had felt anything even remotely resembling relief after Susan, there was nothing like that after Laura. Any sense of liberation from commitment or freedom from future lies, entanglements and complications was replaced by a feeling of regret. What had I gotten myself into? How had it all gone this far?

I never really knew Laura, that's true, but now I never would. I would never see if the wistful, melancholy of her eyes could be replaced by joy. I would never get to know what her face looked like when she was truly happy. In the back of my mind, I also knew that there would be no disappointing her, no arguments and no lies, that was true, but I could see that, on the whole, I had lost more than I had gained.

Any mention of Nebraska still catches my attention. When it pops up on the news, in conversation, on a map, my mind does a sort of subconscious double take. It's not a state that comes up a lot in the public discourse, but you'd be surprised how often you come across something when there's a deeper meaning attached to it. There are movies, songs and artists associated with the state. Fantastic film director Alexander Payne is from Nebraska. Conor Oberst, one of my favorite musicians, is from there too. I feel a special, completely unfounded, almost guilty connection with events and people from the Cornhusker State, like it's a private secret with myself that I choose not to share with anyone else.

The fourth day after Riley's text, I had a meeting with a potential investor that I almost bagged the day before because of how badly I felt. I decided to go to the meeting more out of a desire to get out of the house than anything else. It was with a VC named Trevor at BioBay Venture Partners.

It was the best investor meeting I ever had. The more monotone my voice and clouded my thinking with memories of Laura, halos and my past, the more engaged in the presentation Trevor became and the more questions he asked. I couldn't bring myself to care or be sufficiently focused and so he seemed to care and focus enough for the both of us. He asked excellent questions covering issues and topics that nobody else had bothered to inquire about. He was the first investor who was as excited as I thought an investor should be about the commercial prospects of the recommendation engine. I hadn't spent too much time on this topic in my presentation, since it seemed a little too far afield, but he immediately locked onto a number of possibilities: Deals with the pharmaceuticals, contracts with the enormous vitamins and supplement markets and possibilities in the lucrative diet and weight loss industry. I could only manage to nod along as he rattled off the seemingly endless opportunities.

He asked specific questions about Nina's libraries and reference materials and I opened up a presentation I had started to prepare on the topic (more to organize my thinking than anything else). The deck showed in some detail where the data came from and what it was based on. He understood enough about artificial intelligence and machine learning to have a knowledgeable conversation about it and that same presentation gave us an opportunity to discuss some of those items in detail. He had many of the same questions I did about the source of some of Nina's recommendations. I noted to myself that I appeared to be on the right track.

At one point, we were on my laptop looking at a portion of the deck that had footnotes and references to other papers and articles and he stopped and looked at me curiously.

"Do you wear contacts?" he asked.

"No."

"You can read that font without glasses? That's impressive."

It was a throw-away comment in the middle of a long meeting, but it stopped me cold and served to half snap me out of my doldrums. I did wear glasses. My vision had been getting noticeably worse during the previous few years such that I had begun to rely on them on a daily basis. Except not lately. I had not used my glasses in weeks or months without even realizing it.

We finished reviewing the deck and he called in another partner, Eric, a specialist in the software and data space, to listen in on the last part of the pitch. Normally, I would have been ecstatic at such a positive sign, but my mind was elsewhere and it was all I could do to stand up and smile to greet him. He was a younger guy, probably had just made partner, and he gave me the visual once over when he walked into the conference room. I shrugged it off and reviewed the materials Trevor requested and, for the first time in any of my presentations, Trevor was actually making my arguments for me to his partner. It was surprising and kind of strange to watch. They were speaking quickly to each other, referencing other companies, deals and funds, some of which I knew nothing about and Trevor was talking about Nina as if it were his project. He was excited. And the more calm I remained, the more excitable he became.

We agreed on some follow-up items and to touch base again in a week. As we were gathering our things and walking towards the conference room door, Eric, who had a dual degree in computer science and cognitive science from MIT, asked about my education and where I had gone to school. You could have heard a pin drop when I told him I was an attorney.

"But with a background in programming," added Trevor quickly. "I know it's unusual," he said to Eric. Then he turned to me. "Tell him about all your projects and the applications you've developed over the years."

I started describing some of my programming bonafides, but Eric told me it wasn't necessary. He said he trusted Trevor and that he would review the materials I provided in detail and that would be sufficient. Trevor shook my hand on my way out the door, but not before casting a nervous glance back at Eric.

I couldn't get out of there fast enough. From the car, I called a local optometrist and tried to make an appointment for an eye exam as soon as possible, but I couldn't get anything for weeks. I begged and pleaded to no avail. While driving, I asked my phone to search online for, and call, another optometrist, but was told the same thing: No appointments available. I had reached the freeway at this point, driving 70 mph, when it hit me. I could read every sign on the road for a hundred yards in front of me. The letters weren't blurry, I had no trouble making out details. It was all as crisp as if it were right in front of my face.

That realization was like a bucket of cold water. I made a last-second decision to pull off the freeway on the outskirts of Oakland and stop at an old shopping mall nearby. I drove around for a bit and, sure enough, found a big box vision store. I went in and was able to get an appointment for later that morning.

After a depressing hour of walking through a nearly empty mall past abandoned storefronts and stores that aren't what they used to be, I was able to get an eye exam. To my surprise, my vision was 20/15, better than perfect. I didn't recall ever testing better than 20/20 and made a note to check in with my optometrist. She congratulated me and told me that fewer than 1% of adults have as good of vision as I did.

"It's strange," I said. "My eyesight seems to have improved with age. Is that possible?"

The optometrist thought for a moment before responding. "There are some circumstances, typically negative, under which your vision can improve with age, but you don't appear to have any of those symptoms," she said, taking another close look into my eyes. "You said you had been wearing glasses?"

I nodded. "I was having trouble reading small print but I could always read if there was sufficient light."

"Sounds like presbyopia, but you don't have those symptoms now." She took a third and fourth look in my eyes and at fiddled with her equipment.

"I would recommend you go see an ophthalmologist," she said summarily. I couldn't see her degree on the wall but guessed it wasn't from an Ivy League institution. She was putting away equipment and shutting off machines, giving me the impression that, whatever it was, she didn't want to waste more time with someone that wasn't going to drop five hundred dollars on her overpriced frames. She walked back into her office before I stood up out of the chair.

I went home and rummaged through my files looking for records related to my eyesight. Had my eyesight really improved? When was my last eye exam and where were the results? I used to keep things in relatively orderly fashion until about five years ago. Now the only thing orderly about me was related to my work. My Nina files were meticulous, I could vouch for that. But my medical records?

I eventually gave up on the vision quest and spent the rest of the day digging into Sid's recent data set. Most of the files were well documented and had enough reference information that I could verify their contents online, find similar studies or information or find comparable data that one could consider as an alternative. By the end of the day I had zeroed in on files from one of the sources, which was the outfit called DSL Labs. Not only was the documentation provided extremely poor or non-existent, there was almost no information about DSL available online. They had a barebones website, which provided very little information, and which had a number of broken links and missing pages.

I dug around for more information, but couldn't find any. I sat there staring straight ahead for a while and finally picked up the phone and called Sid. This time, I left him a voice mail.

"Sid, what the fuck, man? Call me. Twenty fucking years and you're just going to blow me off? Call me. It's important. There's weird shit happening. I have to talk to you. Come on. I'm going to have to fly to these places and go see these people for those sources. There are some things that don't make sense. Just call me."

I held the phone tightly in my hand. Maybe I should drive to that mother fucker's house. I could show up at his work. I could stalk him at the few lunch places in Emeryville, where he worked. I was going to have to do something. An abrupt knock on my door interrupted my train of thought. A visitor was out of the ordinary, particularly since it was almost 10 pm.

I got up and slowly opened the door and there stood Juan Pablo.

"Hey, dude," he said. "Sorry, I know it's late, but I saw your light and I haven't seen you in a few days. I wanted to be sure everything is okay."

There's a very specific way the Argentines say "sorry" in English. They do it even when they are speaking in Spanish. They say it with a long "o" and with a slight roll of the "r," almost as if they were claiming that word for themselves. I was focused on the pronunciation and remembering hearing it in conversation in Argentina when I realized I hadn't responded to him.

"Dude? Hello?" he repeated, waving his hand in front of my face.

"Yeah," I finally responded. "Everything is okay."

He closed the door behind him, walked in past me, and went into my living room, looking around. "Are you drunk or high or something?"

"No," I said with a laugh. "Why would you say that?"

He stared at me for a moment and I realized I was still standing by the front door. It was awkward, so I walked towards my desk.

"I'm fine. I was just very busy with work. I had a good meeting today."

Just a moment before, I was lost in a sea of thought and now there was a human in my apartment. I felt annoyed at the disruption but also remembered that this was completely normal behavior, especially in a situation like this where he lived across the hall from me. We were friends, after all, or at least becoming friends. I remembered living in the dorms where it was extremely common for someone to just come into your room and sit down. It happens. It happens all the time. I used to like it, in fact. It was one of the appealing aspects of dorm life, this casual community behavior.

"Your project? The pee thing?" he asked, walking over and making himself comfortable on the couch, like he had done it a hundred times.

"Yes, Nina," I said, still standing at my desk.

He was looking around my apartment and I could tell he had something on his mind, but I wasn't sure how to go about getting him to say it. "Can I get you something?" I asked.

"Dude, I live right there. I didn't come over for some tea, I came to see how you are."

"Oh. I'm fine," I said.

"Have you seen that girl again?"

I looked at him perplexed. "The girl, *boludo*, from the club. The one you said you met."

"Oh, Laura? No, uh. No, I don't think I'll probably see her again."

"Why not?"

"I don't know. It seems complicated."

"Complicated?! Complicated? *You* are complicated." He looked at me intently and then his face softened. "What was she like?"

"She was cute," I began. "She was very sweet..."

"Okay. What did she look like? I'm wondering if I might have run into her too."

He had a strange look in his eye, something probably akin to mildly distrustful or doubtful.

"I doubt it," I said. "I ran into her by the door when you were in the club.

He nodded slowly. "Ok, well tell me about her."

I described Laura to him, but it was only a halfhearted effort. My mind was bouncing around in different directions, on the Nina source code and reference files and I was also still thinking about my eyesight and whether or not it had gotten objectively better. Another part of me was consciously trying to participate in the conversation with Juan Pablo and/or also considering saying something to him about everything. I desperately wanted to talk about the halos and the other things that were happening to me, and maybe he was the kind of person who would listen to me earnestly. Then again, we had really only just met and there was no reason he would trust me and not think I was crazy.

When I finished talking he just looked at me and laughed. "I don't understand you, dude," he said finally. "If she is like you describe, you should just call her."

I could have done it right then, told him everything. It was a perfect segue. But when I tried to form the words, they were too impossible to come out of my mouth.

"*Estás loco*," he said. He stood up, shaking his head but not wanting to continue hitting it against a wall, I thought. So he changed the subject. "I saw Landlord Mike again."

"You did? Did he say anything?"

"He saw me coming and he ran to his truck faster than Bolt. Usain Bolt, you know him, yes? The runner?"

"Yes, of course. Jamaican guy. Sprinter."

"Yes! Yes, that's him. Very fast. Anyway, Mike did a Usain Bolt impersonation when he saw me. Very fast for an old guy. I think I scared him last time."

"He likes to talk," I said. "He probably gets embarrassed and thinks he said too much last time."

He nodded and waved his arms again as if to say, "Whatever."

"I'll let you get back to being alone and working on..."

"Nina," I said.

"Yes. Nina."

He looked at me as the words hung in the air heavily.

"Ok," he said, walking past me. "I just wanted to make sure you were ok, dude." He opened the front door and just looked at me for a moment. "It's not good for you to be by yourself all the time."

I smiled at him weakly. I realized what he was saying and what he was doing. I genuinely appreciated it and I felt bad for not talking to him after we had gone out that night and had such a good time. He walked out of my apartment, crossed the short hallway and opened the door to his apartment. I stepped into the hallway and made an exaggerated motion of looking inside his apartment.

"No more Wanda?" I asked.

"She still comes over," he said. "But no more Mickey. I think she learned a lesson."

"Ciao," he said and disappeared inside his apartment.

The next morning Trevor called and asked me if now was a good time to talk. I said it was. He asked me some questions about the intellectual property rights of Nina and asked what law firm was handling the patent. I was happy to have a response – I knew it had been the right thing to do – and told him. He seemed suitably impressed. "They do good work," he said. I asked him if he needed an introduction and he told me it would speed things up, so I promised to do it right away.

"Listen," he said. "Do you have a law firm lined up to work on this financing?"

"I do," I said, lying. It sounded like an additional test and Trevor wanted to make sure that I wasn't dumb enough to suggest I use a boutique patent firm for a venture capital financing.

"Good. Make sure they're ready. We can move very fast for the right deal and I'm working on getting you a term sheet. I'm fired up."

I thanked him and as soon as we hung up I called Ken to let him know that I would be introducing Trevor by email. It went to voice mail and I left him a message. I thought about calling Julie. She would probably answer her phone – associates usually do – and I wanted to give someone in the firm a little context about what was transpiring, but I didn't want to be annoying and I didn't want Julie to think I was looking for an excuse to talk to her, so I opted to send an email instead.

I emailed Ken and Trevor, with Julie in cc, introducing them all and telling everyone what the introduction was about. Then I called Josh Campbell, a corporate partner that I worked with in my law firm years ago, and left him a message and sent him an email, telling him that I wanted to talk to him about a potential deal.

Everything was finally happening the way I thought it would. When I had envisioned getting to this point in my project, however, I had never imagined having any distractions of any kind whatsoever. There would be a lot more things that I had never imagined.

< 12 >

The Light Brigade

The rejection from Trevor's firm came two weeks later. I was surprised, but, at the same time, not all that surprised.

He called me (very appropriately) to tell me about what happened. At the Monday partner's meeting, where potential new investments are discussed, some partners had expressed reservations about backing a first-time entrepreneur like myself, without the usual credentials, perhaps, and with no computer science degrees on the founding team. He asked me to please call him if I brought on any co-founders or if I found another firm to co-invest with them. He mumbled something about his firm liking to syndicate their investments and that they would be much more likely to invest if there were other investors on board.

His tone caught me so off guard that I almost felt bad for the guy. He had rightly identified Eric as a key partner to bring on board, and it seemed like we had almost got him to the finish line. I hadn't appropriately assuaged Eric's concerns, shall we say, and no doubt he must have had a few back-channel conversations with other key partners to squash the investment. That's life in the big city. Or at least in the big valley.

His last comment to me was meaningless and I have to admire that he didn't even have the courage to say it with any conviction. It must be a VCs favorite thing to say that they'll invest if other firms invest, too. Well, no duh. "Hey, if you find something everybody wants, then we'll want it, too." But Trevor said he was sorry it didn't work out and that he enjoyed meeting me. He seemed genuinely disappointed in a way that kind of surprised me. When he said goodbye, he paused for a brief moment before hanging up.

It was time to face some facts. I looked at my familiar spreadsheet of contacts and VC firms. I had spent dozens and dozens of hours on it, but I tried to look at it with a fresh set of eyes. I had exhausted all of the first and second-tier investors on my list. Everybody had either outright rejected me or was in the process of ghosting me. If I moved into the lower-tier firms, I knew the response rate was going to decrease dramatically since I would be dealing with firms that were unfamiliar with the biotech space.

Sid never called me back and I was at a dead end with the libraries and databases. I was going to have to get on a plane to make progress on that topic. Meanwhile, there was the AI to think about. Maybe something was going on with the artificial intelligence software that I had incorporated into Nina. I thought of pivoting to that as a next step. It was possible that some things would clear up on the investor front as I focused on the AI.

I decided to go for a run to clear my head. It was something I hadn't done in ages, but I had a strange craving to be outside and feel the physical earth under my body. I pulled out my old sneakers, threw on some shorts and headed out the door. I didn't have a good idea of where I was going, I just started to go. It felt good to be outside and my legs felt strong as I headed down Telegraph in the general direction of downtown Oakland.

Maybe Marc with a "c" had been right and I had been mistaken not to use one of the big tech AI products. I needed to ask a lot of questions to see how the AI was affecting Nina and the recommendation engine. Would some startup even be willing to tell me what they were doing with their software? Large companies are much more sophisticated than smaller, young companies when it comes to things like this. A large company knows exactly what aspect of their technology is worth protecting and what they can and can't talk about publicly or with customers. Smaller startups lay an overzealous blanket of confidentiality over everything because they think everything that they do is magic and could be their ticket to becoming the world's first trillionaires. Or, as Shunryu Suzuki said, "In the beginner's mind there are many possibilities, but in the expert's there are few."

Deep in thought, I jogged across a street and was nearly hit by a car. The driver honked at me and gestured wildly as he drove past. Through the window of his '95 Ford Taurus, with music blaring and one almost-flat tire, he screamed, "You're fucking crazy, man!" I realized I needed to pay closer attention to where I was going, so I looked up, but I hardly recognized where I was standing. I was...downtown?

I had run to the end of Telegraph and was crossing Broadway without realizing it. But that was...that seemed impossible. That was at least 3 or 4 miles. I had barely even broken a sweat. I instinctively leaned over to catch my breath, but I wasn't out of breath. I shook my legs and didn't feel a sore fiber in my body. How was that possible? I hadn't lifted anything heavier than a pencil in two years, hadn't run further than the bathroom in all that time and I had just run for 30 minutes with almost no perceptible physical strain.

It's downhill, I told myself, very gradual, but downhill nonetheless. I turned around and started running up Broadway, back towards Rockridge. It wasn't very difficult. I looked at my watch and purposefully picked up the pace a little bit. I had run some 10k's and trained for different sports in high school, so I had a general idea of how fast I was running. It took me eight minutes to run the next mile. I wasn't breaking any speed records, but I hadn't run that fast since I was 19.

I got home and took a shower, feeling that I had yet another issue to track down. I finished and wrapped a towel around my waist and took a long look at myself in the mirror. My eyes naturally went a few inches above my head. Still no halo.

I closed my eyes to keep certain thoughts from creeping into my mind. When I opened them again, I focused lower, on my head and noticed my hairline. Was my hair starting to grow back? That didn't seem possible. I still had a decent head of hair, but was always self-conscious about losing it, like any man in or approaching middle age. I hadn't cleaned hair out of the sink in weeks, months, it seemed. I examined my scalp, but I wasn't sure. Maybe I was just seeing things. Maybe I was just seeing things everywhere.

I got dressed and called my doctor to schedule a routine physical. Maybe that would shed some light on something. I could compare the results to what I was seeing with Nina and see if there were any discrepancies. Plus, it would be potentially useful to have a human look at me. I trusted my machine, of course, but perhaps there was something going on that a human could intuit.

There were no appointments for weeks, of course. Instead of going online, though, I went old school and got in my car and drove up Telegraph towards Berkeley, looking for a doctor's office that I could get into on a random weekday afternoon. It needed to be a certain type of doctor's office, perhaps older and slightly run down. About five blocks across the Berkeley border, I found the perfect spot.

I stopped at a building with fiber cement siding that looked like it had seen better days. It had aluminum windows, a flat roof and a sign that said Berkeley Med in a font that hadn't been updated since people first started lighting up signs on that street in the 1950s. I walked inside and was heartened to see a dingy beige carpet and chairs straight out of a Brady Bunch episode. The waiting room was empty. Perhaps I was in luck.

I walked up to the front counter and a rang the chrome call bell. The frosted window of the reception area slid over revealing a young woman in her 30s with blondish brown hair, a nose ring, and a tattoo sleeve on her left arm poking out from under her green scrubs. She greeted me and I smiled as politely as I could.

"Hi, I'd like to get a physical," I said.

"Do you have an appointment?" she asked. She had olive colored skin and green eyes and I found myself trying my best not to make eye contact with her to make her uncomfortable.

"No."

She did not seem fazed at all as she looked down at her paper calendaring system. I had picked the right spot, after all.

"I have an opening at 2:40," she said without smiling.

"I'll take it."

She gave me a packet of information to fill out before my appointment. I drove down to Bake Sale Betty's, an unmarked joint on the corner of Telegraph and 51st that sold a few cookies, a few pies and the best fried chicken sandwich you'll ever eat. There was a line literally around the block for the first few years after it opened. She (Betty) had even published her damned recipe – here you try and make it – it was that good. You don't even have to specify "Chicken sandwich" when you walk in. "Sandwich," is all you have to say. So that's what I did. I bought a sandwich with a bag of chips and sat down at a table made out of an ironing board and enjoyed the sun and the clouds and the sounds of that town, while filling out the forms and answering an eternal list of mostly inapplicable questions.

I went back to the doctor's office at 2:40. It was my first physical, I told Saanvi, the Physician's Assistant, and I just wanted to be careful since I had recently turned 40, also for the first time. This made her laugh and it all seemed to make sense to her or she didn't care and they ran their tests and ordered blood work, urine analysis and every other kind of test that insurance would pay for.

That night, I couldn't sit still in my apartment. I was restless and anxious and aware of a gnawing loneliness inside me. For the first time since I had lived there, I went across the hall and knocked on Juan Pablo's door, but he wasn't home. I slinked back into my own apartment. I didn't really want to hang out with him, anyway. I didn't know what I wanted, or I did know, I knew very well, but I didn't want to admit it to myself. It's not that I didn't want to be alone. That was only part of the problem. I tried for as long as possible to keep the truth under the surface.

Finally, I had no other choice. It's awful, but there was no running away from it. I needed to come clean with myself and be honest about what I wanted, what I felt in that moment. It wasn't going away and I wasn't going to just be able to fall asleep. It sounds terrible to say, and I know exactly how this will seem, but what I realized was this: I wanted to meet another woman with a halo.

Once that was out in the open, I got dressed and went to McNally's to have a drink. I had a Makers rocks at the bar and sat there looking around and waiting like some pathetic loser. It was stupid and embarrassing. Why me? Why now? Everything had been fine before. But then I thought of the tantalizing feelings and emotions I had felt with Laura and Susan and I slammed down the rest of my drink, closed out my tab and left, with a quizzical look from Tiny. I went to the Golden Bear, where I had met Susan, and then the Swordfish. Same thing happened. Nothing. I went downtown and walked into every bar I could remember, Radio, Tremors, Van Kleef's. When I say I walked in, that's what I did, I'm ashamed to say. I walked in, looked around and then, not seeing a halo, walked out.

I was desperate to meet someone, to have a conversation, to unburden myself. I was pissed off about BioBay and wanted someone to commiserate with my failure, even to feel sorry for me. I was frustrated that I didn't understand everything that was happening and that I was running into so many dead ends with Nina. I wanted someone to tell about all of it. But I didn't want that person to tell me later that I was a dick. I didn't want to be blamed for working late and missing birthdays or anniversaries or buying the wrong present. I didn't want to second guess everything I said and wonder what it was that they meant when they said this or that thing. I didn't want to be responsible for hurting someone's feelings and didn't want to risk anyone hurting mine. In short, I wanted everything that only the halo could provide.

But it wasn't in the cards for me that night. I stayed at Van Kleef's because their greyhounds are legendary. I stopped counting how many I drank after four. There was only indoor seating in those days and so I just sat at the bar, dark as it was. People milled around me, came and went. Luckily, the college crowd doesn't venture that far into downtown Oakland, so I didn't have to deal with their perfect hair and their world-is-full-of-possibility smiles. Not one person in Van Kleef's that night believed they could be anything they wanted to be. Not a single one. I stayed until it closed and took an Uber home. Alone.

Two days later I had my follow-up appointment at the Berkeley Medical Group. I found myself anxiously awaiting the results to see if they could shed light on anything. I rang the call bell when I walked in and the frosted window slid over and the first thing I saw was a light halo over the nose ring, tattoo sleeved receptionist. I was completely caught off guard and only managed to stammer through checking in for my appointment.

She led me to the back and walked me to an exam room herself. My mind raced through possibilities as she smiled at me politely and closed the door behind her. Could I have missed the halo earlier or was it new? I opened the door to the exam room and watched her walking back down the hall. The halo over her head was faint but clear. She turned around and smiled at me again before disappearing around the corner. I couldn't believe it.

Saanvi walked in before I had a chance to close the door and she greeted me with enthusiasm. She was shaking my hand and talking before I remembered to greet her and focus on our actual real-time conversation.

"Mr. Percy, congratulations, you are in perfect health," she said. "Well, nobody is in perfect health, but you are in excellent shape."

She went over the results from my tests and I asked for a printout so that I could analyze it all based on what I was seeing from Nina.

"What do you do for a living?" Saanvi asked.

"I'm a lawyer," I answered. "I'm unemployed right now, or semi-retired depending on how you want to look at it."

Saanvi laughed.

"I'm trying to start my own company."

"An entrepreneur. Fantastic. Late nights?" She asked.

"Quite a few."

"Interesting." She pulled out the paperwork I had filled out before my physical. "It says here you consume 10-20 drinks a week, is that right?"

"Yes, I'm afraid so."

"That's a lot. That's significantly higher than average. You don't smoke?"

"No."

She flipped through the reports, looking a little puzzled.

"I see you used to have high cholesterol, but your cholesterol is almost perfect now," she said.

"My diet," I suggested. She perked up. "I've been focusing on my diet. That's how I do it—why I'm in good health. My company is a sort of diet and supplements company. I'm trying to promote healthy living."

"Well, that's interesting," she said. She half-heartedly went through some health tips for men my age, talking endlessly about diet and exercise and all of the stupid one-size-fits-all crap that had caused me to create Nina in the first place. She actually handed me a photocopied flyer with some health information that had probably been outdated for years. She was a fine person and this was a fine place, but she didn't tell me anything that I wouldn't have preferred reading on the screen of my phone. This experience was inferior to the one I was offering with Nina in every way. Well, in every way but one.

Saanvi wished me well and I walked out of the exam room and headed for the exit, but instead of proceeding straight and through the door, I turned right down the hall and went to the reception area. I walked right up behind the nose ring woman on the other end of the frosted glass window.

"Excuse me," I said, looking around to make sure nobody was watching.

"What is it, Mr. Percy?"

"I have to see you again," I said, sounding even more desperate than I had intended.

She was completely taken aback, and even a bit confused. "Excuse me?" she said.

"What's your name?" I asked, lamely.

"Audrey," she answered, still confused.

"Audrey, I have to see you again. I can't explain it. Can I call you or email you?"

The confusion was gone and in its place was some mixture of surprise and an expression that looked like she was trying to decide between flattery and annoyance, but behind all that I could sense the slightest modicum of intrigue. Or perhaps it was boredom. I couldn't tell, but in any event, I decided to double down.

"Please? Look, I'm sorry for being so forward. I'm not good at this, really, and I never do it even though you won't believe me because that's what I would say even if I did it all the time. But I'm not going to have another chance and so I just thought I'd ask. I would really like to buy you coffee or a drink. May I?"

The art of asking a question. I'm a lawyer. We ask questions all the time. Other professions do it, too, and those people who have no problem with it. Either you are naturally curious or curiosity and inquiry are part of your job, or both. Even though I'm a lawyer, I was not a natural question-asker. I was never comfortable with the ambiguity. I was a question answerer.

There are all manner of questions, open-ended, closed-ended, it doesn't matter. Here, in the reception area of this small, kind of dirty and possibly struggling medical office that may or may not have been a front for some other kind of activity, anxiety building inside me, I remembered you have to just ask the question and wait for the answer. You don't answer for somebody—never do that – and you don't walk back the question.

She looked at me in the face and at once her body relaxed somewhat. She looked around to see if anyone was looking. Nobody was. She turned around and scribbled her number on a piece of paper and handed it to me.

"Sure," she said. "Why not?"

Audrey was a flower dressed up as a thorn. Away from work, she was a completely different person than in the office. She had just turned 30 but was living life with the intensity of a 19-year-old. She had been married once, it lasted 16 months and she was "over that bullshit." She was a perpetually bursting firework of energy, thoughts and activity.

Her father had left her mother when she was 5 and it had scarred her deeply. She missed her dad so much at first that she cried herself to sleep for years. We commiserated on that point. Then, after that, her mom had to work multiple jobs to make ends meet and Audrey rarely saw her. There was a string of boyfriends and the suggestion of something inappropriate or at least unseemly. She was a latch key kid, the kind we used to have before the latch keys gave way to helicopters, I suppose. Someone might take a look at her and say that she was trouble. But I just saw the vitality inside of her and it amazed me.

She was into music and mixed different songs and rhythms on her computer, creating different tracks and playlists for different occasions. She was doing the work of a DJ, but never seriously thought about DJ'ing commercially. It seemed lame, she said.

I saw her on four different occasions and we never so much as kissed. I tried one time, the first night, and she simply said, "No, thank you." I asked her why not and she said, "Because I don't trust you. I like you. But I don't trust you. And I'm not sure why. You're up to something. So until I figure that out, no, thank you." I just laughed because, of course, she was right. I wanted very badly to kiss her, to press my face against hers, feel her nose ring against my skin, but I didn't mind abstaining. I knew how to do that, too. I had her attention and that was more important, I thought.

She reintroduced me to so many things I'd long forgotten, music, authors, tastes, sights, sounds, which had all been hidden away for so long. She loved walking out to the Berkeley shoreline and even more driving to Mill Valley and hiking out to Tennessee Beach in Marin, where she could listen to the waves crash under the bright grey skies.

The halo, dim at first, gradually increased in intensity over the next two and a half weeks. I tried to ignore it as best I could but, in the end, it was hard to miss, I have to admit.

The last time I saw her she stayed the night at my apartment. It was late, we had both eaten gummies and she was too high to drive and didn't want to Uber home. I was a perfect gentleman and insisted I would take the couch and she could sleep in my room, but she wouldn't hear of it. She grabbed a blanket and put up her feet and laid down on the sofa, light as a feather.

At about 3 am I felt her get in bed, under the covers, beside me. I was sleeping on my side and she scooted as close as she could to my back being careful not to wake me up (but I was already awake). It was quiet and cool in my apartment, but warm in bed with her. Under different circumstances, I might have taken that as an invitation to roll over and kiss her. But she had told me no already, and I am nothing if not obedient.

I remembered the last time I hugged my father. It was the summer after my sophomore year in high school, during my second, and final, trip to visit him in Argentina in the house he shared with his then wife. I was waking up very late for me, around 11am (early for an Argentine weekend) and he came into the room where I was sleeping and told me he was stepping out because he had errands to run. I was getting out of bed and he hugged me and thanked me for visiting. That afternoon, I was out, in a neighborhood across the city, with some friends I had made, when we passed a strange looking building with a parking garage door that seemed to appear out of nowhere. That, my friend told me, was a *telo*.

A *telo* is a hotel in Argentina with rooms that you rent by the hour. It is a hotel for casual encounters of the romantic variety. The name itself comes from the word hotel with the syllables reversed, something they do as slang in Argentina to spicen up the language, sort of like using a *rabona* when taking a penalty kick (kicking the ball when the kicking foot goes behind the back of the standing leg). Nobody can tell you definitively why *telos* are common there, it's just part of their culture, but maybe it has something to do with the fact that young people live at home until they're married and a culture that takes infidelity in stride. In any event, right as my friend was telling me this, here comes my dad's car out of the parking garage door. And that, as they say, was that.

But there in Oakland, I sensed Audrey wasn't sleeping and neither was I. The light from the halo was distracting and tying me up inside. I rolled onto my back and lay there, staring at the ceiling. Now that I was awake, she cuddled close to my shoulder and we laid together in silence. I felt far closer to her than the physical distance between us, which was minimal, but I had an intensifying feeling inside me that I could no longer ignore. As close as I was to her, there was one thing that was keeping me from being even closer.

And finally, I couldn't contain myself any longer. I didn't even want to sleep with her in that moment. That wasn't what I felt. We were so close in so many ways that I could no longer tolerate any distance between us at all.

I chose my words so carefully that when I spoke, it felt like English words had never come out of my mouth before.

"Can I ask you a question?" I asked, my voice dry.

"Sure."

"It's one of those stupid, philosophical ones."

"I love those," she said, inhaling quietly, dreamily, her husky voice barely above a whisper.

"What would you do differently, would you do anything different, if you knew…" – it was so, impossibly hard to say the words – "If you knew you were going to die?"

She cuddled closer to me by way of response. I could feel her sweatpants on my legs. I could feel her hand on my arm and her breath on my shoulder, but I couldn't look at her. I stared up at the ceiling only. "Nothing," she said, then rolled over onto her back. "I wouldn't do anything differently." We both lay there now, staring at the moonlight on the ceiling.

"It wouldn't matter, anyway," she said. "I would never want to know."

And there it was. I exhaled a long and deep breath. In retrospect, what I felt, if I had to describe it with one word, was sad. And I also felt resigned. The words of an old friend resounded in my mind.

Theirs not to make reply,
Theirs not to reason why,
Theirs but to do and die.

That was Tennyson. Another guy who understood about following instructions. It was as clear to me as the moonlit, star-filled night. I had my orders and I intended to follow them.

We lay there comfortably in each other's company. At some point, we must have fallen asleep and when I woke up, she was gone. I never saw her again.

The next week, Audrey stopped answering her phone and stopped returning my texts. I had been down that road before, of course, so I kept texting every couple of days. "Hey, have you forgotten about me?" "Did you see who's playing at the Fox?" She wasn't there and I knew it, but for a while it felt like I was talking to her anyway.

Eventually I received a message from her mother. Audrey had gone out with some friends and during a night of heavy partying had overdosed. Did I know her well? What could I tell her about her last days? Could she call me?

I set the phone down. I had known all along that this was coming, obviously, but in a moment like that, it doesn't matter. None of it matters. You follow directions. And you don't ask any questions.

Into the valley of Death
Rode the six hundred.

‹ 13 ›

Continuing Education

I don't remember much about the next week except that I never left my apartment and I didn't answer the door or my phone. It had all gone too far. I could see that now. The halo had provided a unique allure, I'll admit that, but pursuing these relationships was a fallacy.

This one stung, in particular. It wasn't fair. Audrey was young, in the prime of her life. They all had been, to some extent, but she was vibrant. She was one of the most alive people I had ever met, living on the edge of experience, pushing her limits. She was supposed to just gradually stop returning my calls and texts in a few months because I was boring or because I was too old or conservative, or because she found someone her age that was into the same things as she was. Someone she *could* trust. Not this. This was not supposed to happen.

I felt robbed of thinking about her in the future, wondering what she was up to. I would never be able to stalk her on social media from time to time and trivialize some future relationship she was in with an annoying douchebag with fantastic hair. It felt like those things were owed to me and now they had been taken. All the crap that I hated, feeling like her success was a barometer of my failure, being paranoid for months about running into her in places she would never be, waiting for calls and texts I knew would never come, all of it, gone.

There was a sudden and abrupt knock on the door that snapped me back into reality. I stood slowly and walked over. I knew it was Juan Pablo the moment my hand touched the knob, and as the door swung open, he burst into my apartment.

"Dude! What the fuck?! Where have you been?"

"Hi," was all I could muster.

He looked at the clutter and mess all around my apartment, then turned around and looked at me. "Your place looks like shit. You look like shit," he said. "You've lost like 5 kilos, or 10 pounds or whatever stupid thing you call it. Are you sick?"

"I've been sick, yeah," I said, lying, with a subconscious sniffle.

"I must have come over here ten times looking for you."

"I'm sorry."

"You can't respond to the like hundred texts?"

"I don't even know where my phone is. I've been out of it."

"What happened?" he asked.

The weight of everything felt so heavy over me. "There was a girl," I began. I closed the door and walked into the living room and stood next to the couch. I didn't know whether to sit or stand. I was still not totally comfortable and I found myself wondering what to do with my hands, so I put them in my pockets.

"Where is she?"

"I'm not seeing her anymore."

"Again?" he said, incredulous. "You go through women faster than Mike runs away from me in the garden."

I shook my head. "No, you don't understand," I said.

He looked at me inquisitively with his hands out and shoulders in a sort of shrug. You didn't need a gesture translator to know that this meant, "WHAT?"

I closed my eyes. I had to say something. I couldn't go on hiding the truth. "She died," I blurted out.

He stood there, transfixed, his mouth agape, unable to form words, unsure if I was serious. "I don't believe you," he said finally. "I...I can't believe you. You're joking."

"No. No. She died. She overdosed. Her mom called me. We talked for like an hour."

His mouth opened but no words came out.

"Here," I said. I looked on my dining room table for my phone but it wasn't there. I looked in the kitchen, by the couch, all the usual places. I couldn't find it. Juan Pablo watched me tear up my apartment like some sort of lunatic.

"Here!" I said, calling out from my bedroom. I finally found it under a small pile of dirty clothes on the corner of my bed. "Here," I said again, holding up the phone as I walked out of my room. "Here, see for yourself," I said, handing him the phone. "Please, by all means, see for yourself."

He took my phone and pressed on the screen. "It's dead," he said. "Excuse me. I mean it has no battery."

"Crap," I said and then repeated roughly the same search pattern looking for a charging cord. Finally, I realized there would be one at my work station and I walked over and plugged it in.

"It doesn't matter, dude. I don't want to look at your phone. I am so sorry," he said with a truly sorrowful expression.

He put his hand on my shoulder and stood next to me, as if waiting for me to say something, but I had nothing to say. I thought of telling him the whole terrible story, but then I thought maybe just processing one death would be enough for the evening. Instead, he went back to his apartment, made me some tea and stayed with me late into the night. We sat at my small dining room table by the window and took turns talking and looking outside at the trees under the street lights, the darkening early evening sky, and the people outside, coming home from work or headed to dinner. He asked about Audrey and the things we had done and I told him all about how we had met, how I asked her out, what she liked and the things we had talked about. He listened intently as I told him about my conversation with her mom and how thankful she had been to talk to me.

When he left I felt an immense weight lifted off my chest, like I had finally done something I had waited an eternity to do. I had a feeling of clarity and knowledge. The world seemed again full of possibilities and I knew exactly how I wanted to approach everything. It's not like I knew everything in exact detail, but I had a confidence in how I was feeling and in how things were going to turn out.

I felt energized to move forward and get some work done. I ordered food to my apartment and ate twice as much as I normally would. I opened my email and, to my surprise, I had dozens of messages related to Nina. There were responses from investors I had emailed weeks ago asking for a meeting. Even Marc with a "c" and Trevor had both written to me to check in and ask about recent progress.

I set meetings up for the coming weeks and prepared updates to my investor presentations. I opened my dashboard of Nina workstreams and focused on getting to the core of response engine. Clearly something was working very well – I was in the best shape of my life – but I had to know if Nina was also behind the halos and what that meant. The only way to do that was to tackle the issue head on. I needed to get to the sources. Perhaps I wasn't qualified to understand all of the issues and their implications, but I would just show up, do my best and see what happened after that. I began to explore preliminary travel plans.

Juan Pablo came to check on me every day. He asked when Nina would be ready for him to use and, even though the multi-user protocol was finished, I told him that I wasn't quite done with it yet. I felt morally conflicted about letting someone else, particularly Juan Pablo, use Nina until I was sure what was going on with it.

"You use it every day," he said. "How are you feeling?"

"Honestly, I feel better than ever."

"Come on, dude. You don't have to convince me. I told you I'm going to do it."

"No, I'm serious," I said. "Physically, I feel amazing. Some issues have come up that I hadn't foreseen, though, and I want to make sure that you get the best recommendations for you and the best experience possible."

He wasn't interested in details, instead talking about plans for the weekend. I felt energized and confident in myself in a way I hadn't been in years. It was contagious and I decided to seek out situations where I might meet and interact with new people. I'd had my eye on a continuing legal education conference set for the next day, which focused on the latest trends in intellectual property issues. My reluctance to meet and interact with strangers usually acted as a deterrence for me to attend such events, but that was not the case at the moment.

I registered for the conference and looked eagerly at the list of topics and speakers. There were several sessions that looked almost exactly tailored to Nina and the issues I either was, or shortly would be, facing. The speakers had excellent credentials and all looked knowledgeable and interesting. I mapped out which events I would attend and prepared some questions I could ask at each. I went to bed that night with a sense of eagerness and anticipation.

The next morning, I woke up, had a quick Nina-recommended breakfast, and walked to BART. The cold morning air felt incredible and I even took pride for a moment in how smartly I was dressed. Not necessarily how I looked, but I was warm and knew I would be comfortable when I got to the event because I was dressed in layers like we tend to do around here. I felt like I was doing things correctly.

Once on the other side of the bay, San Francisco looked amazing. The winter sky was bright under a layer of fluffy clouds that promised to be gone after lunch time. The bay on those partially cloudy days is an incredible emerald green color and the Berkeley and Oakland hills were a vibrant dark green in the background and the contrasts made the surroundings look even more intense.

Inside the conference hotel, I found the people attending the event to be interesting-looking and professional. People were busy getting coffee and pastries, mingling, speaking with friends or networking. I grabbed a coffee, some fruit and a pastry and headed to the keynote speaking event.

We were all in luck. The keynote speaker was a partner from one of the preeminent IP boutiques in the Silicon Valley, which is to say the world. She had an impeccable resume, Harvard undergrad, Yale law school, and had become a partner at her firm after nearly 10 years at one of the top, white shoe firms in New York. She walked confidently up to the podium and started off her speech by saying, "Webster defines 'crappy introduction' as any speech that begins with the words, 'Webster defines.'" That got everybody laughing and set the mood for the whole introduction.

She began with a fascinating discussion of recent developments in intellectual property law, some unsettled questions that were pending before different Courts of Appeal and the US Supreme Court, and the dramatic impact these could have on the development of the Internet, social media, artificial intelligence and even the entire US economy. She tied different aspects of the cases to the different subject matter experts who would be presenting throughout the day and the different topics to be covered. It was a master class on keynote speaking and professionalism.

She began winding up the speech 25 minutes later, though it seemed she had only just started. It was at that point, I heard a rustling of feet and a moving of chairs beside me.

I looked and was quite surprised to see Julie, the associate from Towers & Gray, the boutique patent law firm that had helped me with the filing of my provisional patent. She was dressed casually but elegantly and her long hair, still a little wet from a morning shower, hung down past her shoulders. I wasn't sure I had ever seen it down before.

She had a smile that encompassed her entire face. Her eyes were smiling, her shoulders were smiling, her entire body appeared to be smiling. When I looked up at her, my expression must have betrayed my feelings, as she smiled even more broadly at me, if that were possible. There was an extra twinkle in her eyes when she looked at me and spoke, just a little out of breath from rushing the way one does when late. "Did I miss anything?"

< 14 >

In the Morning Light

"Julie! What a surprise," I said, moving my backpack and conference papers off of the chair next to me.

"I knew that was you," she said. "I could spot you from a mile away."

The comment was astonishing, but I was too afraid to ask for details. She just smiled at me and sat down, set down her bag and accommodated her things next to her. "What are you doing here?" I asked, very dumbly and with immediate regret.

"Uh, well, I'm a lawyer. This is a legal conference. I need the CLE credits by the deadline, probably just like you."

"Of course. Stupid question. Sorry."

"I love it when people say there are no stupid questions."

"Totally," I said. It was an absolute pet peeve of mine when people said that. "There are so many stupid questions. And that was one of them!"

We both laughed.

"This is Rachel...what's her name," she said looking up at the podium.

"Stroemberg," I said. "Yeah."

"She's fantastic."

"I know. She's been amazing."

The truth is that I had forgotten we were in a room full of people and that there was someone speaking. Ms. Stroemberg was still at the podium, but she was unfortunately wrapping up her speech. I looked at the time and at the conference program with disappointment when I realized that it was almost over. My disappointment, however, had nothing to do with the speaker or the speech, both of which had been excellent. She finished exactly on time at half past the hour.

Despite the early hour and the mundane nature of many of these conferences, the applause was immediate and built up around us, and although Julie had only begun to settle in, we joined in with the clapping. As the response to the keynote speech became more celebratory, Julie shouted out, "Wooo!" and I couldn't help but laugh. I had never seen her like this before. She was so relaxed and easy going.

We followed the crowd out into the main hall to get coffee. They had set out a food line with small, hot breakfast sandwiches and a variety of pastries. I grabbed a mini fruit-filled Danish pastry while Julie went with a small Kouign-Amann that looked like it would melt in your mouth. We both paused a moment, looking at what the other had chosen with approval.

We walked over to the espresso bar, but neither of us liked the look of the espresso machine so we filled tall paper cups with the house coffee, which wasn't bad, and chit-chatted by the coffee prep station. Time flew by and before either of us realized it, the main hall was nearly empty and we were late for the next session.

We had both decided on attending the session on Legal Issues in Cobranded and Jointly Developed Technology, which took place in a smaller break out room, but Julie had left her purse on a chair in the main hall. She had to sneak back in to the main room, while another presentation was already under way, to retrieve it. This was hysterical to us for some reason and we giggled our way to the Joint Tech session, which was excellent, the part that we heard anyway, since we sat in the back and talked over half the lecture. At the next break, we headed towards a crowded session on intellectual property issues in contract drafting.

"You don't have to indulge me by going to this one," I said at the doorway and looking at the program. "Look, there's another session on patent issues pending before the U.S. Supreme Court."

"I've already read up on those," she said. "Plus, Ken could give that lecture himself. And I've heard it. Trust me!" I nodded. He probably could.

"I'm more interested in this one," she said and pointed to a spot in the second row where there were two seats together. I nodded and we went in.

After the session, we walked together to the buffet lunch line and, with full plates, sat at a table full of strangers that we barely spoke to. We were engrossed in our own discussion about the previous session and about how drafting a contract is similar to writing a computer program. They are both self-contained systems that work to control things happening outside the system, and one could derive a kind of pleasure from making a contract as efficient and bug free as possible. She asked about Nina and I told her about the different challenges I was facing and what I had been working on. She seemed to listen intently to everything I said.

During the course of the day, I purposefully gave her ample opportunity to politely go her own way, but each time, she would come back to where I was or come find me. We both saw several familiar faces, acquaintances and former colleagues, but she never broke away from me to speak to anyone else for long. When she would leave to use the restroom, she left her materials with me. When I left to use the restroom, taking everything, I would return to find her in the same spot, waiting for me with a smile.

In some ways, I knew exactly what was happening, but in others, I couldn't bring myself to believe that someone like her could be interested in me. She was attractive without trying to be. She was smart and confident. She'd had a fantastic education. She had a good job. Literally everything was in her favor.

I began to feel nervous about allowing myself to be attracted to her. It had been many, many years since I had felt desire toward someone (without a halo, of course) and even longer since the Christina ex-girlfriend debacle. There weren't a lot of positive memories associated with that time for me. Nevertheless, I felt myself being drawn in further and further by Julie.

Unlike the recent history with Audrey or Susan or Laura, I could sense the possibility of a future with Julie. That's not to say that I was planning the wedding or anything, but in between moments, after a comment or while we were laughing, I could project that image into the future. The thought of it happening again made me even more excited instead of inducing fear, like it might have previously. I referenced places I enjoyed that she had never been to, and I thought of taking her to them. We would talk about restaurants or bars or bands and I would think about the possibility of enjoying those things with her.

We attended the sleepy afternoon sessions together but decided to skip out on the cocktail hour.

"I can only be around that many attorneys for so long," she said with a laugh.

The difference between work Julie and this version of her was fairly dramatic. The law requires a certain level of formality and, with me, there in that moment, she was being very casual. She had her guard down. She was engaging. And she was treating me as an equal, instead of treating me with the deference you might give a client. This took some getting used to at first, but by the end of the day, I was confidently participating in this new kind of relationship we were forming.

I suggested we go to Boulevard for dinner, because it was a classic San Francisco restaurant in a historic building and very near the water. She said she loved the idea. We walked the six blocks down Howard Street and talked about how much this part of the city had changed since the construction of the new baseball stadium in 2000. The South of Market area had been all parking lots and warehouses when I was a kid and now it was full of high rises, first class office buildings, lofts and condos. The old San Francisco saying, "You're gonna grow up to be just another bum on Howard Street," could now take on a whole different meaning.

We were able to get two seats at the bar in Boulevard. The restaurant was buzzing with energy and conversation and I had the feeling that we fit right into the scene at that moment, like a puzzle piece. We were talking about our careers, our lives, just like everyone else. I had a startup, she was a patent attorney, we were coming back from a conference, and I had a sense of belonging that I hadn't felt in many years.

She was from Virginia, the part near Washington D.C., and had grown up in the suburbs. Her dad had worked for the Department of Health and Human Services. Her mother had always wanted to study law, but had given it up in part out of intimidation and in part out of a need to make money. She had become a paralegal and hated it, and gave up on her dream of being a lawyer to start a family and because she had become disillusioned with the law.

With that background, I was surprised that Julie had decided to become an attorney. Sometimes, when you get too close to it, a legal career can lose its appeal because you see all of the daunting problems but you don't necessarily have any of the benefits. I asked her about this and she said, "I feel like when it gets bad you have to focus on the problem right in front of you. You can't think about the big picture or you'll go crazy. But there are so many things that you can find interesting. There are so many different aspects to it."

She was right. That had always been my approach and I felt like my ability to compartmentalize had served me very well in my career.

I asked about her focus on patents. "You seem to have such a variety of interests. Have you ever considered broadening your practice? Not focusing exclusively on patents?"

She couldn't keep a very subtle smile from crossing her face. "I have. We'll see," she said, shrugging her shoulders in a way that I found very alluring.

After a meticulously prepared and delicious dinner, we shared a dessert that was almost as remarkable to look at as it was to taste. Including drinks before dinner and wine with dinner, I had lost track of where I was on my alcohol barometer, but it was high. I was feeling good. She was asking me more detailed questions about Nina and I asked her if she wanted to see it for herself. She did, so we left Boulevard and headed across the bay to my apartment.

My heart was racing as we walked upstairs to my front door. As we reached the top, Juan Pablo opened his door, saw that I was with Julie, said hi and quickly excused himself, closing the door again. He was a tremendous friend.

I opened the door to my apartment and walked quickly over to the kitchen, making sure I hadn't left anything embarrassing out (I hadn't) and turning lights on along the way. I made us an espresso on my home machine and we sipped coffee looking out of the living room window at the street lights on 63rd and Telegraph Avenue.

"This looks like a San Francisco apartment," she said, referring to its small size.

"This neighborhood was mostly constructed right after the quake," I said, referring to the one in 1906 and not 1989. She understood me.

I turned on the lights to my workstation, turned on my computer and opened the development environment, showing Julie the different aspects of the program. It was the first time I had ever shared Nina's source code with anyone. It felt almost like showing somebody the insides of myself and I noted some feelings of self-consciousness about how the program operated and how it was set up and organized. I wondered what about myself I was betraying without realizing it.

"I can't help it," she said, scrolling through different lines of code. "I just really admire this. I really admire you. This is quite an accomplishment."

"It's not anything, yet."

"Are you kidding me? Look at this. Look at everything you've done. It's already a success. You don't need a venture capital investor to validate anything about this, Drew. It's remarkable."

She asked about the sources for the recommendation engine and we looked at the materials together. "You feel like it's working well?" She asked, scooting closer to me.

"It is, I think," I responded. She was gazing intently at me as though she were eliciting the very question I knew I needed to ask. "Do you think you would want...to try it?"

"I'd love to. But don't you normally use it in the morning?"

"Yes."

"Well, then maybe so should I."

My ears filled with the sound of blood rushing to my head and I leaned in and kissed her gently on the mouth. She exhaled sweetly perfumed breath and I thought I heard her sigh, "Oh." We embraced fully and kissed for several minutes, right there at my desk. I felt years of anxiety fall off me with each tender kiss as I floated through waves of happiness, excitement and pleasure. I couldn't believe I was so lucky that this was happening to me.

We walked back to my room. I could feel the decaying outside shell breaking off of me in pieces. My enthusiasm for life and an eagerness to give and accept love grew with each passing moment. I wanted to experience everything again. All of the pain, all of the suffering hadn't mattered, didn't matter. I would gladly trade it all for this.

We spent all night together and it was like a symphony of sights and sounds, feelings and pleasures. Everything was a song, our song, and it was new yet familiar and, in turn, exhilarating and comforting. I fell asleep stroking her hair and woke up next to her, warm, happy and completely refreshed, completely rested.

I woke up because of a strange, but oddly familiar sound. It was something like humming, but not quite that audible. It was more like an audible vibration of air. I had heard it before, but couldn't remember where.

I looked around my room, slowly at first, and then at Julie, asleep on her side next to me, and saw it. It was barely visible but clear, unconscionably, terribly real. There, in the morning light, a faint halo hung above Julie's head.

‹PART 3›

< 15 >

Sid

I jumped backward off the bed and slammed my back against the wall. I was standing there, horrified, no idea what to do, as Julie woke up and her face broke into an easy smile. I was not in good control of my emotions, so there was no telling what kind of contorted expression had taken over my face. I watched as she focused on me, her eyes adjusting.

"I didn't think I looked *that* bad when I woke up in the morning," she said, sitting up, her face changing from a coy smile to something resembling curious concern.

I barely heard her and the humor didn't register. All I could see, all I could think of, was the halo above her head and, "No, no, no, no..." was all I managed to say.

"Drew, what's wrong? What are you looking at?" she asked, waking up more with each moment and looking behind her and above her head. "You're kind of freaking me out."

"No, I'm sorry," I managed to stammer, my mind going a hundred miles a minute. "It's just that...I...I realized I am, uh, I am missing a meeting."

"Oh!" she said sitting upright and clasping the sheets to her chest, as if the conversation, having turned professional, made her current intimate situation somewhat awkward.

I tried to busy myself so as not to betray the flood of thoughts and emotions coursing their way through my mind and body. My brain felt like it was on fire, and something inside me was bursting at my skin, trying to push its way into forcing some kind of movement, any movement, out of my legs, arms, hands and mouth.

I did the only thing that occurred to me. I started looking around for my clothes.

"Can I help you?" she asked, looking around the floor for my clothes, before sitting back up. "Wait, this is your apartment. Shouldn't you just put on some fresh clothes?"

"Yes. Good point," I said and opened a dresser drawer. I stared into the drawer but its contents made no sense to me. My clothes just seemed to be a collection of different colors and shapes and textures, nothing distinguishing one thing from the other. Were they t-shirts or animals or pieces of code? I had no way of knowing or figuring out how to understand. What I was seeing was not translating into coherent concepts in my brain.

"Who is the meeting with?" Julie asked.

The question snapped the correct language model into my brain and I immediately pulled out a t-shirt and went to my closet. "A potential investor," I said. Then I realized if I were going to meet with an investor, I would probably wear a different shirt, so I threw the t-shirt back into the drawer and grabbed a pair of pants and a shirt out of the closet.

I picked up my phone and looked at the time. "Crap," I said for no reason because I wasn't late for anything. I grabbed my wallet and my keys and sat down on the edge of the bed to put on shoes. "Would you mind? I know this is happening fast. I'm sorry. But, can you let yourself out?"

"Of course," she said. She was calm again and relaxed and slightly amused watching me run around like a maniac. I knew the halo was hanging above her head just sitting there almost taunting me and I was terrified to look at it, at her.

"Take your time," I said. "And help yourself to anything. Anything at all. You know where to find the food and everything. Just pretend it's an Airbnb."

She laughed and told me not to worry, that she had to get to work, too, and would be out of my apartment very shortly. She got up and began gathering her clothes while I stood there like an idiot, wanting to leave, needing to leave, but not wanting to go.

"Go! Go!" she urged, generously. "Don't worry about it. I'll figure everything out."

I walked towards the front door, telling myself over and over to just get out of the apartment. Should I try to hug her or kiss her? What would a normal person do or say in these situations? I had no idea. I twisted the doorknob, opened the door and stepped into the hallway. I forced myself to close the door slowly behind me.

In the quiet and poorly lit hallway, I stared down the stairs for a moment, cursing myself, my life, everything. I stood to gather my thoughts. It only took a second before it became immediately clear exactly what I needed to do.

I flew down the stairs, three at a time, barely making contact with any of the steps. Once on the landing, I threw open the front door and ran out into the street. I sprinted to my car, which unlocked automatically as it sensed me approaching. I opened the door and got in. The door made a satisfying *thunk* as I closed it, and I hit the power button, put it in gear, and pressed my foot as hard as I could against the gas pedal, all in one fluid motion.

The car spun its tires briefly and then shot forward, plunging me back into the driver's seat, as it raced the few hundred feet to the end of the street. I made a right turn, cutting hard into traffic on Telegraph Avenue, and the driver of the car I cut off laid heavily on his horn. I barely even heard it. I pressed the steering wheel button for voice control of my phone and when I heard its ready tone, I gave the command. "Call Sid," I said to the computer.

"*Calling Sid Beeman,*" the car responded.

It rang four times and went to voice mail. I left a message: "Call me, motherfucker. Call me now!" I pulled up at a stop light, pounding my hand on the steering wheel.

"*If you're satisfied with your message, press one,*" the phone said.

"Fuck you, bitch!" I screamed, trying to push the END button on the car's center display without taking my eyes off of the traffic light.

The light turned green and I floored it immediately. The car darted left onto Alcatraz Avenue and I went flying down the crowded street. The usual morning traffic was gathering, so I thought fuck it and began passing cars by cutting into oncoming traffic, sending cars veering into the bike lane to avoid hitting me.

"Text Sid!" I yelled at the computer over blaring car horns.

"*What do you want to say to Sid?*" the car responded.

"I don't care what you're doing, what meeting you're in, who you're boning, anything. Call me. Call me right fucking now!" My phone read the message back to me, changing "boning" to "*phoning*," but whatever. He would understand exactly what I meant. "Send it," I said.

"*Message sent.*"

"You mother fucking piece of shit!" I yelled out loud, slamming my hands against the steering wheel.

I drove 75 miles per hour down the last stretch of Alcatraz Avenue, completely unconcerned about police or safety or the wake of honking cars and steamed drivers I was leaving behind me. I wasn't the first asshole to drive 75 down this piece of shit fucking street and I definitely wasn't going to be the last.

I ran the red light on San Pablo Ave., turning left, and floored it again into Emeryville, weaving in and out of traffic the entire time. I drove straight to the BioTechM building where Sid worked, in the heart of the biotech industry of that small, contaminated, crappy little town, and headed for the 5-story parking structure next to his office. I looked at the clock. It was almost 9 o'clock. If I was lucky, I could catch him arriving at the office.

A few minutes later, I got very lucky. I followed the line of incoming cars up several levels of the parking lot, past hundreds of occupied spaces, until we got to the 3rd floor. I found an open space and pulled backwards into a spot and waited. Less than five minutes later, I saw Sid's white Tesla pass me and pull into a parking spot further up on the same level. I watched him get out of his car, staring at his goddamn phone absentmindedly as he walked right toward me. Sid Fucking Beeman, right there in the flesh. I pulled slowly out of my parking spot, turned in the direction of Sid Fucking Beeman, and, after I had straightened out the steering wheel, did the one thing I badly wanted to do. I placed my right foot squarely on the accelerator and pressed down.

There was nobody else in sight. I had a straight shot at him, and I steered my quiet electric car directly at that piece of shit, picking up speed and momentum as I got closer. The distance between us shrank quickly and I gripped the steering wheel in anticipation of a collision. Sid looked up at the last possible moment with an expression of panic-stricken horror, he flailed his arms in an awkward motion that sent his phone and papers flying into the air and just then, at the last possible moment, with my foot firmly on the gas, the car's brakes engaged automatically and the steering wheel turned hard left.

"*Pedestrian collision avoided*," my car said to me as my body slammed forward, hard against the seatbelt.

"You've got to be fucking kidding me!" I yelled. "No!"

If I had been driving my old, gasoline powered, non-fully automated car without the Driver-Assist and Pedestrian Collision Avoidance ^{TM} features, Sid would have been laying on the ground with two broken legs, as he deserved. Instead, he had fallen backward and was laying there, feeling around for his papers and his phone with one eye stupidly on my car, trying to understand what had happened and trying to determine if he should be extremely angry or terribly afraid. I think this must be why so many murders or assaults or kidnappings are successful. The subject, in this case, Sid Motherfucking Beeman, does not realize soon enough the kind of situation they are in – the kind that requires all of your immediate attention and most concerted action. People want to think that maybe their senses are mistaken and that the world is as it was 45 seconds ago. Or maybe it's because, unlike in their favorite crime saga that they're streaming, dramatic music isn't building to a crescendo in the background, alerting everyone that this is, in fact, a life-altering moment.

Well, fuck him. I shifted the car into reverse and drove back about thirty feet. Then I shifted the car back into drive, screamed as loud as I could, and punched the accelerator again. The car sprang forward, Sid's face betrayed the realization that he needed to be terribly afraid and not extremely angry, but again, at the last minute, the car's brakes engaged automatically and my ridiculous electric vehicle veered hard left again to avoid hitting him, and stopped.

"*Pedestrian collision avoided,*" my car said again.

"No! No! Override! Override!"

"*Overdrive, by Drake, now playing.*"

As soft bass-laden rhythms and the sleepy voice of Drake filled the cabin, I screamed, "No, Goddamnit!" and looked out as Sid was up and stumbling into a sort of run.

I shifted my useless fricking car into park and, flinging the door open, got out and sprinted after him.

Sid was in a full run now and looked back at me in horror. "Drew," he said, running. His voice was a cross between "Hey Drew, Good morning," and "Hey Drew, what are you doing here?" But what he actually said was, "What the fuck are you doing?"

"Now you want to know what I'm doing, you piece of shit?" I yelled. I was only a few feet behind him then. "I'm doing *this*!" I said and I threw myself forward and tackled him to the ground.

We hit the pavement hard, my knee slamming into the concrete, and I skidded on top and over him. He hit the ground harder than I did, with an, "Oomph." I felt myself rolling over and off of him, so I caught myself and grabbed his torso to stay on top of him.

"What the fuck!" he yelled from somewhere underneath me.

Using him as leverage, I pushed myself up and kneeled on top of him, pinning his shoulders to the ground. I looked into his face and took pleasure from his distorted and confused expression, like it was feeding an insatiable hunger inside of me. "You're going to talk to me now, motherfucker!" I yelled.

"What?! What?!"

"What is in that shit?"

"Huh?!"

"I'm seeing things, asshole! I see halos around people who are going to die!"

"What?!" he said, looking at me with real fear. "You're insane!"

"You're insane, you little bitch!" I yelled and I slapped him hard on the side of the head.

He screamed, wriggling his hands free and covering his face with his arms, using all of his strength to push against me.

"You are going to tell me what is in that bullshit you sent me," I yelled.

He was wrestling his way out from my grip, so I stood up, letting him slither out from underneath me, and pushed him off. He stood, panting heavily. His pants were ripped and his elbow was cut and bleeding. He had a bright red mark on the side of his face where I had slapped him and a pavement burn on the other side. "Get away from me. You're fucking crazy," he said.

"Yes, I am crazy! I am crazy because I know who is dying. How does that sound? Huh? It is making me crazy!"

He looked at me incredulously like I was speaking a different language and just shook his head.

"I know…," I said again, "Who is dying. I can prove it. I have proved it. Scientific method, bitch. Don't think I don't know what I'm doing or what I'm talking about."

"You need to go to a psych hospital."

"You're going to need the goddamned hospital, mother fucker!" I yelled at him. "Do you want me to go inside your fucking little office and tell you who is dying, you piece of shit? Do you? DO YOU?! Because I will do it. I will fucking do it! I will out every poor, terminally ill bastard you have in that office, even the ones who don't know it. And that's a fucking HIPPA violation if I've ever heard of one and you're going to have the worst medical bureaucrats in your office asking you some very uncomfortable questions. You're going to have HR wondering why you've been looking in their fucking files. How would you like that?"

"You're not even making any sense."

"What was in those libraries and databases?" I asked.

"The usual shit, man."

"The usual shit, huh? Who the fuck is DSL Labs?"

"I have no idea what you're talking about."

"DSL Labs" I said. "Their data was in the files."

"I have no idea," he said. "I just grabbed some data that we had floating around BD," he said, referring to the business development department. "I was trying to get you off my back. I didn't even look at it. It was just a…random assortment of things."

This had never occurred to me before. Assuming he wasn't lying, which I didn't think he was, this was going to be another obstacle. "I need to talk to them," I said. "They reported some findings that I have to follow up on. Nina changed when I plugged her into that last reference set. She was recommending some off-the-wall shit. And things are happening to me, man."

"Holy shit." He was still catching his breath, but now looking at me with something between curiosity and skepticism.

"Yeah, no shit," I said. "So, no special insight into them? Nothing for me to go on?"

"I swear. I had never even heard their name before you mentioned them. I was just trying to get you to leave me alone."

I watched him as he took inventory of his cuts and bruises. "Look," I said. "I know I got a little weird after the BlueLabs acquisition, but that's no reason to blow me off like this. Twenty fucking years we were friends. It didn't have to come to this."

"You got a *little* weird?" he said with a smirk. "You were fucking frightening, dude. You got all depressed. Then you went MIA. Then you started calling me drunk all the time with weird ass shit or some big ideas. I'm trying to raise a family, asshole. I have a wife and children. You know, people who want to see me every day. I know you don't know what that's like," he added.

I had lost focus on him enough that I couldn't even get angry. I was thinking about the nine-figure BlueLabs M&A deal and all the money that had been floating around and my part in all of it. It was like going back in time and revisiting an ancient obsession, an old nemesis and I remembered at once the sleepless nights, the confusion, the remorse.

In a transaction like that, you see, in addition to the hundreds of millions of dollars going from one company to the other (or, usually, the shareholders of the other), there are tens of millions of dollars in transaction fees – lawyers, accountants, bankers, consultants and several others – jockeying for a pay day. Money money money, just going everywhere, in all directions. It all starts to seem like funny money after a while, until you realize, when you're the one keeping track of the terms of the transaction and making sure they are accurately reflected in a written contract, that the words you are writing with your hands have a real life impact on people. How you write a sentence could mean an extra hundred thousand for one person or ten thousand less for another. Putting someone's name on a list, for example, could mean they don't have a job in two months and maybe they have a lot of trouble finding another one. Maybe that person was your friend or just someone you liked running into in the kitchen and maybe that person very sweetly left you a coffee and a pastry one day on your desk because you looked tired. And still, their name was on the list and you didn't do anything about it.

It goes without saying that nobody preps you for this in law school. It's like you're just supposed to know it's going to happen.

"I was under a lot of pressure," I said to him.

"Pressure?" he asked, mockingly. "How much did you make on that deal?"

There was nothing left for me there but a dead end. A dead end and bad memories, so I turned around and began walking slowly back to my car.

"You made more than me, asshole!" Sid kept at it. "How big was your bonus from Jeff for, how did he call it, 'Exemplary work on the transaction'?"

He was referring to Jeff Bloom, CEO of BlueLabs before the company was sold. I flipped Sid off without turning around, holding my middle finger in the air.

"I'm the one who got you that job in the first place, so I think you owe me about 1.5 million dollars, dickhead."

I turned around and ran up to him and grabbed him by the shirt. "No, I earned that money, asshole. I did. But that doesn't mean I would do it again."

"Yeah right," he said, years-old envy finally giving him a trace of courage. "Give it back then," he said. It was the perfect thing to say, of course, and I had no response. "You fucking liar!" he added.

I let go of him and turned back to my car again. He continued talking as I walked away.

"You're all talk, Drew. You weren't acting so tough when you were begging me to come do all the hard work for you and your stupid little startup. 'We would make such a great team,'" he said, mocking me. "What do you want me to do, next, come hold your little dick while you take a piss, you asshole?"

I got in the car, emboldening him further, and as I turned it around, he took big strides towards me. "You're seeing shit, huh? You lying fuck! You're still fucking crazy is what it is. You're as fucking nuts as I thought. And you wonder why I didn't call you, you fucking psycho. If I ever see you again, I'm gonna call the police."

As he said that, an older man walked past us, apparently unaware of the argument he was disrupting. He had a bald head, with a small ring of thin white hair around the base and just barely over his ears. He walked slowly and methodically forward, hunched over. He had a halo, as fate would have it, fairly bright, that illuminated the path before him.

Sid was standing next to the car, breathing heavily. I rolled down the window and the sound and motion made Sid flinch and he took half a step back.

"See that guy over there," I said, nodding toward the bald man.

"Farley," he said.

"He's got about a week to live," I said. Then I rolled up the window and sped away from him and out of the parking lot, leaving him standing there dumbly like the piece of fucking shit that he was.

< 16 >

DSL

I arrived home to an empty apartment that still smelled like Julie. It was distracting, but with my mind full of ideas, I was intent on doing something about it all and doing so immediately. I went through my notes and located an address for DSL Labs I had found during my research. They had an office near Seattle. I knocked on Juan Pablo's door – it was an all hands on deck type of situation – but he wasn't home, so I texted him and drove to the airport.

I called Julie from the car. She was just getting to her office, she said with a guilty laugh. She was surprised to hear from me and I told her that I tried waiting until the next day, but couldn't resist. She laughed a natural and easy laugh that made me feel like the strange events of that morning had already been forgotten. That's what it's like when you find the right person, I thought, minor transgressions and misunderstandings are easily swept aside instead of being focused on intently and analyzed for clues and potential hidden meanings.

She asked me how my meeting went and I felt a twinge when I lied and told her it went okay.

"Listen, I'd really like to see you again," I said.

"Me, too," she answered, extending the o's in "too."

"I'm on my way to Seattle."

"Are you serious? Good thing you woke up when you did!"

"Well, I didn't know I was going this morning. I guess you could say it was a product of my meeting."

"Sounds like the meeting went better than okay," she said.

"We'll see." I could almost hear her smiling through the phone line. "I'll call you when I get back?" Framing statements as though they are questions is high on my list of absolute, redline faux pas, but I wasn't in complete control of my emotions. I managed to say something else completely mealy-mouthed, like, "Maybe we can go out this weekend." It's the kind of thing you should never say in this situation because it shows neither confidence nor conviction. But, like I said, I wasn't in control of myself.

"That would be great," she answered, generously forgiving my stupid half-question. "I'd like that."

I was relieved. I felt like I could do no wrong with her, that I could say dumb things and she wouldn't even notice or she'd dismiss them as an irrelevant or even a charming part of my personality. "Talk to you soon," I said.

Another call came in and I said goodbye to Julie and answered.

"Drew, hey, my name is Max Sherman. I think Sid has probably mentioned me to you before?"

I instinctively looked at my phone to check the number, as if the call couldn't be real. Max was Sid's friend from BioTechM. Finance guy, Wharton MBA, the typical kind of dude investors drool over and love to see on a founder team. Back when I had tried to talk Sid into joining me on the Nina project, I asked him if he knew anyone looking to take a risk and get into a founding team early. Max's name had come up, but Sid told me he wasn't interested. Max was having too much fun leading corporate development for BioTechM, lining up companies, technology and assets for the company to buy.

And now here was Max on the phone, calling *me*. I was caught as much off guard by the call as I was by his Australian or South African accent, I couldn't tell which at first.

"Max, hello," I said. "Yes, he's mentioned you. Nice to speak to you."

"Likewise, mate. Listen, I just spoke with Sid. You're fucking crazy! I love it. I love the intensity. It's off the hook. He doesn't know I'm calling you, by the way. I understand you two have a history. Regardless, he told me about some of things you said about your Nina product, and, if any of that's true, you might really be onto something."

He paused there to give me a chance to speak, but all I could manage to say was, "Thanks." It didn't matter, though. He had plenty on his mind.

"Do you have investors on board already?" he asked.

"No, not yet. I'm working on that."

"Fantastic," he said. It was South African. That word and the a's sounding like eh's gave it away. He was still talking as I was cataloguing his accent, so I only caught the tail end of what he said. "So, I'd love to get together for lunch over the next couple of days and talk to you about how BioTechM could be a great spot for your technology. We could really make this thing take off."

"I'm not interested in selling."

"No, of course you're not. You're on a rocket. I get it. But listen, I just want to talk to you. Sometimes we invest in companies and let them grow," He said. "We have access to so much data, contacts at all of the key companies in the industry and sources of funding to help your company achieve its goals. We can be a partner and not just an investor."

Yeah, I thought, while calling all the shots and potentially destroying the very company you've invested in. "Of course," I said, "I know that."

I was having to force myself to remember all of the excitement I'd had, just 24 hours ago, about Nina. "Listen, I'm pulling into the airport. I have some meetings in Seattle, but let's get together when I'm back."

"Fantastic. That sounds super," he said. "So you'll give me a chance for a lunch? On me, mate."

"Sure, yes. It couldn't hurt," I said.

"Awesome," he said, trying to copy California jargon. I wished he would stick with the South African. "Look, I'll send you some dates and times and you can pick one."

"Sounds good," I responded before hanging up the phone.

I parked my car and boarded a nearly empty shuttle to the terminal. I reflexively pulled out my phone and checked my email. To my surprise, in the last two hours, I had received several emails from investors, some of whom had already blown me off, asking for meetings about Nina. They were all time stamped after 9:45 a.m., about 15-30 minutes after I had left Sid's office. It couldn't be a coincidence. I read through them with curiosity but didn't respond to any. I needed to focus on finding some answers first.

A minor detail about my encounter with Sid was annoying me and kept resurfacing in my mind. I had insinuated to him that I had *proved* the relationship between the halos and death when I knew that, scientifically, the premise that a halo meant that someone was going to die could only be called a hypothesis or a theory at this point. In order to assert it was proven, I would have to organize research and that research had to be replicable. I would have to develop procedures, conduct various studies and document the results. I would have to stop taking Nina's recommendations for a while to see if it had any effect on the halos, for example. It would all have to be done in a way that the theory could be disproven. But, I couldn't risk it. If Nina was somehow causing or allowing me to see the halos, it was a humanity-changing moment and I needed to keep pressing forward.

I just wanted to shove something down Sid's throat, that's why I said it, but it bothered me to think that I had played fast and loose with science. We live in a society where hyperbole is king and nothing breaks through the noise of social discourse unless it's exaggerated. Someone being 20 minutes late becomes "hours late," someone raising their voice a little becomes "yelling," and on and on. I didn't like participating in that kind of trend, especially when it was about something as important as scientific facts. But it didn't matter in the end. Sid wasn't going to believe me no matter what and he obviously wasn't going to help me. Somehow, though, information about this morning's encounter had leaked out and was making the rounds through the Valley.

I had become used to traveling in business class, even for personal trips, so the trip up the west coast was short and uneventful. We landed in Seattle and I took an Uber to Redmond, home to Microsoft, hundreds of other tech companies, and the only address I was able to track down for DSL Labs. It was sunny and bright and I found this extremely annoying. That city can be so dishonest with people. You visit on a day like that and it's the most beautiful place on the planet, with the lush green mountains and the deep blue of the Sound. You move there and next thing you know, you're popping Vitamin D supplements and buying sun lamps to stave off clinical depression.

My game plan, once I got to DSL, or what I was looking for, exactly, wasn't at all clear to me even then. I only knew enough that I had to go looking. DSL hadn't published anything and there was simply not a lot of information about them to be found online. The files I had received from Sid weren't accompanied by a comments file or annotations, just the name of the author (I presumed), P.B. Harlowe, in a small text file. There was absolutely nothing that was of any use to anyone using the data. It was such a careless, unprofessional, haphazard and, in the medical context, dangerous way to go about your fucking job. But I was convinced that I needed to talk to them if I wanted to understand why I was seeing halos and what they really meant.

Never far from my mind, and what was behind my frustration and urgency, was the need to help Julie. I didn't know how much longer she had to live. I wouldn't let myself consider the possibility that she could actually be dying. What if the future could be changed? What if she had a condition that was operable, for example? How long before the end did the halo appear, exactly? Did Audrey have the halo when I first saw her, or did I only notice it the second time I saw her? If she didn't have it at first, then that gave Julie 2-3 weeks.

I got to the address for DSL, hopped out of the Uber and went inside. It was, of course, a dead end.

DSL had moved out of the building two months ago. Where did they go? The security guard at the front desk had no idea. He was of no use and had no interest at all in helping me. They'll hire anybody these days to work one of these buildings. In the old days, being a doorman was an entire goddamned profession, but the Future Doormen of America are all attempting to kickstart their careers as influencers instead of learning how to deal with actual real people with real problems.

I went to a coffee shop across the street and looked around. I was going to have to get creative. While I waited, I gave the espresso machines the visual once over, ordered coffee and sat down, keeping an eye on the building across the street. I looked up the building office management and found that it was on the sixth floor. I had my coffee and waited for a lapse in the attention of the security guard, which took no time at all.

Within fifteen minutes I walked into the building and piggybacked with someone else up the elevator.

The button for the sixth floor wouldn't light up without a key card. So, I asked the 28-year old looking dude with a shirt that didn't fit him and worn sneakers if he wouldn't mind please hitting the button for the sixth floor. I told him I couldn't find the security guard when I walked in and I was late for a meeting. He just nodded at me, swiped his card and hit the button for the sixth floor.

"Thanks," I said.

He again nodded and said, "No problem," while only raising his eyes halfway to me.

The building management office was a small unit on the back side of the building. I walked in and saw an empty reception desk and two offices, each with two desks. The carpet looked like it had needed to be replaced five years ago and the office smelled like the cheap morning brew had been on the burner since the day before.

"Excuse me?" I called out.

A couple of moments later, a middle-aged man with a significant beer gut and a short sleeve, collared shirt walked out of one of the offices, looking as though I had just interrupted him doing something trivial and unnecessary.

"Can I help you?" he asked.

"Yes, I apologize for the interruption. I'm trying to see if I can locate DSL Labs."

"Uh-huh. They moved out six weeks ago."

"Yes, I'm aware of that. Unfortunately, though, I don't know where they went. Did they happen to leave a forwarding address?"

"I don't know," the beer gut man said.

"Look, I wouldn't normally ask. I know it's not totally appropriate, but it's actually a matter of significant medical importance. They published some information that is critical to the patient of a doctor I'm working with."

"Oh, I see," he said. I had gotten his attention and I thought that it was to his credit that he actually had attention to give me. There was a trace of professionalism and dignity beating within his slightly bloated body. I decided to focus on that.

"I know it's a little unusual. I could get the information from you with a subpoena, but that would take me a lot of time that this patient doesn't have and then you'd probably have to hire a lawyer to respond to the subpoena and make sure the building owners don't get into any trouble. And really, I just need to know where I can find them."

I shrugged my shoulders as matter-of-factly as I could and I stood looking at him as he looked back at me. I could tell he was waiting to see if I would flinch and retreat, but he didn't know me. Wait for an answer, Drew, I told myself. A few moments passed and I bit my lip to prevent myself from even thinking about speaking and I stood "calmly," waiting for him to respond.

"Yeah, I think I have it," he said after a moment.

He disappeared into his office and came back, handing me a piece of paper with a handwritten address in downtown Seattle.

"Thanks," I said. "I really appreciate it."

"Will that be enough? Are we, like, done?"

"Yes, this is everything I need. I won't trouble you again."

"Good," he said and walked back to his office without waiting for me to leave.

I had to wait ten minutes for the Uber and the 30-minute drive to downtown Seattle was annoying. Of course, the building wasn't near the

Amazon headquarters or the new and hip parts of town, it was a decrepit building that was clearly in the lowest quartile of rental prices for office space in Seattle. For that price, you don't get security and you don't get a doorman. I walked inside and took an elevator to the 2nd floor, *sans* keycard. I found the DSL office easily and walked right into a reception area that had yet to be unpacked. There were boxes everywhere.

Like people, companies have life cycles. Also like people, the life span of a company can vary dramatically based on what it does and who is doing it, how they handle changing markets and economic times. Take IBM for example. In the 1980s, it was a computer company. Today, it doesn't sell computers and it's worth three or four times more than it was back then. That's a pretty remarkable change and it took a tremendous amount of skill to undertake. Most of their competitors died out long ago.

The office I walked into had one of the hallmarks of the dying stages of the corporate life cycle: Dramatic cost cutting. And from the looks of it, it was done without the care and conscientiousness of a company that was going to pull an IBM-type turnaround. The office was littered with things that were out of place, in temporary locations or broken. The reception desk didn't fit well into its allocated area. Someone had obviously just moved it from the other building without a thought to how it would work, how it would look in the new space or whether or not they would keep it or replace it. Further down the hall there were empty desks and filing cabinets, more unpacked boxes and a few empties.

It was an ominous sign and I began to wonder if the office had been abandoned altogether. However, a few steps into the office, I saw a desk that appeared to be occupied, meaning that there were pictures, a coffee cup, a computer and other obvious signs of life. There was a heart there that was still beating, I thought, however faintly, and I was hopeful that would prove to be sufficient for my purposes. As I was about to call out to ask for help, a young woman in her early 30s came out of a random interior door that apparently led to the bathroom. She walked almost straight into me.

"Excuse me," she said, looking up at my face with obvious surprise. "Can I help you?"

"Yes. I'm here to see P.B. Harlowe."

"Paul doesn't work here anymore," she answered.

"Well, can I speak to the person who replaced him?"

"Yeah. Um, nobody replaced him," she said, with her voice rising in intonation towards the end of the sentence in the most annoying way possible.

"Okay. Can I speak to someone in sales?"

"We don't have sales a sales department. It's called a customer success group."

I bit my lip so hard I thought I tasted blood. "Someone from there would be just fine," I said.

"Ok. Who are you?" she asked.

"I'm a client."

"Oh!" she said with some surprise and then directed me to a junky conference room with a table so big and ill fitted to the space that you could hardly walk around it to the far side of the room. Even if you could, however, your path would have been blocked by the stacked columns of moving boxes that leaned heavily against each other all along the wall.

"Have a seat," she said. "Someone will be right with you."

The chairs were some of the nicest pieces of furniture in the office, large black leather numbers that probably cost over a thousand dollars apiece. They would have been nice to sit in normally, but they were cramped together and gave the opposite impression of the luxurious effect they were designed to exude. In this office, in this room, they just added to the air of desperate depression that hung everywhere, a reminder of better days and better times. The whole stinking office was miserable.

Being around dying companies is almost as depressing as it is being around dying people. I've never really been around babies, but I can imagine that young parents might hold a baby in their arms and swell with pride thinking about all of the fantastic things this new human can someday accomplish. It's the same way with new companies. There is a tremendous amount of energy created by new ideas and enthusiasm and a certain lust for the prosperous future that awaits everyone involved. It can be a heady feeling. But all of that passion and zeal were gone from DSL Labs, replaced instead by aluminum framed conference rooms with cheap, broken metal blinds.

The DSL Customer Success representative walked in through the cheap metal framed door of the conference room. I stood up to shake his hand. He was a man in his late 30s who looked like he had already accepted that his best days were behind him. He was lazily dressed and walked and moved like it was, like everything was, an afterthought. He wiped his mouth with his hand and introduced himself as Stan.

"Sorry, I didn't mean to interrupt," I said.

"No problem," he responded in a tone that indicated he did consider it to be a problem. "How can I help you?" he asked, sitting down.

He was surprised to hear that I was a paying customer of a set of their digital libraries and reference sets, what he referred to as a beta version of one of their digital products. He was able to verify this information on his laptop and seemed intrigued. There weren't many users yet, since they were still in beta. He asked how I had come across them and I told him about Sid, without telling him what I had done to Sid as a result. He seemed excited that a company like BioTechM knew about them.

He asked how I was using the files and I told him about Nina and how I plugged their library into my program. He was typing into his laptop, either taking a significant amount of notes or responding to personal emails. It was hard to tell which, because he kept typing long after I was done talking. To fill the silence, I told him I was looking into their data because of some unusual results I was seeing and I was hoping to better understand the product.

He looked up at me with an expression like he was trying on some new clothes. He took a deep breath and began. DSL was an aggregator of information in the biotech space, he said, a new business model the company was transitioning into. What was their original business model, I asked. He told me they had been more of a supplements company, focusing on a recently discovered flowering plant called *Dulcinea Galdamesiana*. He confirmed for me that this plant was only found in the Panamanian rainforest. They thought it was going to be the next acai berry, he said, with tremendous potential since DSL owned it and had applied for a patent on the genome of the plant.

"You can't patent something naturally occurring," I said.

"Yes, that turned out to be a problem."

"You raised money behind that idea?" I asked, perhaps a little too incredulously.

"Yes," he answered, annoyed.

I would have been curious to see the metal-framed conference rooms of the investors that had lost their money in DSL, but I didn't have time to ask about them because Stan was still talking. As they got bogged down in trying to exploit the supplement, he continued, they realized there was money in connecting the sources of data about naturally occurring supplements all over the world. They had a head start because of the research they had done along the way and there was tremendous movement in the market towards big data, of which they thought they could take advantage. And when competition sprung up for their supplement, with no way to own production, they shifted business models.

"It's going to take us some time to get off the ground, but we think there's a lot of potential," he said, unaware that by the time they got to where they were headed, the next big thing after big data would already be under way.

"So who can help me get more information about the medicinal properties of these supplements?" I asked him finally.

"I don't know," was his response. "The entire medical research division was laid off."

"Who would lay off the medical and research staff of an aggregator of information about supplements?"

He shrugged. "It's all in the data now. Everything you need to know is in the libraries and files."

"Well, not everything," I answered.

"Everything."

"Okay, but you realize that how you present and provide access to data can provide as much information as the data itself," I insisted.

"It's all about the data," he said.

I admit I was getting frustrated. "I can't help but think you don't really know what you're saying," I said, unfortunately. I immediately regretted it.

"I'm sorry if you don't think I can be of more help," Stan said. He shifted topics and immediately began asking about my connection with BioTechM. Who did I know there? How were they using DLS's information? Did I know if the project was going well? Did they seem likely to buy more licenses? I kept trying to steer the conversation back to their supplements and the way their files interacted with Nina, but he was having none of it. Eventually, he excused himself, left for an embarrassingly rude length of time and then finally came back to tell me that he was sorry but he needed to take another call and wouldn't be able to continue our conversation.

I didn't like it, both that the meeting was over and the way he went about telling me, but I got up nonetheless and Stan walked me toward the door. Down the hall, I could see a handful of people walking around slowly, without pride or purpose it seemed to me. Stan was asking me more questions about BioTechM and I happily gave him Sid's contact information.

"He'd love to hear from you guys," I said. "Be persistent."

< 17 >

Artificial

In the Uber on the way back to the airport, I looked at my email and saw that my inbox was exploding. I had an email from Max with some options for a potential lunch to talk about a BioTechM-Nina venture. I also seemed to have an email from every investor I had ever contacted, including an email from Trevor asking if we could touch base.

I had always known that word traveled fast in the Silicon Valley. For all of its formidable innovation, perhaps its biggest export is one thing: Hype. But was it possible for news to travel this fast? And news about what? Something I said to Sid?

As I was sorting through my emails, my phone rang. It was Marc with a "c."

"Congratulations, Drew," he said in a big voice, like he was welcoming to the podium the hallowed headline speaker everyone was there to see. "I heard you're making terrific progress with Nina. The word is out!"

I had no idea what he was talking about, but I played along and told him that it was the product of hard work and the feedback of brilliant people like him.

"When can we meet?" Marc asked. "I talked to the partners and they're pumped. I'm confident I can get you that term sheet this time around."

"Are you serious?"

"Completely serious, man. This thing has legs now. But we have to get moving. Can we meet tomorrow?"

This was the phone call I had been expecting just a few short weeks ago. Back then, nothing would have made me happier than to fulfill what I thought was my destiny with Nina. I would have dropped everything to take a meeting like that. But I couldn't stop looking for answers now. Julie, and to some extent I, depended on it. "I'd love to, Marc, but I'm on the road. I have a couple other stops I need to make before I come back to the bay."

All of the air came out of the conversation in an instant. There was a long pause before he spoke again, and when he did, his voice was different, terse. "Who else are you talking to? Are you in negotiations with another firm?"

"I've had some meetings, but..."

"Are you talking to Sequoia?" He blurted out.

"What? No."

"You have to be honest with me," he said. "Drew, if you're not honest with me, that's not the basis of a productive long-term relationship."

This was coming from a person who had lied to me repeatedly since I first met him, and said as guilt free and frankly as if he were telling me the formula for calculating internal rates of return. But I didn't see the benefit of pointing that out at the moment. "I swear, Marc. I've had discussions, but I'm not at the term sheet stage with anyone else."

"Okay. Okay, good," he said. "Call me the minute you're back in town. Promise me."

"I promise."

I went straight from the airport to Cupertino. I was at a dead-end with DSL, but I needed to keep looking, so I turned my attention to Nina's

AI layer. Perhaps I could find something between the AI and the libraries that could give me some indication as to what was happening, why, and what I could do about it. From the Seattle airport, I set up a meeting with GLO AI, the startup from which I licensed the AI software for Nina.

To some degree, everything in tech is urgent. Every time anybody asks you to do anything, it's urgent, so extremely urgent. When you have something that's actually urgent, like this was, you have to find a way to break through this fake urgency culture. Fortunately, I was able to do so and get a meeting for that same afternoon.

The purpose of the artificial intelligence layer in Nina was simple. The AI took the feedback provided by the recommendation engine, considered the impact on the daily sample results, and, combined with the DNA, used that data to improve daily recommendations. It was not a complicated system and, for that reason, I had not been too picky in the AI selection process. The software could get more sophisticated as the product developed, of course, and I would have been able to switch AI midstream, if necessary. At the time, I needed an inexpensive, shrink-wrap, out-of-the-box AI that could do basic data science for me.

And I found that in GLO AI, a smallish startup with a technical team that had decent credentials and which had raised $15 million from some fairly relevant software VC investors. They weren't making the front page of any industry journals, but they were one of the hundreds of VC-backed companies in the industry, out there trying to grow big enough to be acquired or go public themselves. The Silicon Valley is a machine for churning out companies like them.

GLO AI's offices were in a modest office park in Cupertino, full of other mid-sized startups and tech companies. I sat waiting in a small conference room with a whiteboard that still had notes from a previous meeting. It was obviously a sales meeting, and from the looks of it, sales weren't going great. As a result, everybody's sales targets were increasing by 8%. Ah yes, the well-worn management strategy of writing bigger numbers to solve problems. Hey guys, we're not selling enough, so I'm going to write a bigger number on this piece of paper and that will fix everything for now. What some management types lack in creativity, they supplement with a lack of logic.

At the meeting, Scott the Sales Rep seemed distracted. I wanted to like him, but he looked like he would much rather be finishing up the game of online poker he had left at his workstation, or maybe it was some proposed fantasy football trade he was mulling over. I needed to understand how their product was performing its analyses and feeding the recommendation engine. "It's impossible for me to tell you without knowing more about the reference sources. It's a database issue," Scott said. "The AI isn't going to return any values that aren't in the input variables. It's not going to make anything up."

"I understand that."

"So talk to your database people," he said.

"I have. Look, let's assume I understand the data set. What I need to know from GLO AI is more about the model, more about how it is learning from the database and learning from the inputs and creating the recommendations."

"We can't tell you that," he said.

I tried a different line of inquiry but got the same results. He couldn't or wouldn't even answer my most basic questions. "How many engineers did GLO AI have?" "I'm not sure, I think that's confidential." "How much open source is in the source code?" "I don't know." "When is your next release scheduled?" "I'd have to ask someone."

I predicted Scott was going to have trouble meeting his 8% increased sales target, but I couldn't worry about him. I needed information.

"Scott, I know that there are limits to what you can tell me. But, I'm a customer. I'm building a product based on GLO AI. I have to know this stuff if I'm going to keep GLO AI in the stack."

"Yeah. I'm not sure what to tell you. Let's see," he said, poking around his phone.

"Look, I have a term sheet in my hand," I said, lying, but with the kind of lie everyone around here understood. "I need to be able to roll out quickly when we close the round. You could sell one million dollars worth of software licenses to me. One million."

He looked up at me, suddenly making eye contact for perhaps the first time in thirty minutes.

"I have to know," I said. "You have to let me peek under the hood here."

"Let me get the Sales Director," he replied. He had been dying to say it for a half hour and I had finally given him a valid excuse to do so. I kicked myself for wasting so much time.

After about five minutes, Scott came back with a young woman who, I could instantly tell, did not have an online poker game or fantasy football page up on her workstation. She smiled professionally and looked me in the eyes when she shook my hand, unlike Scott had. Her name was Sheryl. She left the door open behind her, and a few moments later, someone else walked in.

The newcomer was Travis Lawson, the founder of the company. The energy in the room changed immediately when Travis walked in. He was dressed casually, but smartly and comfortably, in clothes I had seen recently in dozens of targeted online ads. He had a big, warm and magnetic personality. His mere presence in the room somehow attracted attention. It wasn't difficult to see why someone would trust him with $15 million (of someone else's money, at least.)

As we congregated around chairs at the table, everyone had big smiles on their faces and I was hopeful that perhaps, now, this group of people could give me the answers I needed. "Don't mind me," Travis said, taking a seat at the far end of the conference table and pulling out his phone. "I'm just going to observe. I love hearing from customers first hand."

We all sat down and Sheryl the Sales Director spoke first. "I hear you might increase the size of your order," she said, smiling. "We always like to hear that."

"I hope so," I replied. "I'm very happy with the way your product has integrated with mine. I just need to make sure the specifications are consistent with my long-term objectives," I replied.

Sheryl nodded. She asked me intelligent questions about Nina and the AI integration and it was clear that the difference between her and Scott was a chasm much bigger than their four-year age difference and online poker. She understood software. She understood the industry and she knew her own company. She seemed to believe, in the same way I did, perhaps, in what was happening in tech and its ability to be a transformative factor in human life and in her role and the role of her company in all that. Which is to say she was engaged. She cared about what was happening in the room at that moment.

After discussing at some length the product integration, she asked who had built the AI model. I told her GLO AI had helped me with it. It was one of the reasons I went with GLO AI – their ability to help provide a turnkey solution. She nodded. "I guess at the end of the day, what I'm really after, what I really need to know is this: What is GLO AI's differentiating factor? What makes you different from all of the other AI tools in the market?"

Sheryl looked at Scott. "We have a Confidentiality Agreement in place, right?" she asked.

"There's one in the license agreement you had me sign," I interjected.

"Good point. Right," Sheryl answered. She was about to continue when Travis set his phone down on the table and stood up.

"That's a great question, Drew. Thanks for asking. I love hearing from customers and I love the opportunity to talk to the people who use our product on a daily basis," Travis said.

He drew a breath to continue speaking and when he did, his body went through a very subtle, yet impressive, minor metamorphosis. His chest puffed out, his shoulders broadened and his posture improved, all in the fraction of a second between breath and speech.

"When I started this company," said the founder, looking almost a full inch taller than when he'd first stood up, "It was on the belief that there were some core needs in the AI space that weren't being adequately addressed by the products in the space." After being in tech long enough, I knew inherently what this meant without needing to do a conscious translation. It was almost as though he were speaking a different language now, one which I understood perfectly. He meant that his research had shown that the AI market was growing faster than the ability of the companies in the industry to keep up.

He went on. "We have investors that believe in us. They saw the market opportunity and invested before our product was fully developed." This meant that he had found a group of VCs who had not yet invested in AI and were desperate to get a piece of the AI action somehow. FOMO (fear of missing out) had gripped these VCs. Perhaps their limited partners were asking them what portfolio companies they had in the AI space, or perhaps all of their friends at other VC firms bragged incessantly about the AI companies in their portfolio. The internal and external pressure on them to find and invest in something (almost anything) related to AI was overwhelming.

"But why you? Why this space?" I asked. "Do you have a background in AI? Why did you start the company?"

He smiled. "We saw a market opportunity and we're exploiting it," he said. I nodded. My translation had been accurate and it was exactly as I had understood.

He paused and looked at me, from which I perceived, in this secret language that we were speaking, to find something vague and non-committal to say so that he could keep talking. "There's no question there's a good fit between our companies."

"Absolutely," Travis said. "I was meeting with Sheryl when Scott came in to talk to us. When I heard your name, I texted a few buddies and, man, you are generating a lot of buzz recently. I love it. In fact, can we put your logo on our website?" He turned to Sheryl. "We can get their logo up quickly, right?" Sheryl nodded in agreement.

"I don't have a logo," I said.

It was a record scratch moment. "You don't have a logo?" I may as well have told him that I didn't brush my teeth. "Dude, you have to have a logo. You have to have a strong brand, be top of mind. Branding is key. How are you going to stand out in the market? How are you going to differentiate yourselves?"

"The quality of my product?" I said to myself and only in my head. I couldn't offend this guy, not now, so I kept it to myself. And besides, he had managed to raise $15 million and I had raised zero millions and so maybe he was right who the hell knows. In any event, I needed to get to the point. "I'll get there," I said. "But, what I'm here to find out, what I really need to know first is why GLO AI? What makes you different?"

Travis exchanged looks with Sheryl and then looked back at me. He pulled up a chair at the table directly across from me and sat down. "It's the Lisp," he said, leaning forward. "Our AI is based on Lisp. That's our secret sauce. That's what is going to give us the edge, the market advantage."

Lisp is one of the oldest programming languages still in use, I knew. It was used in some of the original AI applications, but had since been surpassed by a number of other programming languages for various reasons. However, Lisp still had a hardcore group of followers and believers that continued using it long after it had fallen out of favor in the trendier computer programming circles. I found this connection intriguing.

"I'm familiar with it," I said. "Where do you get it? Which version?"

"We use Lisp Factor. They're in Berkeley. Hardcore engineering group."

"The technology is impeccable," Sheryl added.

"We have our own engineers here, of course," Travis continued. "But using Lisp Factor, it's like we have our own back office R&D team. Those guys are incredible."

I nodded. "But you couldn't use their product alone," Travis added, hurriedly. "Lisp is just the language. It's the tool. We're able to productize the technology and turn it into something a company like yours can use in your tech stack."

We talked more about their implementation and how the Lisp was important, but the more he spoke, the more impatient I became to leave. It was clear that I needed to go back across the bay and get in front of the Lisp Factor engineers. I was at the cusp of understanding what was happening inside Nina, and inside of me, for that matter.

I told them to send over pricing for a conservative expansion of the license after we closed a VC round. "I already emailed you the names of two brand consultants," he said holding up his phone, showing off one of the many "efficiencies" (i.e. lack of focus) so widespread in tech.

"You've gotta get on it. It's gonna set you back you a couple hundred grand, but it's well worth it, my friend."

A few firm handshakes and slaps on the back later, I was in my car driving back across the Dumbarton Bridge to the East Bay. I hoped to make it to the Lisp Factor office before everyone packed up and headed home for the day.

During the drive to Berkeley, my phone buzzed like crazy. A text came in from Sid, of all people. "Hey, man. Give me a call." The nerve of that guy. I was mildly curious to speak with him so I could understand what was happening with Max, Marc and the VC community, in general, who were suddenly hot on my tail, but I didn't have time to waste. I needed to focus on finding answers.

A second text came in from Trevor, the VC from BioBay, saying he was clearing obstacles and he thought he saw a path to getting me a term sheet. Normally, this would have been incredible news. There is nothing like having two investors competing for you to ensure you get fair terms in a venture capital financing. But my mind was too focused on the upcoming meeting to give it much thought.

The trifecta was a text that came in from an unknown 650 number a few minutes later. It turned out to be TechCrunch, *the* tech news website in the industry. I'll never forget flying up the 880 as my phone read the message to me: "Hi Drew, this is Eric from TechCrunch. We've heard you've signed a term sheet with PA Bio Ventures and I just want to confirm the terms so we can report it."

< 18 >

Lisp

Lisp Factor was a small company that had been around since the 1980s, founded by a group of hard-working Cal and Stanford engineers years before the trend of doing so was unleashed by the flood of venture capital in the 1990s. The company had grown and expanded at a reasonable pace until 2000, when growth stalled. While many of their contemporaries had rang the bell on the Nasdaq or been acquired by bigger companies and cashed out, Lisp Factor had, in the last 20 years, quietly shrunk back down to a few dozen employees.

It is an oft repeated pattern in the area. Fortune smiles on some more than others and the Lisp Factor business declined when trends shifted in a different direction (and nobody from IBM showed up to advise on a turnaround strategy). The growth of open source computer languages like Python and Java, which became more widely adopted with the world wide web, had pushed their licensed Lisp programming language from the mainstream. Lisp Factor still had paying customers and a niche business that paid for office space, employees, mortgages and college tuitions, but their star-studded aspirations to close a mega acquisition and retire to tech paradise were no longer realistic.

The fog was beginning to roll back into Berkeley as I pulled into a parking garage next to a long, non-descript five-story office building on University Avenue. Downtown Berkeley is grimy, but it's alive with people, students, professors, retirees, punks and all kinds of other assorted individuals. Walking down the sidewalk is an international cultural exercise more than anything. In the half block I footed it to the office, I walked past a small Greek café, a burrito shop and a Pakistani restaurant.

I walked into the Lisp Factor office unannounced, hoping someone would still be around to talk to me. It was an extraordinarily quiet office for its size, neatly divided between cubicles and offices, that could fit about thirty people. The sound of servers humming was louder than any human voice I could hear. There was no real reception area and no receptionist. The first person who came out to greet me was the head of HR. She asked if I wanted to speak to a sales rep, but when I described my situation and interest, in as complicated of a manner as I could, she shifted gears and introduced me to the CEO himself.

Brian, the CEO of Lisp Factor, was the kind of person that you could pick out as an engineer if you saw him in line at the grocery store. In his early 60s, he had a full head of white hair that was just wiry and tangled enough to give him the professor emeritus look. He had two large computer monitors in front of him and the pale white complexion to match. His office was quiet and messy in a way that I was certain made perfect sense to him. There were stacks of books, disorganized (looking) stacks of paper, magazines and industry journals all around him. He stood up to greet me without moving out from behind his desk, and motioned for me to sit in a chair, which I was more than happy to do. I wondered if I could find the answers to the questions about Nina and Julie that I was looking for somewhere in those stacks of papers.

He seemed to sense my curiosity and anxiety all at once. I could tell he was in the middle of several different projects and yet had a certain calmness to him that, in turn, served to calm me somewhat. After a very brief introduction, he looked at me pleasantly, but intently, with an expression that contained a mixture of curiosity, amusement and interest. He spoke just one word. "So..."

It was the perfect segue. I began a monologue that lasted probably ten minutes. I gave him a brief history of Nina's origins and raison d'etre. I told him about the recommendation engine and my recent integration with GLO AI. I spoke vaguely about needing more information and trying to better understand my own product. He listened with precise attention, nodding. He occasionally jotted something down in a journal he kept open in front of him (and I noticed about 40 similar journals in the bookcase behind him). He asked all the right questions, speaking carefully but quickly, and zeroed in on all of the right issues. At times I felt a little embarrassed about my lack of technical training, but he was forgiving and kind. At the same time, I had the feeling that he could forgive lack of knowledge far more quickly than he could forgive lack of competence.

"What I need to know is," I said, getting to my point at last, "What is it about Lisp that makes GLO AI work as well as it does?"

He smiled like a teacher might smile at a middle school student and began speaking slowly. "A program is only going to work as well as it is designed, but I think I know what you're asking. You want to know, out of all of the AI out there, what is it about Lisp that makes the GLO AI product special? What makes it different?"

"Precisely," I said, appreciatively. It is no small thing to know what question to ask and how to ask it, but it is entirely another thing to know what question someone else is trying to ask, so this was next level intelligence at work and I admired him for being so perceptive. Brian took a breath before speaking and I felt like I could see his brain working and firing behind his eyes.

"Computers are machines, right?" he asked. I nodded and he continued. "They can't understand human language. You need a human to understand human languages, not counting the training of certain animals, of course. The brain of the computer is the CPU, the central processing unit, and what the CPU understands is binary code, 1s and 0s, each of which corresponds to a specific task depending on the circumstances. You follow me?" I nodded again.

"But humans are incapable of writing the 1s and 0s in a way that a computer could recognize," he continued. "At least not anymore. Back when Alan Turing came up with his theoretical basis on the way computers work today, he had in mind step-by-step mathematical computations which were easier to write, but with the code we have today, forget it. Humans couldn't do it, couldn't efficiently communicate to the computer.

"So we have computer languages," he continued. "You have a technical background. You know this. Computer languages are a way for humans to interact with the CPU in a way that humans can comprehend instead of with the binary code, yes?"

"Right," I said. It was refreshing to speak to someone so obviously brilliant. His clarity in communication and his conviction were the product of years and years of study and rigorous scientific application. There were no shortcuts, no catchy slogans, no pretension. Just pure knowledge.

He went on. "But the computer, the CPU, still can't understand even this computer language. So you need something to convert the computer language that the *human programmer* knows into the 1s and 0s that the

CPU knows. That is the job of the compiler. Every computer language has a compiler, are you familiar with this?"

"Basically," I said, afraid that he was at the precipice of surpassing my level of expertise.

"Not all compilers are the same. Some compilers are more efficient than others. Lisp is a very special language," he went on. "It's an old language. But the language itself is actually much closer to the compiled result of a computer language than is the case with any other language. The genius of Lisp is that you're much closer to speaking the CPU's language. This is very powerful and it has many advantages. There are certain things, for example, that can be done only in Lisp."

"Really?"

"Yes, of course. NASA, for example…the Hubble Telescope, it uses an observational scheduling system that was created using our Lisp. There are many complexities involved in space travel and satellites and now you're getting into quantum physics, but what they needed couldn't be done with any other computer language. Well, perhaps it could be done but it would take millions or tens of millions of lines of code to do what we could do in just a few thousand lines. And of course, lines of code is equivalent to memory, which is equivalent to physical size and you can imagine that in a telescope that is in high demand."

"That's incredible," I said. "Since I started using your Lisp in GLO AI, after combining it with my DNA and a number of different health databases, libraries and reference sets and following its recommendations, the product's recommendations seem to have dramatically improved."

"In what way?"

I told him how Nina's advice seemed to change over time and how it had evolved into recommending special order supplements and different and novel vitamins and other products that were somewhat obscure and not easily obtainable. "As a result of all of that, my health, in general, is much better."

Brian looked at me, somewhat skeptically.

"My eyesight is better, for example. I no longer need to use glasses."

He raised an eyebrow. I had to weigh what I told him very carefully. Brian struck me as a very open-minded person who obviously believed in the power of technology, but he was also a man of science, a man of facts and figures, a man of peer-reviewed industry papers, a man who would rather wait 6 months to have something properly published in a scientific journal than blurt out something that was only 95% correct. "I can run farther than I have in years," I added.

He squinted his eyes in a way that told me I had missed the mark; my observation was very subjective. "I had a physical," I added. "Lab work, everything. I'm in extraordinary physical condition."

"That is impressive," he said. "You would want to, of course, verify all of this in a scientifically sound way."

"Of course."

"But it could be, it *could* be, right?... It could be that the AI has fine-tuned your recommendation engine in a way that is harmonized with your DNA."

"I think so," I answered.

"And the result *could be*," he stressed, "That you are consuming nutrients and supplements in a manner that has been more or less perfected, for lack of a better term, for your body in a way that was never before possible."

I nodded along with him. It was all making sense.

"Western medicine is obsessed with a one size fits all mentality," he continued. "Here, take this aspirin, take this medication, no matter your DNA or the chemical makeup of your body at that particular moment.

That will seem primitive to us by the end of the century. Absolutely primitive.

"But your machine," he went on, hands in the air as if he was forming the objects in the air in front of him, "Combined with your DNA, your internal biological system, and AI, could allow you to do what no other human has ever done."

He sat there, looking up and weighing all of this information for a moment before continuing. "It could allow you to be, not only as healthy as humanly possible," and then he paused, and when he spoke again, he did so very slowly. "But as healthy as scientifically possible."

He fell back into his chair and I realized only then how far he had been leaning forward the entire time. He leaned back now with the weight of a potentially meaningful scientific discovery sinking him back down into his chair. He smiled and shook his head as if trying to understand something tricky, then he looked back at me.

"Congratulations, Drew," he said. "You could be about to become incredibly wealthy."

"I don't know," I said. "Honestly, I'm a bit over my head."

"Nonsense." He seemed very surprised by my feelings of inadequacy. "You shouldn't feel that way at all. Even if you didn't find what you set out to discover, that doesn't invalidate its incredible potential and import. Some of the most profound scientific discoveries of our time were accidents," he went on. "The discovery of antibiotics, for example. Alexander Fleming neglects to clean up his lab and leaves out a dirty petri dish. When he comes back after a nice weekend in the country, there is mold in the petri dish and no bacteria around the mold. *Voi la*, Penicillin."

There was a brief pause as he relived, in his mind, such a significant scientific milestone.

"But this isn't about the AI," he said, after a pause. "Artificial intelligence isn't causing this."

"How do you know?"

"Are you eating the AI?"

I laughed.

"Of course not. You are taking supplements and vitamins and foods in the real world. This is what is driving the change. Artificial intelligence isn't really intelligence at all, in many ways, it is very dumb. Computers can only learn through repeated trial and error. The advantage of the computer is that it can learn so quickly because it can run billions of trials and find billions of errors every day. That's how it finds the right answer."

"I know, I understand," I said. "But, I haven't told you the whole story. There's more," I added carefully.

"More?"

It was just the two of us in that room, but it felt like it was only the two of us in the universe. The word "halo" seemed like it wouldn't fit in my mouth. It was just a word but it was too big for me, too big to say. Too impossible. I felt dizzy. The walls around us were holding us in space as we floated through the solar system at 67,000 miles per hour, and as the solar system rotated around the center of the Milky Way galaxy at 514,000 miles per hour. And yet there we were sitting in the impossible miracle of his office, and I felt that possibly, just maybe, if I could manage things in a certain way, I could find an answer, not just to the halos or Nina or Julie or even me, but to everything.

"I'm seeing things," I said finally.

"What kinds of things?"

"It's hard to describe, really. Rings."

"Rings..." he said, staring at me closely, and a little differently.

"Yes, they're like rings of light. In the air."

He paused for a moment. "It could be a hallucination," he posited.

"Could be," I said. "I don't think it is, though."

He leaned in and looked at me intently for a moment and the room seemed impossibly quiet. The only sound was the hum of the servers in another room. I felt the weight of everyone on my shoulders. I thought of Susan and Laura, Audrey and Julie. I saw the faces of the Grey Man, the Red Jacket Man, the Lonely Man, the Navy Suit Woman and all of the halos I had seen along the way and all of their children, parents, husbands, boyfriends, friends and everyone affected by their deaths and it pulled at me intensely. And as soon as I had decided to continue, I would say even the impossible word, he spoke instead.

"It could be a bug," he said.

"A bug," I said flatly.

"A bug. A problem or an error in the code."

"Yes, yes, I know what a bug is."

"Don't get distracted by these low-probability scenarios," he said, sitting up and preparing to stand. "Focus on the tangible, what you have in front of you." He looked at his watch. "The AI is certainly helping discard billions of possibilities a day, but I have a feeling that the answers you are looking for are real world answers. You need to look in the real world, what you're ingesting."

"I need your help to figure it out."

"We'd love to help," he said, relaxing in his sitting position again. "Can you pay for our time?"

"I don't know," I said. "We're a pre-seed…I mean I am, or it is… just a pre-seed company. We haven't raised any money."

He let out a sort of laughing smile.

"We have a term sheet, though. Two, actually. And we're getting noticed by the press."

Brian sat forward again. "Do you see these stacks of papers?" he said, pointing to different piles of papers, magazines and books on his desk.

"Yes."

"These are all paying customers. They are all paying for our time. You have no idea how many people ask us to do free research for them with promises of a big payback down the line."

"I could give you a percent of the company, stock in Nina."

"Stock won't pay my staff," Brian answered. "Look, Drew, it's going to take hundreds, if not thousands of hours to go through your code, go through the databases, go through the AI model, all of that, just to understand what is happening. And then, I'm not a doctor. Even when we get up to speed on the technology, we have no way of understanding how it is affecting you. I know how computers work. People? Now that's a different story."

"We could figure it out."

"No. No. That's the beauty of computers, see. There is an answer. It's in black and white. It's a 1 or it's a 0. Now, people? We are a far more complicated system."

I was speechless in a very inopportune moment.

"In any event, technology is not your product, humans are. The most successful tech tools are only a substitute for a real-world need: information, knowledge, connection. The things you are ingesting, that's what you need to focus on. The real world. I suggest you turn there."

He took the opportunity to stand up and extend his hand toward me.

"It's been great fun chatting. I have a call in a few minutes. I wouldn't worry too much about the bug," he said, shaking my hand. "You can solve it later. Focus on what is working well. If you get funding, you can come back to us and we can work together."

"Ok," I said.

"Plus, you'll have to buy more licenses if you get funding. That's good for us, too. If GLO AI sells more, we sell more. But, if you ever have a problem with them, you can come to us directly," he said. "We're partners right now, Lisp Factor and GLO AI, but we're also competitors in a way."

He thanked me for coming by before I could get another word in. He told me that he had a busy evening of programming and meetings and programming meetings and I heard myself say thank you.

I was still dazed as he walked me out the door and closed it behind me. I mechanically took the elevator down and walked outside. I stood alone on the street, engulfed in the fading sunlight, no closer to understanding what was happening than I had been before.

< 19 >

The Rainforest

I walked up the stairs to my apartment. Feeling defeated, a familiar voice inside my mind was telling me to give up. It was hard to resist the overwhelming urge to go where I knew my mind would go next: desolation, anger. But this time, a new feeling (or at least a feeling I hadn't felt in many years) kept me from sliding into that dark space. It was like a small flame, this feeling I had about Julie, and I needed to protect it from the gale-force wind. I couldn't give up on her, I couldn't give up on either of us. Negativity would only cloud my judgment.

My mind worked on the Rubik's cube of problems, issues and potential solutions. I had created something with Nina, something potentially valuable to the scientific community and to the world. At the same time, I had found something, someone, valuable to me who was caught in the crosshairs of the exact same creation. Each possible line of action with one felt like a move directly against the other.

I couldn't turn to the investor emails and calls that were piling up, for example, because that felt like giving up on solving the problem of Julie's future. I didn't have that kind of time. Julie and the halos, what they were, what they meant, needed to remain at the forefront of everything I did. I wanted to just call Julie, be with her, tell her everything, and solve the problem together, but I couldn't imagine a scenario where that led anywhere. She would react like any sane person would react to the possibility of seeing into the future: with incredulity. It would destroy the possibility of a relationship with her in its infancy. Of course, if I didn't do it, the possibility of a relationship with her was likely also doomed. I was in an impossible bind, a catch-22. Joseph Heller didn't write poetry, but he wrote a hell of a book.

As I reached the landing, key in hand, Juan Pablo opened his front door with a big smile on his face.

"What's so funny?" I asked.

"Where's Julie?" he countered.

"How do you know about her?"

"I heard you leaving your apartment a few days ago, so I opened the door to say, 'hi,' only it wasn't you, it was this Julie."

"Oh. Yeah."

"She was very nice. Very pretty. Congratulations. This was the first one of your friends I actually met, you know. I was beginning to wonder."

I opened the door to my apartment. "Sorry, I've had some tough meetings. I'm not in the mood for joking around."

He followed me into my place. "Who's joking?" he said with a smirk.

I collapsed onto my couch and must have had a very concerned look on my face because Juan Pablo's expression changed from light-hearted to more serious.

"Sorry," he said. "Look I found what you were looking for." He handed me his phone and I looked at it only to see a paradisiacal looking beach with flawless pale cream-colored sand and, bright, sky blue water. It looked like a magazine spread.

"That's Bocas del Toro," Juan Pablo said. "Panama."

"This doesn't look like a rainforest."

"Sorry, that's one of the other islands. The area has a very unique geography," he said. He took his phone back and brought up a different image.

I looked at it again and there it was, a plant, the *Dulcinea Galdamesiana*. It appeared to be the main ingredient in the Nina-recommended supplements I had been taking. This is where Brian seemed to be indicate I needed to turn my attention. My last thread of hope was a strange looking tropical plant on an island in the Panamanian Caribbean?

"Why is it so important?" he asked.

I took a deep breath. I was desperate.

Nina had uncovered a potentially life-threatening condition in Julie, I told him. I described my pursuit of answers, including all about the last 24 hours, from my wild run in with Sid, to the crumbling DSL Labs in Seattle, and finally the CEO of Lisp Factor and his clear-headed visions of science and technology, but focus on real world solutions.

"What did the doctor say?" he asked with real concern.

"Doctor?"

"For Julie's condition."

"She hasn't, uh, seen one yet."

He looked at me, confused.

"I haven't told her."

His hands went immediately to his head with a look of extreme disbelief. I wouldn't have blamed him if he had just walked forward and punched me in the face right then and there. Instead, he sort of spun around and hopped up and down once or twice before saying, "Whhaaaat?!"

"Look, it's not like that," I said, but I could tell I wasn't very convincing. "I don't know what it is exactly and I don't want to alarm her in case it's nothing. This is just experimental technology. I'm not a doctor.

What do I know about any of this shit, after all? I'm in over my head. I saw something concerning, yes. But, I was hoping to get real answers first before I freak everybody out."

He nodded. That's what a good friend does. He believes you and doesn't ask a ton of fucking questions you don't want to answer or give you some bullshit advice.

"I thought DSL was the key to everything," I said. "Everything started changing when Nina plugged into that new reference set and when I started taking this supplement. But they couldn't tell me anything. Nobody could. I've just been chasing my tail. All I have left to go on is the plant itself."

"If it is so important, let's go get it from the bull's mouth," Juan Pablo said.

"Horse's mouth," I corrected him.

"No. The bull's mouth," he replied. "Bocas del Toro means 'mouth of the bull' in Spanish. Let's go get that shit!"

Of course! He had put into words what had been lurking in the back of my mind. There was one link in the chain I hadn't yet examined and it was the source of the supplements itself. Every other potential source of information had proved fruitless. It was time to go straight to the bull's mouth.

I had no idea what I was hoping to find other than an answer of some kind. I was desperate and action, any action, felt like the only course of action. We would go see the plant and the solution would somehow present itself to me, I was sure of it. I had to believe in something, after all.

Early the next morning, Juan Pablo and I headed to the airport. The presence of my new friend served to increase my confidence, my belief in a potential solution. I sent Julie a text asking her out to dinner later that week and telling her I was off to Panama. She replied with surprise face and ocean wave emojis and said, "Of course."

I was feeling in good spirits as we headed to security. While standing in line, I received another call from an unknown 650 number. I answered and the caller introduced himself as Trent Sullivan, a reporter from Fast Company Magazine.

"Fast Company is one of the largest magazines focused on technology and business," Trent began.

"I know who you are."

"Fantastic. I'm not sure if you saw my email, but I'm calling because you were referred to us for an article I'm writing on the Top 10 startups likely to make the biggest impact in the next five years. Do you have time to talk? I'd love to ask you some questions."

I thought briefly of how I would have reacted a month before if I had received a call like that. However, the call couldn't have come at a worse time. I was putting my belongings in a bucket that was going to go down a conveyor and get examined by a different sort of computer. I told Fast Company Sullivan that I was traveling and he agreed to send me times for us to speak in the next day or two along with a list of questions and potential topics for discussion.

As I went through the metal detector, I wondered what it was that Sid had told people, exactly. What were people saying? Or perhaps it was something else, I thought. Maybe there had been some sort of investor conference and predictive biotechnology was identified by some presenter as the wave of the future. Either way, the timing was terrible.

We flew into Panama City with its modern high rises, colonial old Town and lush green surroundings. Panama divides North and South America and is home, of course, to the Canal, one of the most significant shortcuts humans ever invented. In fact, I have long said that keyboard shortcuts should be called "Panamas" in its honor. Computers have so spoiled us and driven us to the point of a lazy, self-absorbed narcissism, that it is difficult to conceive of such tremendous engineering feats being completed entirely by hand (with the help of prophylactic quinine for the malaria, of course), and yet there it sits, ushering dozens of ships a day between the Pacific and the Atlantic. Unfortunately, we didn't have time to explore the canal or the city or even leave the modernized, duty-free shopping mall of an airport. We had a connecting flight on a small propeller plane to the island.

As we waited for a shuttle to take us out to the small plane on the tarmac, a small brown man with leathery skin and a white Panama hat walked past us, a halo above his head.

"You see that guy?" I asked Juan Pablo.

"Yes."

"What do you see?"

"I don't know. Typical older Panamanian gentleman, it looks like."

"But do you see anything else? Anything around him?"

"Like what?"

"I don't know. Does he look different in any way? Look a little above him and to the sides."

Juan Pablo looked hard. "His hat?"

"Well, no. Above his hat."

"Above his hat??"

"Kind of. Just anything. Anywhere."

"All I see is him. His hat. He looks normal."

"Okay."

It was just a short, 45-minute flight to Isla Colón, the main island in the small archipelago in the southwest Caribbean known as Bocas del Toro. We landed in the airport, a small and rustic outpost that was the polar opposite of the glamour and glitz of the capitol airport. Everyone and everything moved much more slowly here, a combination of the heat, the tourism industry and the fact that there just wasn't a lot happening.

A few taxis loitered in the heat by the airport and we took one a short way into town. We drove along the bumpy streets to a small, bright, two-story hotel on the pier overlooking the bay where Juan Pablo and I got a couple of rooms for the night. We dropped our bags and went out to a small restaurant café on the same block on a tip from the driver. We each had a plate of tender snapper with flavorful rice and beans and a small bowl of fruit with a scoop of ice cream for dessert. We walked back to our hotel, the air still hot from the day, and retired to our rooms, exhausted from a day of travel. As excited as I was, it didn't take me long to fall asleep.

The next morning, we took a water taxi to the island Juan Pablo had identified in his research as our best option. The island contained a large grove of the *Dulcinea Galdamesiana* and a small production facility belonging to a supplier of DSL and many other new supplement companies. Juan Pablo showed me the information he was able to pull together from various sources. It filled me with a sense of gratitude to have a friend like him who did things for me like that and was willing to go on elaborate scientific adventures that could alter the course of human events (and also the very personal fate of one or two humans).

It was hot already at 9 am, with the morning sun shining down on us as we moved steadily across the sea in a little motorized skiff. With no relief from the sun and the heat, beads of sweat dripped down my sides under my shirt. The sky was a bright blue, with hot white clouds along the horizon. The water was a crystal blue to match. It looked beautiful, but it was so hot I had to focus on how it looked to keep from being too uncomfortable. The driver stared ahead, uninterested in us, steering the boat absentmindedly as it skipped atop the small waves. We passed, and moved through, all manner of different islands and land formations, big and small, lush with green vegetation, rocky coves and sandy beaches.

After 20 minutes, we turned towards a large, long and narrow island a short distance from a series of other islands. It was lush with green vegetation and a few dirt roads that led to what appeared to be some sort of makeshift farming and production facilities. The pilot beached the skiff and identified the man in charge, a tall, dark-skinned man wearing tan pants, a light blue short-sleeved, button-down shirt, a white Panama hat, and holding a cigar in his mouth. His name was Felipe and he took us back to his office, a desk and a chair in the corner of an open-aired warehouse.

We sat down and Felipe motioned to a woman who brought us glasses of cold water with condensation dripping down the sides. Juan Pablo told Felipe in Spanish that we had come from the U.S. in search of new supplements for a line of protein shakes. Felipe seemed unsurprised and asked what we needed and Juan Pablo told him we would like to see as much information as possible about the plant. Felipe nodded and wrote down an address on a piece of paper and motioned for us to follow.

Felipe gave us a brief tour of the impressive facility. It was impressive because it had been built on a relatively remote island, with no heavy machinery in sight. This was one of dozens of islands for them to exploit, he said, with a license from the government, of course, he said with a side-eye to Juan Pablo and a glance back to me. Juan Pablo simply nodded and kept looking straight ahead.

They would replant everything they harvested so that they could return to harvest again in two years. The plant was cut in the field, driven to a large facility, dried, then sent by boat back to Colón for further processing. The facility in Colón is where the records were that we wanted to see, he said, and gave Felipe the paper with the address.

I looked around to see if there was anything that could be gained from an examination of the farming operation. I thought of Laura and her family's farm in Nebraska and momentarily wished she could be there with me. Everything was low tech and unremarkable. The plant was cut in the field, loaded onto wheelbarrow-sized carts and brought down to the main storage unit, where it was air dried. A small dock allowed for a large boat to come, load up the plants and move them to Colon.

"Do you mind?" I asked Felipe, my hand on a drying plant.

"*Por supuesto,*" he said with a smile.

I tore off a portion of the plant's large, fan-like frond and examined it. I guess I thought I was Sherlock Holmes and would be able to decipher some clues with a careful analysis of the evidence but, of course, nothing stood out to me. After a few minutes of "examination," holding it up to the sun, holding it down below my head, and feeling the leaf carefully with my fingers, I folded the leaf and put it in my pocket.

With smiles and handshakes to our host, we took our skiff back to Colón and a taxi to a relatively modern looking warehouse in a small commercial sector of the island. The heat was unbearable but nobody else seemed to notice. We were greeted at the front by a thin, petite attractive young woman in a knee-length plain skirt, who was expecting us, and she led us back to an air conditioned conference room that was already full of dozens and dozens of bankers boxes. It was organized the way a due diligence project might be and it was apparent they were accustomed to dealing with people like us.

With a glance at each other, Juan Pablo and I began poking around. We first did a cursory examination of the boxes to get an idea of the contents. Juan Pablo took the initiative and pulled out a pad of paper and began an index. There were ledgers and schedules with details about their operations and similar materials, as well as binders and folders full of photographs and information about the plant. I went through a high level overview of the contents of each box and he wrote it down in his pad.

A different young woman came in and asked us if we would like coffee. We said yes and she returned with two small espressos and small glasses of mineral water. We thanked her and took the opportunity to take a small break from the tedious work. It felt good being inside the air conditioned room and besides, the whole process made me feel somewhat nostalgic.

"I used to do this a lot when I started out as a lawyer," I said, taking a sip of coffee.

Juan Pablo nodded.

"Now everything is digital of course. But we used to go through so much paper we would wear those little rubber protectors over our fingers to avoid paper cuts. Hours, shit, days we would spend going through everything sometimes. It was quite an ordeal. Sometimes we would travel and hole up in some hotel room. It was fun, I guess. A lot of bonding with your fellow associates."

"I bet," Juan Pablo said and took a sip of his coffee. He nodded appreciatively at the flavor, set his cup down and looked over at me. "If you don't mind my asking, what are we looking for, exactly?"

"I don't know. I kind of get the feeling that I'll know it when I see it."

We finished the coffee and continued hunting for information. This company began processing the plant about five years ago and built an impressive list of customers, DSL among them. I looked through sales records, invoices, purchase orders and similar information. It looked like the types of backup records you would accumulate when going through an audit. It was legitimate.

We sorted through most of the boxes by early afternoon. I felt like we had been given visibility into the company's operations but the information I was after was still tantalizingly out of reach. DSL had locked up exclusive rights to distribute the product in the US, but only for two years. Two years after they had launched in the US, various other suppliers stepped in and the operation grew from there, and was still growing. It was, at the moment, becoming one of the trendier "exotic" supplements in the US and certain markets abroad.

After a late lunch, we were given access to a virtual data room online with dozens of folders containing even more information. My heart skipped a beat when I came across a folder containing findings of the DNA sequencing done on the *Dulcinea Galdamesiana*. There, surely, I would find what I was looking for, answers to the questions that had been evading me for so long.

The positive feeling was fleeting. As I looked through the DNA materials, I felt a flush come over my face and an overwhelming sensation of insurmountable embarrassment and impotence. I quickly realized I had no way of interpreting or making any sense of the data. I wasn't a doctor, I didn't have a degree in genomics or biology or any kind of scientific degree whatsoever. My experience with DNA in Nina began and ended with the swab needed to get my DNA into the model built by GLO AI to run the AI algorithm and the software I had licensed to fit into the stack.

I was overcome with the realization that had been gnawing on me since we landed, but which was now a painful reality: We had traveled all of this way for nothing. Presented with all of the data there was and everything I needed, I was unable to do anything useful with it. I wasn't even sure what I had been thinking. I looked over at Juan Pablo who was clicking through different folders, making notes. Wonderful, but futile. Meanwhile, I was looking at lab reports that I needed a different degree to understand. There, within those files, was potentially all of the information I needed to make an important discovery, but I was incapable of extracting the necessary knowledge.

I had been staring at the screen like this for hours, perhaps, when an older man with streaked grey hair, very elegantly dressed in a tan suit, walked into the office and introduced himself as Gerardo, the General Manager of the operation. He smelled like coffee and sun and had white teeth that contrasted with his light brown skin.

"Has the information provided been to your satisfaction?" Gerardo asked in English.

"It has," I said. "Thank you very much. This is very thorough."

"We have been doing this long enough that we know what you want to see," he said, smiling.

"Forgive me. I'm not a doctor and some of this DNA-related information is quite complicated," I said. "I didn't see any studies about the effects of the plant in humans."

"We simply own the land and harvest the plant," Gerardo said. "We aren't selling to the public, so we do not undertake the research."

"I see," I said. "Are you familiar with the benefits attributed to the plant, though?" I asked.

"Yes, of course. We have read the published materials, and some unpublished ones, but we do not undertake these studies ourselves, at least not yet."

"If you were to summarize the benefits, what would you say they are?"

"The plant is extremely high in antioxidants, of course. Is that what you mean?"

"Yes."

"It has anti-inflammatory properties, also. This is what it was traditionally used for on these islands. It has been reported to be good for the brain, the hair, the skin, and it is high in fiber, of course, so it is good for the digestive system."

"How about eyesight? Can it help with eyesight?"

"I have not seen anything specifically about that," Gerardo responded.

"Anything unusual that you have seen? People reporting any side effects?"

Gerardo shook his head.

I probably should have pressed him, just gone ahead and said it, but it seemed so futile at the time. After some more general questions along these lines, which did nothing to further the extent of my knowledge, we thanked Gerardo and headed back to the hotel.

"We can keep looking," Juan Pablo said to me later that evening, as we headed up the stairs to our room. "But perhaps it would be helpful if we had a better idea what we were looking for."

"I know," I said. "We don't need to waste any more time. I think I know what I need to do."

Before going to bed, I unpacked clothes for the next day. I wanted to be ready to leave as early as possible. I saw the Nina prototype sitting there in my canvas bag and I took her out for a moment and looked at her in the moonlight coming in through the window. I sat down on the edge of the bed and turned the prototype, every inch of it now so familiar to me, over in my hands. I studied its familiar contours, remembering every step I had taken in the project and how everything had evolved up until that very moment. The ceiling fan blew a gentle breeze against my body.

Let me not to the marriage of true minds
Admit impediments

What the old Bard was doing in my mind that night was difficult to tell. I was in a difficult place, I guess. I was officially out of options. I knew there was only one way out, but that didn't make it any easier. It wasn't just the thousands of hours I had spent working on the project, but the years of thought and my personal journey that had led me there. I had given it everything I had, and more.

I retraced the steps in my mind searching for clues but, of course, there were none. This was well-trodden ground. I had gone over everything a thousand times already. I remembered the initial concept I had, how the project developed, my excitement at assembling the first prototype. It seemed so long ago now. At the same time, it seemed like yesterday. I couldn't imagine my life without the project, but I was aware of the impossibility of my current situation.

I picked up my phone and stared at it for a moment. Methodically, I clicked over to my email inbox, searched my email, found the phone number and called Max Sherman.

He was happy to hear from me. South Africans are always happy. I've never heard a sad South African in my life. After some brief small talk, how happy he was to hear from me, etc., Max and I agreed on the principal terms of an acquisition. BioTechM would acquire the Nina technology from me for $500,000 in cash up front, which was roughly double what I had put into the project up until that point. In addition, I would be paid another two to five million dollars over the next four years, depending on certain milestones. As a BioTechM employee, I would be paid a nice salary, be eligible for bonuses and receive stock in the company. It wasn't on the scale I had been hoping for, but it was a fine deal. The whole conversation took less than 30 minutes. He told me that I would have a term sheet in my inbox, waiting for signature, by the time I got home.

"Good deal, mate," he said. "You won't regret it." Then he hung up.

My body felt like a thousand pounds but my head was as light as a feather. Lying in bed, I set down the phone with one hand and held up Nina with the other. Her familiar shape looked somewhat new in the Panama moonlight. I stared at the object hard and looked at it as though, with just the sheer force of my gaze, I could unravel its mysteries. It was all so complex, yet also very straightforward. My questions were really very simple. What was wrong with me? Why was I seeing things? And what did it all mean?

And in those thoughts, I fell asleep, the prototype there next to me in bed. It wasn't the first time it happened. I had fallen asleep a hundred times working on Nina, at the computer, planning, programming, researching or writing, in bed reading. Hundreds of times it had happened before. But this time would be the last.

< 2 0 >

On the Inevitability of Fate and the Plight of Good Intentions

I woke up to the sound of Juan Pablo knocking on my door. I was still in bed, fully clothed, and Nina was lying right next to me on the pillow. I looked at my phone. Our flight was leaving in less than an hour. Luckily, it's a small island.

I didn't have time to change much less eat anything and for the first time in a year or more, I didn't start my morning by urinating in a cup and taking whatever food or supplements were recommended to me by a computer. We hopped onto the little 20-seat airplane and made the short trip across the water to Panama City, where we had breakfast. I had a cup of good coffee and a pastry looked that good to me at the time. It felt strange to choose for myself without any sort of technical indication.

I upgraded us to business class for the flight home because I didn't have the energy to deal with sitting in the back of the plane, plus I was rolling in dough again. Ok, that's an exaggeration, but I was going to have an income for the first time in a few years and so I splurged. I also felt the need to think: Where had I gone wrong? How could I possibly have started a project that I was so spectacularly unqualified to finish? I wanted time and space to ponder the thin veneer in life that always kept me from crossing to the other side, to the euphoria, the joy, that life had to offer.

Once in the air, I sat quietly, eating warmed nuts and being served mediocre food on a tablecloth, as if that made it taste any better. I stared at my laptop, clicking from one window to the next, over and over again, in circles like a television show I'd seen before but couldn't turn off. I went over the same line of thinking I had been going over for weeks, only this time from a detached distance, as if I were reading about someone else's life or emotions. Maybe BioTechM would be able to help? They perhaps held the key that could unravel this whole mystery. That was the theory. At least people there would know how to parse a DNA database, that's for sure. I would have access to doctors and scientists of every degree and specialization (assuming they were willing to pour the types of resources into the project that Max had promised).

What other options did I have? I had exhausted every possibility in my mind. Well, every one except perhaps the most obvious. Juan Pablo was mostly quiet sitting next to me. He spent some time watching a movie, but turned it off. He read his book and then set it down. He tossed and turned in his seat as the minutes and hours ticked by. He would occasionally glance over at me and then look away. A couple of times, I thought I noticed him gather himself as if to speak, but then he would think better of it and look away.

About halfway home, though, he finally spoke up. "Did you find what you were looking for?"

"No," I said, shaking my head slowly. "Well, yes and no. I don't know. Maybe."

He looked disappointed but in a way that I understood he hadn't been expecting anything other than disappointment. Yet, still, he had gone all that way to support me. "I'm sorry to hear that," he said, finally.

"I agreed to sell Nina to BioTechM," I told him.

"So soon?"

"Soon? It's been over a year," I answered. "Besides, it's too much for me. It's too big of a project. I'm not qualified to handle it. I don't know enough of the science."

"You could bring in some co..."

I cut him off. "I've tried it. I've tried everything."

He nodded his head in a sort of acquiescing agreement.

Two things were available to further my understanding of the halos. The first, I had taken care of the previous night by agreeing to sell my company to someone who could help me with the science. And the second was right next to me. It had been the one thing I could have done all along. It was so simple, but sometimes the simplest things are the most difficult.

"Listen," I said, gathering as much mettle as I could under the circumstances. "I have to tell you something. Something serious."

"Ok."

"You're not going to believe me. It's...well, it's incredible. Fantastic even, but, in a different sense than that word probably means in Spanish."

"I understand."

I gathered my breath. The hum of the plane's engines filled the cabin with white noise and I thought of the miracle of the two of us, flying through the air at such speeds. We may as well have been at home on the couch. "I see things," I said, finally.

He looked at me curiously.

"I think Nina has been making me or helping me see things."

"What kinds of things?"

"Things no one else can see," I said and stopped there. I looked over at him and his face was serious. He was taking me seriously. What more could I ask for? Nothing. He simply nodded.

I closed my eyes. There was only one way through. "I see halos," I said, at last.

"Halos?" he asked, confused.

"Halos."

"Halos, like above the head of Jesus or an angel?"

"That's right. Specifically, I see halos above people who are about to die. About 2-3 weeks before they die, I believe. Those were the earliest ones I saw, anyway."

Juan Pablo looked at me unflinchingly, waiting for there to be more, for there to be something to explain this bizarre confession. "You are serious?"

"Very serious."

He looked ahead and so I looked ahead, both of us staring at the back of the seat in front of us. There was only the white noise of the engine and the tinkling of ice in somebody's glass. Juan Pablo shifted uncomfortably in his seat. It was his right to ask the questions. He had earned it, or at least I owed him that much.

"Do I have a halo?" he asked me.

"You do not."

He nodded. A lot of time passed, although I can't say for certain how much. Five minutes? Ten? I sat next to him, quietly, knowing it was important that I not be the person to speak next.

"Can I ask you," he said at last, pausing and weighing very carefully what he had to say. "The Panamanian gentleman you wanted me to look at."

"Yes."

"I remember that conversation because it was very strange," he said. I nodded in response.

"He had one of these...a halo?"

"Yes."

He nodded slowly. After a moment, he pursed his lips and squinted his eyes, and then relaxed his face again. He brought his expressive hands to his face and rubbed his forehead. "And, excuse me if this is too personal, but..."

"Go ahead," I said. "Ask me anything you want. You can literally ask me anything. I am aware how insane this sounds."

"Well, maybe, but it explains some things. For example, it's very complicated, but...The girls you have been bringing home recently...the women. Your relationships. They had halos, too?"

I paused for a moment before answering him. It was true. It was all true. And for the first time, it seemed worse out in the open than it had ever felt in my head. "Yes."

"That's why you were involved with them?"

"No, no, not exactly. At least it didn't start that way. It was an accident," I said and I wasn't lying. I spoke quickly to clarify the point. "The first one was at a bar and I was very drunk and upset and we were just talking. She spoke to me first. She was even hitting on me, or pursuing me it seemed like. I don't know. It's hard to tell in retrospect and I can't even call her to ask her because she's...she's...well, she's dead. It all happened so fast."

He nodded and I think I saw that he genuinely understood me. I don't want to say he believed me, because I don't want to put words in his mouth, but he understood.

"It felt so good to have that kind of attention from someone," I added. "You have to understand, I hadn't slept with anyone in years. Years! And in a way it seemed harmless, right? Who got hurt? Well, she did, but not because of me, you know what I mean? It was something that was going to happen and so I was there in the meantime."

I was babbling and he forgave me for it. "But after that," I said. "I will admit that it was more conscious. After the first one, yes."

"And Julie?"

"No, not Julie," I said quickly. "Well, yes, she has a halo now, but she didn't at first. I've known her for almost a year. I really like her. Her halo came after the first night we were together. It was completely unforeseen and it made me panic. That's when everything started to unravel."

He nodded again and fell silent. "Thank you. I appreciate that you did not...put me on the pee machine. I would not have wanted that."

"I know."

"Can you explain it to me again, how it works?" he asked.

I pulled all of the equipment out of my carry-on in the overhead compartment and we went through everything, from the source code to the app, to Nina itself, and finally to the vitamins and supplements.

"You take these every day?" he asked, looking at the supplements.

"I just do exactly what Nina tells me to do," I said. "Some days one pill, some days another. Some days, only certain foods."

He nodded. "But you haven't been able to find what is causing it?"

"Right. I keep thinking there's something I haven't tried yet. I felt like if I worked on it hard enough, I would come up with the solution, the silver bullet."

"Silver bullet?"

"It's symbolic. In the old movies, they had to use a special weapon to kill supernatural creatures like werewolves or monsters. It was usually a silver bullet."

"You realize, of course, that this symbolism is very bad for you now."

He asked more questions and for the rest of the flight, I told him about Nina, the history of its development, my interest in the mysteries of the body and what I was trying to accomplish. I told him about how the sale to BioTechM could help me understand the science and, although I would lose virtually all control over the future and direction of the project, it was my last chance to see if I could understand the halos. I know it sounded like giving up, I told him, but it's not exactly giving up, it's just like changing course to continue moving forward. He listened attentively and asked questions until I felt almost completely unburdened.

I was in a slightly better mood when we landed in San Francisco. Talking it over with Juan Pablo made me feel better. I was relieved to finally tell someone about what was truly happening to me. Plus the arrival into SFO is dramatic from the south, as you fly over the rolling coastal hills and land on a small pad of cement jutting out into the bay. I think it's enough to turn any mood into a positive outlook. How can you not be in a good mood when you live here?

We walked purposefully off the plane and through the airport toward the designated Uber pick-up area. Juan Pablo was on his phone, arranging for a ride, and I was looking around, appreciating the cold bay wind and the rolling grey clouds after the stifling heat of Panama. It had to be at least fifty degrees cooler than Bocas del Toro and the air felt refreshing against my face and body. I was wearing the same sweat-stained clothes from the day before and I was looking forward to getting home and taking a shower.

As we crossed the street through the arrivals terminal roadway, something bright caught my attention. To my left, there was an overweight, middle-aged man walking down the sidewalk. The brightest halo I had ever seen hovered menacingly over his balding head. Or perhaps it was the reflection from a large window, it was difficult to tell for some reason. He was agitated, dragging an old carry-on case behind him. The bag was missing the cover from one of its wheels so it didn't roll properly. He had a heavy backpack hoisted precariously just off of his right shoulder. Sweat stained his back and was beading on his face even though it couldn't have been more than 60 degrees. He was staring down at his phone, ear pods in his ears, having what seemed to be an urgent conversation with someone far away. He was completely oblivious to the world all around him.

"There!" I said to Juan Pablo, hitting him on the shoulder.

Juan Pablo looked up. "What?"

"That guy," I said.

"A halo?" he asked quickly.

I started to answer, "I think so," when I noticed a large shuttle bus heading down the roadway right in the Distracted Man's direction. There was something about the way he was walking, or where he was exactly on the sidewalk and the length of his stride, or the combination of everything, that made me certain that he was about to cross the street, right into the path of oncoming traffic and the rental car shuttle.

Without even answering Juan Pablo, I dropped my bag on the ground and sprinted towards the Distracted Man as fast as I could. It was an instinct, to be sure, and I would like to think I would have done it even if he didn't have a halo. Since we're being honest, however, I'll confess that as I sprinted down the sidewalk, with a million things flying through my head, one of them was that this was potentially a moment of scientific significance.

If he did have a halo, I was about to learn about destiny. If I could save the Distracted Man, I could prove that a halo was not a definitive death sentence. Something could be done to alter the course of history. Suddenly, my work, my project, Nina, would have tremendous scientific and human value. It would be the most important acquisition in BioTechM's storied history. I would receive immediate notoriety at the company and Julie, Julie would have a chance to live her full life, perhaps together with me. The halos could be the ultimate warning sign, a last chance to improve your outcomes, and not a harbinger of doom.

I heard nothing but an onrush of blood in my ears as I reached the Distracted Man just as he stepped off the sidewalk and right into the path of the onrushing courtesy rental car shuttle. The shuttle driver laid on his horn instinctively, turning the wheel as I grabbed the Distracted Man by the back of his dark grey cotton hoodie and pulled him back as hard as I could onto the sidewalk and off the street. I felt the air from the passing shuttle as it swerved past us, smashing the Distracted Man's backpack, which had flung off his shoulder, into pieces and sending papers, containers and a water bottle flying through the air.

The Distracted Man hit the ground hard, his ear pods flying off and bouncing down the sidewalk. He landed on his butt and rolled backward, hitting his head softly on the pavement behind him. As he came to rest on the ground, the shuttle bus skidded to a halt and Juan Pablo and a crowd of Samaritans and onlookers ran over. Everything at the airport came to a screeching halt.

"Holy shit, man," I heard someone say from the crowd. Several people came forward to offer assistance. Somebody helped me up. I heard someone else ask the Distracted Man if he was alright.

He sat upright and shook his head, taking inventory of himself. He smiled a meek sort of smile and opened his mouth as if to speak, but didn't. He raised his eyebrows as if to say, "Whew!" and tried to stand up, but struggled. Someone from the crowd told him to take it easy and not hurry anything. A couple of hands appeared on his shoulders from behind him.

He seemed to relax again for a moment and he wiped the sweat that had gathered on his forehead. His forehead! I looked up and noticed the halo was still there above his head. Was it fading? In a way it was, but in a way it wasn't. It appeared to be as bright as ever, but it wasn't like any I had seen before. It was not a continual, persistent light like the others. This one was like an autostereogram – one of those pictures that hide an underlying image that you have to relax your eyes to see. The halo sort of zoomed in and out of my focus. I looked back down at his face because the glare from the halo was hurting my eyes and just as I did, the Distracted Man's mouth closed tightly shut, his eyes rolled into the back of his head and he fell hard back against the ground, making a grunting, gurgling sound.

"Oh, no," a middle-aged woman said, and burst forward through the crowd, rolling the distracted man onto his side. "Somebody call 9-1-1!"

"Calling," Juan Pablo said from next to me.

The woman was feeling for a pulse and looked back at me. "Do you know this man?" she asked.

"No, I don't. I don't know him. I just..."

The Distracted Man began convulsing rapidly and then went limp. "This man needs an ambulance," this doctor, or at least she seemed like a doctor, said and rolled him onto his back. She felt his neck for a pulse. Then she leaned over and put her ear next to the Distracted Man's nose. She popped up and rolled him onto his back and began chest compressions.

"No, no, no," I said.

"He's not breathing. He has no pulse!" she shouted at Juan Pablo and I could hear Juan Pablo repeat this into the phone behind me.

I heard the sound of a siren in the distance. Someone in the group of onlookers began to cry. An older man with a gentle face and a soft expression pushed his way through the crowd and came up behind me. I turned to look at him and his face had an expression of such extreme compassion that it was only at that moment that I realized I had tears streaming down my face.

"You did everything you could," he said. "I saw it. I saw it, too. You did everything you could."

"Wait, what? You saw what?" I asked, but I was mumbling or blubbering through my tears, I think, and people were starting to come in between us.

"What did you see?" I cried out, as more people pushed between us. "What did you see?" I yelled out over the din of the traffic and chaos, but to no effect. He was just smiling at me sorrowfully. When the paramedics got there a moment later, I had lost track of him entirely, the Compassionate Man.

I stood up next to Juan Pablo, trying to keep track of him in the crowd. Juan Pablo put his arm around me, though, and I turned and watched with him as the paramedics worked on the Distracted Man for some time, before putting him on the gurney and pulling a white sheet over his face. He was dead.

Police officers showed up to disperse the crowd and speed traffic through the front of the terminal. One of them came over and asked me some questions. He thanked me, took my name and phone number and told me to go home and get some rest.

I don't remember anything about the ride home. I'm not even sure how we got there. But when we did get home, Juan Pablo followed me into my apartment solemnly. BioTechM was buying Nina, but had said nothing about the vitamins and supplements I had been taking.

I gathered everything I had been taking into a bag and went outside, Juan Pablo beside me. I walked over to the garbage can, opened the lid, and dropped everything inside.

He patted me on the shoulder as we stared at the random assortment of bottles lying in the garbage bin on top of neatly tied compostable garbage bags full of our garbage. "I believe you now," he said to me. "I believe everything."

I wasn't sure whether he was saying that for my benefit or for whom, but it didn't matter. He patted me once more and turned to leave without looking at me. He walked into his apartment through the patio door, closing it softly behind him.

I went inside and signed the BioTechM term sheet without thinking about it twice. All the terms were as promised and everything was exactly as Max had said. I clicked the bright yellow "Sign Here" button and my signature was digitally applied to the agreement and sent directly back to Max without any further action on my part. I closed the lid of my laptop and went into the bathroom and threw up. I had no idea what to do after that, so I took a shower and changed clothes, without even unpacking my bag, and waited in my apartment to see if Max or anyone else would call me.

< 21 >

Penumbra

When I was 14 years old, I played in the championship game of the area rec soccer league. I still remember my dad driving me to the game. It was one of the last times we were together in that sort of father and son way before he moved.

What I remember most about that car ride, though, was the feeling inside my chest about the event that was about to take place. It would be too generic, too simple, to say that I was "excited" about the game. It was a lot more complicated than that, and the feelings that were moving in me were about more than just a game.

It was the first time I remembered feeling that there was something big, something important, that I wanted – to win the championship — and where I had the ability to affect the outcome. The feeling of participating in the creation of my future, of having agency in my own life, was something I had never felt so palpably before. I knew the game was within my control to influence and how well I played would have a direct impact on the result. It seems simple, but at the time it was a revelation.

I remember my uniform on, my cleats on, the window down and the air flying through my hair. Everything in the whole world seemed possible to me at that moment because I could sense, like the smell of something sweet but distant, the ability to control my own life. If I could affect the outcome of a game, then logically I could influence other things, too, guide my life the way I wanted. It was up to me, I could do it. For the first time, the ability to shape my future seemed bigger than the death of my mom and the other things that had shaped my past.

Staring out of the window at the passing buildings and trees, it felt like I was flying. I was flying into my future and into my destiny, into a world that I could create for myself. Gone were the days of the tragedies of the world acting upon me, of things happening *to me*, I could now act on the world. I could make things happen. The feeling of anticipation and possibility was almost overwhelming. It was exhilarating. When we arrived at the parking lot, I burst out of the car and ran to meet my friends and teammates on the field to warm up for the game. I felt like I was doing exactly what I was supposed to be doing. I felt like an adult.

I had a similar feeling on my way to see Julie the next night. I considered postponing the date out of a sort of anticipation or dread, but time was still of the essence and there wasn't any way to prepare for the meeting as much as I would have liked. I was simply going to have to get ready, go out onto the field, do my best, and accept the consequences. Would I tell her about the halos or not? Would I tell her about Panama and the supplements? How would I explain the twisted story of the last few months in a way that she would believe?

We agreed to meet at Ocean Beach in the City. My sort of loosely held plan was to walk south along the sand near Golden Gate Park for a while and then have sushi in the Avenues. Nobody takes the Sunset District seriously because it has terrible weather – socked in fog nearly all of the time – and for that reason, it actually feels like a city apart from the City, and a perfect spot to see her again. I picked a place with tremendous sushi and fish and within walking distance from the beach, but which was rarely crowded because of how far it felt from the rest of San Francisco.

In addition to the butterflies in my stomach, the day was unusual for other reasons. I woke up at 9:45 in the morning, which was the latest I'd slept in years. It was only the second time in over a year (the first being the morning prior in Panama) that I hadn't started my day by urinating in a plastic homemade filter and it felt strange. I had a nagging feeling all morning that I was forgetting something or missing something or not doing something I was supposed to do.

It was also only the second time, in all that time, that I hadn't started the day with vitamins or supplements or a particular dietary instruction. I felt like a child whose parents leave him alone for the first time. I wasn't sure what to do, what to eat, where to go. But I didn't interpret that feeling as being relieved of a burden or freed from a rigorous routine of monotony. Instead, I'll admit I was a little worried.

Sure, I could eat whatever I wanted, but when you become accustomed to being told the *right* thing to eat or drink or do, then this kind of freedom of choice is not relaxing. For weeks after I stopped using Nina, I wondered if the food I was ingesting was perhaps not what my body needed at that time and then I had to remind myself what I was moving from and what I was moving toward. For all of history, humans had eaten whatever they craved or what was available to them or what they could catch and find, and what had it gotten them? This mess, sure. But the alternative had proved too terrible for me, or at least too terrible for me right now.

After staring at my refrigerator for several minutes, I fried myself an egg, with the yolk over medium, the way I used to like it. I toasted a bagel, buttered it, and placed the finished egg on top. I sprinkled some sea salt on the egg and added two turns from my pepper mill. Then I layered two slices of turkey bacon on top and grated some cheddar cheese over the whole thing.

I made myself an espresso. *Doppio.* I steamed some milk and poured it slowly in. I sat down at my table and ate it all quietly, enjoying every bite and sip as if I were tasting food for the first time.

After breakfast, I turned with dread to the mountain of necessary clean-up work that I knew was waiting for me. There were too many emails and messages to appropriately respond to. Marc with a "c" was texting, calling and emailing me. Trevor, same. They had both heard about the deal with BioTechM and were asking if there could still be a chance for them to step in. Twenty million dollars at a $50 million valuation is what they were both offering me now with promises and guarantees of this and that. I let them down easy even though they didn't deserve as much. I also had emails or texts from virtually every venture capital investor I had ever met with and the occasional reporter. My inbox looked like a Who's Who of everybody I had wanted involved in my life for the past year. Only now, I was walking away from it.

With all that emotional baggage behind me, I drove out to the beach to meet Julie. Crossing the bay, the water was as blue as it ever gets, with the sun angling down toward the horizon. Through the Golden Gate, though, I could see a tremendous bank of fog a mile or more off the coast. I wondered what that meant for a beautiful, romantic sunset encounter, but hoping for a miracle is not the same thing as expecting one.

As I pulled into the Ocean Beach parking lot, I immediately spotted Julie out on the sand and I steered quickly into the first space I saw. I had the door open and a foot out the door before I even set the car into park. I tried to play it cool as I half walked/half jogged in her direction but I was overwhelmed with the need to see her and the state of her surroundings, shall we say. The closer I got to her, the more I began to run and the less I walked.

She was standing in a bright trail of sunshine, so I had difficulty seeing. As I moved forward, I took off my sunglasses and squinted. I ran faster, but the faster I ran, bumping my feet on the lumpy sand, the less clearly I could see. I didn't want to slow down but I needed to know as soon as possible. Could it be true? Could I really be seeing what I was seeing? By the time I reached her, I was almost in a dead sprint.

As I reached her, I grabbed her shoulders to steady myself and she shrieked happily as my momentum knocked her backwards a step or two. She had taken off her shoes and it looked like she had been walking in the sand for some time. She had a big smile on her face like someone with their lungs full of fresh air and her face had the warm color of the sun. She laughed as I held her shoulders in my hands, with my arms straight forward, looking at her.

"What is it?" she said, as we clasped arms. "Why do you always look over my head?"

In this case, it was because her halo was gone.

"Oh my God. Oh my God. Hi!" I managed to say, breathless. "You look great!"

"Hi!" she responded looking at me, trying to understand the look in my eyes. "Thank you."

I was aware that I didn't have control over my expression, so I spun us toward the horizon and looked out at the sky before the tears released themselves from my eyes and rolled down my cheeks. The sky above the thick layer of clouds and fog was still a bright blue, no hint yet of the yellows and pinks. "Isn't it beautiful?" I said, quickly wiping my face.

"Oh, that!" she said, looking at the sky, the water and the crashing waves. "It never gets old, does it? Too bad about the clouds."

I took the opportunity of her facing west to steal a couple of additional glances over her head. There was no question that the halo had vanished. Where had it gone? Was it coming back? These questions seemed important, but less important than the fact that it was gone, that I had her there with me, and that I could begin to think that she wouldn't be taken away.

We walked on the beach and talked about everything and nothing at the same time. She was in a fantastic mood. We talked about our favorite beaches and she told me about her favorite spots on the eastern coastline, summers in Virginia and people she grew up with and where they were today. We talked about Ocean Beach, about the origins of the Burning Man festival there, and about San Francisco beach culture, and how this spot, this one spot, is where the two great natural aspects of San Francisco come together – the park (Golden Gate Park) and the beach (Ocean Beach) – like a river emptying from a mountain into the sea.

Even though it was cold, we sat close enough to the water that the occasional wave came up and kissed our feet. We laughed like kids at the waves that came too close to us. I felt her warm body next to mine with my arm around her. I felt her form, her shoulders, and basked in her and the golden glow of the sun as it moved its way closer to the horizon.

We walked to the restaurant and sat by the window. We ate and talked until the world outside through the window disappeared in the dark and became a glass wall that reflected the light and the view inside. We ate sushi and drank Asahi and talked and laughed as the restaurant emptied and the waiters began cleaning the tables around us.

When it was clear it wouldn't be long before we were asked to leave, I invited her back to my place and, for the first time, her face broke from its expression of joy and happiness into an expression that was at once dreadful and sweet. In my head, it was as though a song that had been playing softly the entire evening was only now being turned up loud enough so that I could make out what it was. I wasn't surprised, exactly. After all, as the saying goes, thousands of actors have played Hamlet, but Hamlet always dies.

"Look, I've been meaning to tell you, but I don't know how to tell you and I've been having such a good time that I didn't know if I wanted to tell you, but I'm just going to come out and say it." She said it all so fast and in such a very nervous and cute way that I forgave her immediately for what she hadn't yet said and almost didn't mind what was about to happen.

"I'm moving," she said quickly.

"You're what? Where?" I took a long drink of water.

"I'm moving. Back to Virginia. Northern Virginia. I got an amazing offer to be head of Intellectual Property at Bright Star," she said, referring to the hottest tech company to IPO in the last five years. "It's a great opportunity for my career. It's the perfect job."

"Wow. Congratulations," I tried to say it in a way that sounded authentic in part because that's how I wanted to sound, but also because I was genuinely impressed and in no small part truly happy for her.

"Thank you. I'm so excited," she said, and then seemed to sort of catch herself. "In a way, I have you to thank."

"Me?!"

"Yes, you could say that. I was so impressed with what you were doing with Nina and how much you were enjoying it that I thought maybe I needed to go in house to actually enjoy my legal career. You know? To really achieve my potential."

"It's a great move for you, I think. It's the right one. Really. Congratulations."

"Anyway," she said, extending the "way" for several beats. The next part she said as though she were walking on eggshells. "I don't think we should get too serious, you know?" She paused for a moment, but I knew better than to say anything stupid, so she kept going. "This could be big for me and I want to start clean. I like you, but I would hate to start a new life and be torn because of a relationship out here. That sounds awful, I know."

"No it doesn't," I said quickly. "It makes perfect sense." This time it was her turn to remain quiet and hear what I had to say, so I continued. "I'm disappointed. I'm not going to lie. I haven't met anyone that I've liked in a long time. A long time. And, I've been through a lot…" A genuine look of sadness came over her face and her shoulders slumped slightly forward. "But, look, I probably shouldn't go into more detail than just that. You're doing the right thing."

She laughed. "You're very sweet."

"That's kind of you."

"I also don't think I've ever met someone so concerned about my health before. That's so cute! You asked me so many questions and your check-ins were hilarious. It must be because of your work."

"I guess so," I said, hastily drinking more water.

"Maybe you should have been a doctor?"

"Ha."

She emptied out her water glass with a big drink. I sat there soaking in the last sight of her, trying to memorize her features and burn everything about her into my memory.

"Also, I think you're really onto something with Nina," she said, as an afterthought. "So your life is going to be changing fast."

"How do you mean?"

"I can't believe I haven't told you! I've been thinking about it so much but obviously today has been crazy."

"I'm not following."

"When you left me in your apartment, last week, I hope you don't mind...we had talked about me trying Nina. So, I got into your laptop and saw you had created an account for me in the cloud. I looked at the filter you used and it was very rudimentary. I made one myself at home, I synched them together and I've been using it ever since. Nina II!"

I tried to say something, but nothing came out of my mouth.

"It's fascinating," she continued. "It feels incredible to really know what's going on inside your body, to feel confident that you're doing the right thing to be the healthiest person you can be."

"Yeah," was all I could say.

"I hope that's okay?"

Five thousand different things flashed through my mind. "I haven't thought about it, to be honest." I looked around for the waiter, hoping to get a refill of my water, but he was purposefully avoiding eye contact with me.

"I'm such a loser for not having told you! You're not mad are you?"

"Don't say that. You're not a loser. It's not that I'm mad. I'm just very surprised."

"I'm your first customer!"

"I guess so."

We left the restaurant and walked in the dark back down to the Pacific Coast Highway and crossed over to the beach parking lot. The wind had picked up, but the moon was reflecting off the crest of the waves and creating so much light that it was easy to see.

There was so much more to say about us, but also everything had been said. And regarding Nina, what was I going to tell her that she wasn't about to discover on her own? Why bother mentioning BioTechM? She would see the changes herself or get bored and quit using the product. The bottom line was that she was leaving and that was it. There was nothing I could say, nothing I *should* say, to change it. Everything else was just noise.

"Look at the moon's penumbra," she said, pointing to the sky. "It's so bright that you can even see the part of the moon that's in the earth's shadow. Like a big ring."

We stared at the moon from the parking lot for a long time with the sound of traffic and the waves crashing ashore.

Finally, abruptly, as if she had finally garnered the courage and didn't want to lose the momentum, she thanked me for everything, kissed me on the cheek with something between a sigh and a giggle, got in her car and drove away.

Inside the car, her face was illuminated by a street light as she turned onto the highway. She had a big, but bittersweet smile, and she was as perfect as she could be. Her whole life was ahead of her, or at least that's the way it seemed to me. And then she was gone.

The next day I ran into Juan Pablo and told him what happened with Julie and he gave me a big hug even though I told him I didn't really need it. He had some friends coming over for an *asado*, so we went to the Uruguayan butcher and bought meat and went to the wine store for wine and a produce shop for vegetables.

He set up the grill in our backyard and took his time getting the charcoal and wood briquettes just right. "It's all in the fire," he said, smiling.

As the flames went up, he told me that he had seen Landlord Mike that morning and that our apartment complex would be listed for sale next month. We were going to have to find a different place to live and I was overcome with a mild melancholy at the thought of not living next to my best friend.

"Have you seen the house for sale on Colby Street?" he asked me.

"The brown shingle with the studio in the back?"

"Yeah, that one."

"I did. I saw it the other day."

"You should buy it," he suggested.

Before I had a chance to respond or even think much about it, his friends began to arrive. It was a group of people from different parts of Latin America, mostly, some other Argentines, his good friend, Jorge, from Chile, a Peruvian, two Brazilians, some people from Mexico and a German couple, just to keep things honest.

We spent the afternoon eating, drinking, laughing and had a great time. I felt like a bit of an outsider, sure, but it didn't bother me. I appreciated the company and Juan Pablo was kind enough to make sure I didn't feel left out. At some point that evening, it occurred to me that this is how friends are made. Juan Pablo and I won't ever need to talk about those crazy days again and yet they will always be there, we will always have it. It's part of the foundation of our relationship.

Believe it or not, I have no idea what happened to Julie. I never heard from her again. I never looked her up, either, and have no desire to do so. Am I curious? Sure, I'm curious. But I like thinking of her in Virginia, rising through the ranks at Bright Star, or maybe getting an offer to be General Counsel of some startup somewhere that makes a big splash. Married to someone nice maybe, a few kids eventually. And that image makes me so happy, I find it so peaceful, that I don't ever want to replace it with anything else. And so I leave it there, like a painting in my house that I can look at forever.

As for me, we lost that championship soccer game when I was 14. And in the pain of losing, I had forgotten the incredible feeling that I had that morning driving to the game. I searched for reasons, had blamed myself for not playing better. Eventually, I quit playing soccer altogether.

But that evening of the *asado*, with a chill in the air, I sat with my jacket on, burrowed into my lawn chair and remembered. I closed my eyes and with the soft sounds of conversation all around me, I thought of my friends, my teammates from long ago. I remembered romping around practices and get-togethers with them and remembered the feeling of flying to that last game.

This time was going to be different. I wasn't going to forget the feeling of endless possibilities, no matter how painful some of them are. So, these days, whenever someone refers to Nina as my "failed venture," I correct them. I didn't fail with it, I'll say. I just came to the end of my success.

Epilogue

About three or four months later, I was at McNally's before the start of a Warriors game. It was going to be crowded that night because it was the playoffs and what better place to watch a Warriors game than a bar in Oakland (before they moved to San Francisco).

I was in escrow on that house on Colby Street. Juan Pablo had agreed to rent the studio in the back. He wasn't sure how much longer he was going to stay in the country, but it was going to be good to have him around. He had become one of the better friends I'd ever had.

I was still working at BioTechM at the time. The Nina project was slow to get off the ground. Big companies are terrible at innovation; that's why they buy small companies. About a year after the deal closed, after all the code had been reviewed, after all the ground work had been laid to really develop the science, the economy hit a mild blip. At about the same time, another bioanalytics startup, this one based on analyzing blood, went down in a blaze of scandal-laden glory after raising a ton of money. As these things go, BioTechM was looking for places to save some cash and Sid convinced them to shelve the Nina project. He was very political and well-connected in the company and he managed to scare everyone into believing there was a PR risk for any bioanalytics product until the dust settled from the blood company.

I had no heart to put up a fight, having long before let go of the true motivation that had been driving me. I still got the full five million, though, because I am a lawyer after all and I didn't fall asleep while reviewing the final transaction documents that came after the term sheet. It's up to you to decide who got the last laugh, Sid or me.

I never saw another halo, and I thought less and less about them over time. The whole episode seems like a feverish dream. Of course, I'm curious about what caused them and what they really meant, but I'm also curious about the origin of life, the nature of consciousness, the conflict between the Theory of Relativity and Quantum Mechanics and other aspects about the universe that I'll never understand. The halos led me where I am today and that is all I need to know, really.

Through the process, I also learned to forgive my father. I eventually called him (he's back in the States), and we see each other for coffee now and then, the holidays and the other usual times. He apologized to me, I mumbled through an apology to him for leaving abruptly and not responding to his many attempts to contact me. We get along fine.

In any event, on this particular night in question, I was sitting with Jim from Google. It turns out he went to McNally's to watch the Warriors games because he didn't have a television at his house. He and his wife have two young kids and they don't want them to know that television exists yet.

"You can only hide from the truth for so long, my friend," I said.

"Yeah, but the longer the better," was Jim's reply.

About an hour before the game started, I noticed the brunette whom I had seen the night at McNally's after I first saw the Grey Man. Back then, even Tiny had noticed her looking at me and had tried to get me to buy her a drink, but I had (foolishly) declined.

She was by herself for some reason, no blonde friend this time, and she was nearly done with her drink. I looked at her, staring even. She seemed out of place in a way, fidgeting with the cocktail straw in her drink. She had the same long earring in her left ear that I remembered from the previous time, a feather of some sort, and straight, short dark brown hair that was cut in a bob just below her ears.

I got Tiny's attention and he came over to me and nodded. I motioned over to the woman. "Another round, on me," I said.

"Right away, boss," he said, and immediately grabbed a glass, flipped it, filled it with ice and started pouring. There was no snide comment, no smart ass remark about better late than never, none of it, although maybe I did detect the faint hint of a satisfied smile on his face. I freaking love that guy.

Tiny took her the drink and I could see him nod towards me and say something. She smiled at me the way she did that first day and I walked over and touched the top of the chair next to her. "Mind if I have a seat?" I said. In some ways, that's the easiest question in the world to ask.

We chatted and I had the distinct feeling that I was going back in time to correct a previous mistake, something only the luckiest of us get the chance to do. She told me she went to McNally's every few months to meet an old friend, but, on that evening, her friend had called to cancel after she had already arrived and ordered a drink. The friend had a sick kid and couldn't come out after all. "What about your kid?" I asked her.

"I don't have one," she said.

I confessed to her that I had seen her there before, but had been too afraid to introduce myself on that other occasion. She smiled and completely floored me by reciting a line from that old John Burroughs poem:

> *I stay my haste, I make delays—*
> *For what avails this eager pace?*

I stand amid the eternal ways
And what is mine shall know my face.

"Yes. Exactly like that," I said. We touched glasses in toast.

After we had finished our drinks, I asked her if she was hungry. "I know a place that serves a great burger."

She looked at me and I wasn't sure if she was trying to ascertain my intentions or trying to figure out what kind of a place we could get into that would serve decent food in the middle of the dinner rush without a reservation.

"They have other stuff, too. It's a good place, always crowded," I added by way of clarification. "But I can usually get a seat at the bar."

She smiled and told me that she'd like that.

Outside, College Avenue was just perfect. It was an unusually warm spring day for Oakland, the kind of day that makes you wonder how people can ever choose to live anywhere else. The sky was wanting to turn from blue to purple and the twilight lit the street and the shops and the trees in warm hues.

We stood outside McNally's for a moment, soaking it all in.

"How should we get there?" she asked.

"We can walk," I said.

"Are you talking about Black Tavern?"

"Yeah, that's the place," I responded.

"Isn't it going to be packed?"

It was a good question. It was very likely going to be packed, but I was willing to rely on my friend at the bar and the luck of the evening. Things had a tendency to turn out alright for me there. "I don't know," I said. "Maybe."

"I've always wanted to eat there. My friend keeps promising to take me."

I nodded. "It's a good place."

"Do you actually think we can get seated?"

I shrugged and she gave a sort of laugh, not knowing what to make of either my confidence or nonchalance. "You know, there are apps for that," she said. "They can tell you how crowded a place is or whether there are any tables available."

It was not so much what she said as how she said it. She said it in a way that was less a suggestion or an accusation, but instead she said it as a question, a sort of ink blot test, to see what I could see in an image she was showing me.

"Yeah, that's true," I said. "But these days I prefer not to know. It always spoils the fun."

Her eyes brightened and her face softened into a smile. "I think so, too," she said.

Off we went. We walked down the street together, the five or so blocks to the restaurant, to our seat at the bar, and in the general direction, as it turns out, of the sunset.

Made in the USA
Las Vegas, NV
07 March 2025